Evernight Publishing

www.evernightpublishing.com

Copyright© 2015

Liv Rancourt

Editor: Melissa Hosack

Cover Artist: Jay Aheer

ISBN: 978-1-77233-614-6

ALL RIGHTS RESERVED

KING STUD

DEDICATION

This book is dedicated to my in-home King Stud, who even now is starting our long-awaited kitchen remodel, complete with solid surface countertop. (Yay!) Thank you so much, my dear, for giving me the foundation I need to write.

The book is also dedicated to the two most fantastic teenagers any mother could ask for. You guys are so patient with me, and I appreciate your willingness to put up with all the time I spend at the laptop.

It doesn't matter what story we're telling, we're telling the story of family.

—Erica Lorraine Scheidt

I'd like thank Evernight's Stacey Adderley for putting her faith in this story. I'm so happy King Stud found a home with Evernight. I'd like to thank my agent Margaret Bail of Inklings Literary for sharing her skills and talking me off the ledge more often than I should probably admit to.

I'd also like to thank Melissa, my editor with Evernight, who is an amazing mix of knowledge and flexibility, and their fantastic cover artist Jay Aheer. My beta readers for this project were Michele, Debbie, Amanda, Shannon, Rhay, Ruth, and Ellen. I could not have done it without your eyes and minds and patience. You guys rock!

And finally, I'd like to give a shout-out to Margie Lawson, whose Fab30 and Immersion classes taught me so much. King Stud is a much better novel because of Margie.

KING STUD

An O'Connor Family Novel, 1

Liv Rancourt

Copyright © 2015

Chapter One

Ryan jogged down the stairs and grabbed his sweatshirt from the post at the bottom. Stress had a chokehold on his shoulders, and as he pulled the sweatshirt over his head, he paused to stretch his neck and shoulders, but couldn't loosen up.

"Come on, bro. We'll grab a couple o' senoritas and teach 'em to mambo." Chubb lounged against the bannister, his white-boy dreadlocks trapped in a ponytail holder.

"Are you trying to sound like a douche?" Frustration added an edge to Ryan's tone. Times like these he wished he could afford his North Seattle house without a roommate. "Because you've pretty much got it nailed."

"Shut up," Chubb said, with all the concern he'd give a snarling puppy.

Pulling a black watch cap over his dark curls, Ryan opened the door and gritted his teeth against the near-freezing air. "Gotta keep moving, man, me and the sharks." Gotta keep moving to keep from thinking. To keep from feeling. To keep from making the same mistake. No way he'd go crawling back to Cherry. No way.

Chubb didn't give up. "We'll go to the Pig and have a couple beers, and if the Toxic Twins are there, we'll go somewhere else."

The Toxic Twins were Ryan's very recent ex-girlfriend Cherry and his sister, Maeve. They were best friends and pretty much the reason he had to stay on the move. "You're on your own. I'm going to go to Home Depot to grab some pavers for that Sanderson job."

"What job? It's a holiday." Chubb smacked the bannister like he was really irritated, but they'd been friends for too long for Ryan to buy into his bullshit.

"I'll see you later." Ryan cut off Chubb's protest by slamming the front door, pretty sure his roommate would find himself a senorita before Ryan had the truck warmed up enough to drive.

The Ford truck's engine rumbled a chorus of growling bass notes, the only soundtrack Ryan was in the mood for. He'd been planning the break-up for weeks, and three days later his bones still said it was the right thing to do.

But a low-grade, irritable queasiness said some part of him noticed the loss.

In the ten minutes it took him to get to Home Depot, Cherry left him three voicemails and Chubb sent him one final whiney text. Ryan jammed the phone in his pocket without listening to the messages, though he came close to caving in to Chubb's request. The combination of the dark, half-empty parking lot and the shitty weather made hanging out in a friendly pub more appealing. His knuckles tightened on the steering wheel. He could be talked into it if Chubb would agree to go somewhere besides the Pig n' Whistle.

A woman walked behind the truck, heading into the store. She had straight ginger hair, long legs, and something familiar that Ryan couldn't place. She passed the scope of his rearview mirror and he shifted in his seat to watch her stride through the big sliding doors of the store.

Okay, so he might only be seventy-two hours past the worst break-up on record, but he could still appreciate beauty when he saw it. Ending things with Cherry had beaten him up, but it hadn't killed him. He climbed out of the truck, shrugging his shoulders against the cold.

It'd be a lot easier to keep moving if he had a pretty girl to chase.

* * * *

Faced with the drafty interior of a big box store on a Sunday evening, Danielle did what any other single woman would do. She whipped out her cell phone, scrolled through her contacts, and sent up a prayer to whichever god was listening. She'd been back in Seattle exactly three days, just long enough to have figured out things at her grandmother's house were a lot worse than she'd anticipated.

Maeve picked up on the third ring. "Why aren't you here?"

Relief trailed out on a sigh, and Danielle eyed the rack of lumber, each six foot piece as wide as her hand. Those boards wouldn't fit in her Mini Cooper, which might not matter since she wasn't sure they'd fix the problem. "Because I'm here."

"Where?" The brew-fueled babbling on Maeve's end of the call made her location obvious: her favorite hang-out, the Pig N' Whistle.

"Home Depot."

"You nerd," Maeve said, then hollered 'Home Depot' to the crowd around her. A surge in the general hubbub gave Danielle's location a big thumbs-down.

"Do I want to know what you're up to?" Maeve's voice dampened, as if she'd cupped the phone to cut out the background noise.

"Well, the kitchen floor's kind of a problem." It topped the list of challenges at Danielle's late grandmother's house, right ahead of 'no heat' and 'intermittent electricity'.

"That whole house is a disaster."

"Shut up. There's nothing a little elbow grease can't fix."

"Wishful thinking," Maeve said over a swell of crowd noise. "You don't believe that any more than I do."

Danielle scratched the hairline at the back of her neck, wanting nothing more than a long, hot shower. "Guess I got a couple months to prove us both wrong, then." Maeve had been her best friend since high school, her go-to phone call when things turned to shit in L.A. In the three days Danielle had been back in Seattle, Maeve had been her rock.

She rested against one of the orange metal stepladders employees used to reach the top shelves. The whole thing shifted, zapping her with fear the top boxes would come tumbling down on her. Why not? The oversized store, the oversized project, hell, the oversized change in her life could very well squash her flat.

If Maeve had been at home, painting her toenails or paying bills, Danielle would have invited her down to the ol' Home Depot right off. But now? No way could she interrupt Happy Hour.

To her right, a man pushed one of the store's big dollies up the wide aisle. He wore a black knit cap pulled down almost to his brows, allowing just a fringe of dark curls and long sideburns to show.

"Just come have a pint with the rest of us," Maeve said. "The floor will be there when you get home. Tomorrow's Veteran's Day and the place is packed."

"Honey, it's the kitchen floor." Danielle gave Mr. Sideburns a 'privacy please' grimace, then almost made a fool of herself double-taking his return smile. His dimples and blue eyes had a familiar feel.

"Don't 'honey' me," Maeve said. "You can't cook there anyway. Nothing works. Did you call my brother yet?"

"Not yet." Danielle rubbed her forehead, pushing back the headache that wanted to take over. *Focus.* She was in no shape to play with Mr. Sideburns, no matter how sexy he looked in his paint-splattered UW sweatshirt. "Last time I saw Ryan O'Connor he was a ten-year-old with a dirty face and holes in the knees of his jeans."

"Call him. He knows his stuff." Maeve said. "And you're family, babe. There's nothing more important than family."

Danielle had to smile. Maeve's family – her rowdy brothers and generous, loving parents – had been Danielle's ideal since she was a kid. In comparison, her own mother had relied upon a principle of benign neglect when it came to raising Danielle, her carelessness contradicted by a perverse inability to approve of any of Danielle's life choices.

"You're a good sport to help me out like this," Danielle said.

11

"I figure if I'm nice enough, you'll stick around."

"Yeah, my boss'd love that." Right now, her job was the best part of life in L.A.

Mr. Sideburns pulled a couple sticks of lumber from the rack, angling them across the top of the bags of concrete and box of tiles already in his cart. He lifted them with no more effort than if he was pulling a box of cereal off the shelf in the grocery store.

Danielle dragged her eyes down to the floor. No more ogling the other shopper. The buffed and gorgeous other shopper. Who probably had all kinds of women admiring his dimples and sideburns and whatever was hiding under his worn-out jeans.

Danielle convinced Maeve this wasn't a good night for drinks with the gang and tucked her phone away. Like any L.A. woman worth her yoga studio membership, her usual approach to home improvement meant calling a local contractor. She could have done the same thing this time, except she'd given in to the impulse to get her hands dirty.She refused to look too deeply at that decision, because it probably meant something significant. Why else would someone with a great job, a gorgeous condo, and a busy life drop out for a three-month leave of absence?

When the project was done, she ought to take a long vacation and figure out why she'd chosen to come home to Seattle, why she wanted to do the work herself. Until then, she needed to leave off the introspection and go ask one of the orange-vested employees for some help.

"Must be bad to get you into Home Depot on a Sunday evening." Mr. Sideburns leaned on his cart and gave her an appreciative once-over, his almost-cocky baritone mellowed by a hint of laughter.

Hitting on me? Not until I've had a shower, dude. Danielle jumped up from the ladder, ready to run. "I'm good, thanks."

"Got that right," he said, mostly to himself. "Sounds like you need a carpenter." A wry grin tweaked the corner of his mouth, just enough to show a dimple. "Ryan O'Connor."

"Ryan?" The wheels in her head burned rubber tracking back through the conversation with Maeve. *How much did he hear?* "It's been what? Fifteen years?" She raked a strand of hair out of her face, torn between embarrassment over her woefully unwashed state and stupidity for blushing like a teenager. "Danielle Jacobsen."

"Figured." He smiled wide enough to show both dimples. Yep. Definitely related to Maeve. As a kid he'd had freckles and a snub nose. His nose was still rounded at the end and it looked like he'd broken it at least once, and his jeans had the kind of shredded wear at the knees that L.A. hipsters paid big dollars to copy. Her reserve melted until it warmed parts of her anatomy that had no business heating up in a Home Depot store.

"So … um … you're Maeve's little brother." Danielle offered her hand, covering her momentary fluster with a glossy SoCal smile.

He wrapped her in a grip so sure and strong she didn't want to let go. "Yep. I heard you were back from L.A."

Danielle loosened her grasp to keep from giving him the wrong idea. Or to keep from giving herself the wrong idea. "Got here Thursday."

"Shouldn't you be at the Pig with Maeve?"

"Well, my grandmother's house is kind of run down, and there's this hole in my kitchen floor." She gave

13

a weak laugh, the banks of glaring fluorescent lights turning their conversation into a stage play.

Ryan stuffed his hands in his pockets and shrugged like he'd already seen worse than anything she could show him. "Before you spend any money, let's go take a look."

"Not tonight. I mean, it's a holiday weekend." If he was anything like Maeve, there was a bar stool with his name on it somewhere. "I'll call you and get on your schedule."

He gestured to his cart. "I just gotta pay for this stuff and we can go. Don't buy anything 'til we know what you need."

"But you must have plans."

"Yep. I'm going to help out a pretty woman." He lifted his eyebrows in a clear gesture of approval.

It's like that, is it? She pinched her lips to stifle a grin, aiming for stern with a helping of skeptical. "Pretty *older* woman."

"What do you expect from a kid with holes in his jeans?" He gave his cart a shove in the direction of a checkout line.

It would have been rude not to follow.

* * * *

Grandmother's house was on Perkins Lane, at the westernmost edge of the Magnolia Bluff, an area best known for breathtaking views and devastating mudslides. Danielle parked her Mini Cooper in front of the garage door, because she didn't trust the rickety building not to collapse if she pulled the car inside. The house had gotten shabbier in the hour she'd spent at Home Depot. It crouched low on its lot, avoiding its neighbors, ignoring the view of the Sound.

She waited for Ryan on the small front porch, the headache dancing around her temples, not quite settling in. A six foot laurel hedge shielded the house on the street side. The shrubs blocked the streetlights and covered the yard in murky shadow. Standing there in the dark, Danielle had time for some stern self-talk. She had too much going on to be distracted by any guy, let alone someone so young, so scruffy, and so closely related to Maeve.

So why was she so fluttery?

Finally a huge black pick-up pulled into the driveway.Ryan climbed out of the cab and surveyed the yard as if he'd already started a to-do list. "Nice pink Mini." He gave her car a careless nod on his way to the front door.

Her eyes narrowed. Was he really going to make fun of her car? That was asking for trouble. "It's cream."

"Looks pink in this light. Only a real princess would drive a pink Mini." He stood with his arms crossed and grinned up at her from the front walkway.

She squashed an answering smile. The O'Connors valued teasing more than anything, and if she didn't dish it right back to him, she'd be in trouble. "And I suppose only a real man would drive a monster truck."

"Ford F250."

"Don't you mean F150? I've never heard of a 250."

His half grin hinted at all kinds of inappropriate thoughts. "It's bigger."

Her stomach did a triple flip, and in self-defense she reached for the doorknob. *I guess he's old enough.* "Compensating?"

"Don't need to."He put his foot on the lower step, his tone casual, his eyes hot.

She jerked her gaze away, convinced her blush would leave permanent burns on her cheeks. "Come on."

Ryan didn't move right away. Danielle gave him time to get a good look at the cracked 1930's siding, the grass sprouting from the gutters, and the moss clinging to the shingles.

"Have you thought about tearing it down?" he asked.

"Come on, now," she said, halfway laughing. "This place has great bones."

His gaze worked her over with the same intensity he'd given the house. "Can't argue with that."

She managed to get the door open without combusting, and he followed her through the foyer into the living room, snickering when it took her three tries to coax the corner lamp to turn on. Uncle Jonathan had arranged for the estate sale people to come, and except for a few of the nicer pieces Gram had specifically left to family, the room was bare.

Danielle winced at the overall shabbiness. The old wool rug she'd played on as a kid had gone to the dump – the parts of it the rats hadn't eaten, anyway – and the walls were mottled and stained. The big stone hearth was still in place, though, along with the arts and crafts mosaic tile surrounding the firebox.

Built-in bookcases flanked the fireplace and most of the original wainscoting remained. Ryan ran his fingertips along the mahogany chair rail, moving slow, as if he could read the wood's story by touch. "This is the shit."

"Come see the kitchen." Dropping her purse on the lone wing-backed chair, she led him past the dining room with its antique cherry wood table and four ratty chairs.

A single fluorescent tube hung from the kitchen ceiling. She flipped the switch, and for once it turned on. "Ta-dah."

The linoleum floor was a lot older than the 1970's vintage olive green appliances, and there was an inch-deep well in the floor in front of the sink. "Sonofabitch, you put your foot through the floor," Ryan said, kneeling down to pick at the chunk of linoleum missing at the center of the depression.

"Hey! It's not like I meant to."

"Right." Ryan stood and straddled the hole, focused on the generous window with its view over the edge of the bluff. "Turn the light off again," he said.

Without the glare, all of Puget Sound spread out underneath them. Danielle eased up alongside Ryan, not quite close enough to touch him. Behind a tugboat, a single row of lights skimmed the water, marking the progress of a shipping barge. The twisted arms of the back yard madrona tree made a velvet silhouette against the darkness. Across the Sound, random bright spots pockmarked the dense shadow of Bainbridge Island.

He pulled himself up against the sink, hitting about mid-thigh and looking down over the windowsill. "What's out there?"

"A porch."

"Is it safe?"

She made a disgusted sound. "Nope."

Easing down carefully to avoid the pit in the floor, he nodded at the light switch.

She almost said something about why it was important to say please when asking someone to turn on the light. Instead, she flipped the switch and bit her tongue.

He gave the room another inspection. "This place is a time capsule. You cook in here?"

"Not really, no. The power's iffy."

"Right on." He stood up, heading for the back door. It also led to the basement stairs. "What's down here?"

"Cellar," she said, both nervous and intrigued by the idea of crawling around in the dark with young Ryan O'Connor. "We'll need a flashlight."

"Scared of the boogeyman?"

She couldn't decide whether to be irritated at his condescension or nostalgic about getting teased by an O'Connor. "Don't make fun of me."

He made an obvious effort to stop smiling and came toward her. She caught a trace of his scent, musky with a hint of mint, like maybe from brushing his teeth, like maybe she'd taste it if he …

Embarrassment froze her, allowing him to move into her personal space, close enough to feel the heat from his skin, close enough for the low buzz of his energy to brush against hers. Close enough to kiss her.

The voice in her head stammered from a combination of surprise and desire, anticipation and embarrassment.

"Um, I've got a flashlight in the truck, and if you let me by, I'll go get it."

"Mine's in the…" *Bedroom.*

She backed up quick, because if she accidently touched him she was likely to on-purpose drag him upstairs.

He jogged across the living room, leaving the door open on his way out to his truck.

She did some quick mental arithmetic. He'd been about ten when she and Maeve graduated from high school. That meant an eight-year age difference, and since she was thirty-three, he must be twenty-five. Okay, old enough that she wouldn't be arrested for child molestation.

Still, Maeve would kill her.

A moment later, Ryan came back with a heavy-duty flashlight that gave off more light than any lamp in the house. "Let's go check out the foundation and make sure this baby's worth saving."

"Are you always this bossy?" She made it light, teasing, with just enough snark to let him know she wasn't a total doormat.

"Yep." He rubbed his mouth with a knuckle, though the gesture didn't quite hide his smile. "I've been told it's one of my better qualities."

Danielle hurried to the cellar door, because right then if Ryan O'Connor had told her to do anything – get on her knees, bend over, drop trou – she'd have done it without a second thought.

Random skittering followed their footsteps as they headed down the squeaky wooden stairs. The cone of light from Ryan's flashlight swung left and right, up and down, exploring the four small rooms. The place smelled of wet cement and old metal. The dirty floor looked solid, though there were a couple cracks where white powder ghosted along the seams.

When he made a quick turn, Danielle almost bumped her nose on his chest. "Whoa, Princess, give a guy some room." His free hand wrapped around her waist, gently moving her back.

She stayed where he put her, the echo of his touch vibrating through her shirt, through her skin, down to her core.

"This place ever get hit by a slide?"

Ryan's question jerked Danielle back into the grubby basement. "A what?"

"Mudslide."

"Yeah, a few years ago. The road was closed for a couple weeks." Danielle tried to remember the year by linking disaster with her favorite heels, favorite hairstyle, favorite song. "I was, like, a sophomore in high school."

Ryan thought for a minute, frowning. "I would have been about second grade."

Oh. Right. Good to remember. Not something to dwell on. Instead, she made a mental note that Ryan was cute even when he frowned.

"Where's the electrical panel?" he asked, interrupting her naval gazing.

When she managed to speak, her voice was higher than normal. "You mean the fuse box? Underneath the stairs, I think."

He moved past her and she followed along, feeling like the sidekick on this adventure. His proximity brought to mind the details Maeve had mentioned over the years. He liked boxing, he'd gone to a community college, and he had a girlfriend. *What was her name?* Some kind of fruit. Apple? Clementine? Cherry? *Oh yeah.* His girlfriend's name was Cherry.

The breaker box's gray metal door squawked like a wounded crow when he opened it. "Looks like someone stuffed cotton where a couple of the fuses should be," he said, his face angled close to the box and his voice tight. "Total fire hazard."

He flipped a toggle at the bottom of the row of fuses and shifted to meet her eyes, though in the limited light she couldn't read his expression. "You want the bad news first, or the good news?"

"Bad news."

"That's no fun." The flashlight cast shadows in his dimples as his smile broadened. "The good news is, the foundation's solid and the woodwork rocks."

Okay. Things weren't hopeless. "And…"

"The bad news is, I just cut the power, and you cannot stay here until you get an electrician to pull a permit and rewire the place."

"Damn it." Aggravation punched through her momentary peace, tightening the headache around her temples.

Ryan took a couple steps in her direction, and Danielle had to stop herself from putting her hands on his chest. She fought the uncharacteristic urge to lean into him and let him take over. Even more ridiculous, she had to cope with a gut level clench at being close to him. *I don't have time for this kind of bullshit.*

"C'mon. We'll go find some dinner and come up with a plan."

She took a deep breath and blew it out loud. "We, as in you're joining Team Jacobson?"

"Yep." He rubbed his hands together, cracking the knuckles on one hand in the palm of the other. "All the original trim in this place it's making my dick hard."

Relief disabled her filter. "Dude, you're what? Twenty-five? A gust of wind makes your dick hard."

He shot her a sly grin. "Twenty-four, and, well…"

Maeve was *so* going to kill her.

Chapter Two

The bartender gave him his change, and Ryan stuffed his wallet into his back pocket. The bar at Taco Diablo was a hole-in-the-wall plastered with Harley logos, punk rock posters, and grinning skeleton caballeros. He palmed the pair of margarita glasses, holding them close to his chest to avoid getting jostled by the crowd.He didn't want to waste a drop, because he had every intention of getting Dani tipsy.

A pretty woman in a place like this? A guy never knew what might happen.

He sidestepped a table full of happy tequila drinkers, heading back to where Dani perched on a stool in a back corner. Her thumbs flicked across the screen of her smart phone and she sucked on her upper lip, an action that might have aided her concentration but completely destroyed his. He flashed back to when he was nine years old and caught up in his first crush. He'd wanted Dani Jacobsen bad, though at nine he hadn't had much of a clue about what he wanted her for.

He sure as hell did now.

"The hostess said it'd be about fifteen minutes for our table." He handed her the drink, keeping his eyes on her face instead of her body.

Her naughty-older-woman smile boomeranged through him.

"I'm cut off after this," she said.

"Lightweight."

"I'm serious." She took a long draw off the straw and swallowed, eyes closed, head tipped back, forcing him to shove his hand in a pocket to keep from running his fingertips down the line of her throat. She'd been pretty in high school, but age had taken her to a whole other level.

"If Maeve asks, dinner tonight didn't happen," she said. The restaurant's sound system played an old AC/DC album loud enough they had to raise their voices to be heard.

Ryan took a drink of his margarita so he wouldn't pop off with the first thing that came into his head. After Cherry, any woman who tried to maneuver him into something stupid jumped right onto his last nerve. He'd done a good job swallowing down his earlier irritability, and fought like hell to keep it from reviving. When he could sound like a grown-up, he responded. "Can't stand games."

Dani tapped her glass slowly, her mouth pinched as if remembering some past Maeve-interaction that hadn't gone her way. "Her world. Her rules."

He stamped down an automatic refusal. "Maeve's always been the problem child."

Danielle's dark hazel eyes held his gaze for a couple beats too long. "Survival strategy."

Damn, but he wanted to take a bite outta Dani's apple in the worst way. He liked her wide mouth and pretty lips. He liked the way she carried herself, all polished and classy like a model or actress or something.

If only she wasn't Maeve's friend, and if only he hadn't just been ripped raw by another one of his sister's friends. He and Cherry had dated all through high school, but once she was old enough to go out to clubs, she turned into Maeve's BFF. He'd have to be stupid to make that mistake again. Stupid or flat-out crazy.

"All right, then. Dinner tonight is our secret." Ryan raised his glass. So did Dani. The clink of their glasses cued a goodly portion of his blood to head down south, leaving him light-headed. "Right." He exhaled hard. "The house…" He fought to get back on track, because he really wanted to have a conversation with her before his cock completely overrode his communication skills. "You kind of grew up there, didn't you?"

Danielle swirled her straw, making a spiral in the slush. "More-or-less, and Gram always promised she'd leave it to me when she died."

Ryan braced himself against the brick wall where he could keep an eye out for the hostess and still watch Dani. "She leave you a hundred grand for repairs?"

"Enough to get started." She gave him a too-bright smile, as if he'd insulted her but she was too polite to say anything.

Ryan raised his hands palms-out. "Sorry, that was dumb."

"No, it's okay." She shrugged, the graceful movement calling his attention to the curve of her breasts under her loose sweater.

He jerked his gaze away, but her raised eyebrow hinted she'd busted him.

"Maeve said you're into old houses, and you need to know I'll pay you for the work you do."

"Hell yeah. You hiring? I can hook you up with an electrician and all, guys who can do the stuff I can't."

She raised her glass. "As long as I leave you the fun parts?"

"Yep." He let his gaze slide over as many of her fun parts as he could see, gratified beyond belief at the rising color in her cheeks. "Just don't stay there 'til after the power's fixed."

Before she could flip him shit, the hostess interrupted them, and by the time they were settled at a dinner table, her good humor was back.

"Between the head-banging music and the Day of the Dead stuff, this place is making me homesick," she said. "It's got a very L.A. vibe."

Ryan leaned in closer. "You went down there for college, right?"

"Good memory." She broke a tortilla chip into tiny pieces. "UCLA for undergrad then Palo Alto for my Masters and a few post-grad classes."

Ryan kept his expression bland, wincing internally at the comparison with his hard-won Bellevue Community College associate's degree. But he wasn't insecure about much when it came to women. He knew how to flirt with pretty girls. He knew how to chat up smart girls.

The combination? Dani studied her cocktail and he studied her. That was one lesson he'd love to learn.

"L.A.'s a pretty cool place." Her voice trailed off and she went back to swirling her straw through what was left of her drink.

He wanted to keep her talking, but before he could come up with a good leading question, AC/DC faded into Metallica and the waiter arrived, his black-tattooed-cool fitting the scene down to his ironic head bob in time with the music.

"You should get chicken enchiladas." Ryan tapped Dani's menu. "They're the house specialty."

"Quesadilla, please."

"Chicken, pork, or carne asada?" the waiter asked.

"Carne asada … and extra guacamole."

Ryan scuffed a hand through his hair, ordered a burrito with a couple of tamales on the side, and switched out his empty margarita glass for the promise of a beer.

"Are you always into giving orders, or is it a new thing?" Danielle caught the tip of her tongue between her teeth, like she knew exactly how her flirty tone would get to him. "You tell me I can't stay in my own house, and then try to tell me what to get for dinner." Her grin veered toward naughty. "I thought the oldest child was the bossy one."

"Hey, wait a minute. Your electrical system is an explosion waiting to happen and the enchiladas here are awesome."

She covered her mouth with her napkin, but he could tell she was laughing.

"Besides," he said. "Niall's a cop, so he does kind of have the bossy angle covered."

"What's your excuse, then?"

"Dunno. Somebody had to stand up to Maeve." He hitched his shoulders in an apologetic half-shrug. "Niall's older and didn't care, and I swear Eamon's got the Asperger's."

"Yeah, Eamon always was a little odd. Maeve said he's working in some research lab now."

"Dude's a freak, and I can say that because I'm his brother." Ryan stuffed a chip in his mouth and rubbed stray salsa away with his knuckle. "And when we were kids, Joey didn't do much more than ride shotgun for me."

"I bet it helps you out at work. Your boss probably likes a take-charge guy."

He sputtered a laugh, because it was easier than thanking her for the compliment. The waiter brought Ryan his beer. True to her earlier prediction, Danielle didn't want more than one, and judging by her flushed cheeks, Ryan figured she knew what she was doing. "I work for a general contractor, but I do stuff on the side, too, and your grandmother's house would be awesome."

"Oh, the job's yours."

Score one for O'Connor. Ryan muzzled as much of his grin as possible. Not only would he get to work on an old house, he'd get to hang around Dani Jacobsen at the same time. He wiped his hand on his jeans and offered it to her. "Shake."

Her grip was stronger than he'd anticipated. He liked it. A lot.

* * * *

"I feel like an idiot," Danielle said, rubbing her cheek to get rid of the weird numbness that signified she'd reached her alcohol limit.

"You don't look like an idiot."

Ryan's smile had all kinds of things to say about how she looked, most of them R-rated.

Danielle hid behind her glass. "Because my uncle calls and says, 'the house is yours', and I turn around and tell my boss I'm coming up here."She slurped up the remains of her margarita and waved the waiter away. "I've put more thought into grocery lists."

Dinner better arrive soon, or she might segue from self-disclosure to maudlin. Before the airport shuttle dropped her off, Danielle imagined her grandmother's house would need a couple coats of paint and some new appliances. Nothing had prepared her for the level of deterioration she'd found. Or the guilt she'd felt. *Perhaps if Mom actually spoke to me, I'd have had a clue.*

"What do you want to do first?" she asked.

Ryan smirked into his cocktail.

"What?" Danielle said, half-hoping she hadn't misread his wicked dimple. "Where do we start?"

Ryan relaxed into his seat and crossed his arms, his biceps bulging in a most appealing way. She bet he'd be enjoyably rough in bed, forceful and strong and demanding. The combination of her imagination and the tequila made her lady parts melt.

She had no business thinking that way. *Maeve's brother. Maeve's brother. Maeve's brother. Maeve's brother. Don't touch.*

"Well, there's always…" He stopped himself and his mouth twisted. She hitched in her seat, hoping he was headed somewhere fun. Finally, he let go of a deep breath. "You need a functioning electrical panel and plumbing, along with a weather-tight roof."

Danielle guessed he'd been about to say something different, something dirtier, something that would totally displease his sister. Better to keep him on the subject of the house. She widened her eyes and nodded, encouraging him to go on. In either direction.

Fortunately for her libido, he kept to the house, lecturing her on safety until she yelped. "Yeah, yeah, I get it."

"You'll have your chance to play designer. First you need to know if the roof leaks."

She had so much catching up to do. "It hasn't rained since I've been here."

"Um, Seattle in November? It will."

Point to O'Connor. She lifted her hands, conceding defeat. A smart girl would just sign the checks. "You really are going to make me take care of all the boring stuff first."

"Have you thought about moving walls around to take advantage of the view?"

"No way." She played with her fork and hoped he couldn't see the calculations going on in her head. She'd lived with an architect and had an insider's view of how much time and money such repairs added to a project. "I've only got three months to get this place ready to sell—"

"Selling? I kinda figured you'd be moving in when the project was done."

"Nope. The unit will fall down if I'm gone for more than three months."

He leaned in on his elbows as if searching for the joke. "Unit?"

"Cedars-Sinai Neonatal I.C.U." She dropped into her professional persona. "Assistant Nurse Manager."

He rubbed his lips with the side of his thumb. "Your timeframe should work, and you can always leave someone in charge to finish up after you head back to L.A." He paused to examine his margarita. "Someone like me." His expression turned brighter. "At any rate, you're going to need a place to stay tonight."

"I'll call Maeve."

In a room full of people, all she could see was Ryan – his dimples, the hitch in the bridge of his nose, and the way his sideburns faded into a dark shadow suggesting he needed a shave. Braden, her ex-boyfriend, former live-in lover, and intermittent fiancé, was years older and several universes away. He had a quick wit and a good job, and most of their L.A. friends assumed she'd say 'yes' when he proposed.

He dumped her instead.

She'd had no warning, no sense that things were weird, and as a result she'd spent the last six months trying to figure out what the hell happened. Inside, she had a dead spot where Braden had been, one she hoped would just scar over and go away.

When she called Maeve, Danielle ducked her head and covered both ears to hear the phone. Maeve's voicemail picked up, but Danielle didn't leave a message. She'd turned down the invite to The Pig, and she couldn't really justify having dinner with Ryan instead. No message meant nothing for Maeve to question later.

"There's always Motel 6." Danielle made a half-hearted effort to stick to the high road.

"I've got a three-bedroom house and my housemate's out for the night."

The crowd noise surged, as if everyone was laughing at her for holding out. Her unabashed female nature was dying to jump right on Ryan's offer.

But there was Maeve.

And the nine-year age difference.

And the three-month time limit.

"What about your girlfriend?" Those other things were tiny hurdles compared with *Thou Shalt Not Mess With Another Woman's Man*.

Ryan's lips curled like he wanted to grin but just couldn't do it. "Broke up."

Tiny? Had she said tiny *hurdles?*

Danielle ran both hands over her head, smoothing her grubby ponytail. She was about to take a huge risk, and blood pounded through her tequila-warmed cheeks. "I really need a shower."

"I have one of those." One corner of his mouth lifted, showing a victory dimple.

"All right, but you have to *promise* me you won't ever tell your sister."

It must have been the tequila talking.

His dimples deepened. "Promise."

* * * *

Danielle parked her Mini on a gravel parking strip in front of a boxy split level. Ryan's big Ford truck was already in the driveway. She got out and pressed the key fob to lock the car, and gulped to slow her speeding heart.

Ryan climbed out of his truck and pocketed his cell phone. "C'mon. Chubb isn't home so we've got some privacy."

"Cool." Or nervous, depending on who was asking.

Ryan put his shoulder against the front door and gave it a shove. The entry was about six feet square, with a slate tile floor.

He hitched his head towards the downhill stairs. "Chubb's cave is there." He headed up, taking the stairs two at a time, and glanced back over his shoulder when he got to the top. "Be best if you stuck to the main floor."

Danielle made it to the top step but couldn't go any farther without bumping into Ryan. He had one hand on the railing and his other elbow cocked, and his sly grin dared her to pass.

"Guest room's down the hall, and the bathroom's next door." Ryan nodded off to the right.

She didn't move.

Neither did he.

"Um, are you going to charge me a toll?" *Because that didn't sound at all flirtatious.* Danielle screwed on a smile, though inside she was wincing. She was just there because she needed a place to crash, and hadn't meant to lead him on. *Seriously.*

He waited another long minute before answering. "Maybe you'll just owe me one."

He stepped aside, and Danielle slid past him into the hall. She opened the first door she came to, but the shabby comforter and pile of hand weights said "guy's room" so loud and clear she backed right out.

"Try again," he said. "It's next to the bathroom."

She found a room with an empty bookcase, an old desktop computer, and a futon bed. She dumped her bag on the futon and headed for the shower, wondering if she should lock the door or secretly hope he'd sneak in.

Half an hour later, Danielle's clean hair hung in a mostly-dry curtain down her back, and she'd shaved the important bits. She'd changed into clean jeans and a bulky knit sweater nearly the same shade of green as her eyes. With her I-can-smell-myself problem solved, she still needed to figure out the how-am-I-going-to-keep-my-hands-off-this-guy problem.

She paused in the kitchen doorway, fingers barely touching the wall, waiting for her fluttering nerves to settle. Ryan sat at the dining room table, a laptop in front of him. The décor was classic '90s Colonial-Rental style, which meant a blue and coral color scheme, lots of cabbage roses, and few accessories that hadn't come from the landlord. *As if twenty-something guys would ever hang copper pots on the wall.*

"Did you leave me any hot water?" he said without turning around.

"You didn't tell me I had a time limit."

"Nah, just messing with you." He kicked a chair in her direction. "Sit down."

A cat jumped up on the chair behind her as she sat, claiming the space before Danielle scooted all the way back. Apparently this was the cat's chair, although from the proprietary way he surveyed the kitchen, Danielle guessed it was all his. She perched on the edge of the seat, afraid of annoying the feline.

"You want anything else to drink?" Ryan tipped his beer in her direction.

She pressed her cheeks, testing for residual margarita buzz. "I'm okay."

He took a long pull on the bottle and closed the laptop. "I'm off work tomorrow. I could come by your grandmother's house in the daylight and take a better look."

The intensity in his eyes had her swallowing hard. "That'd be great."

"Do you want to watch a movie or something? TV's downstairs."

"Sure." But only if he picked something G-rated. Watching on-screen romance might just send her leaping into his lap.

"Throw Barnabas on the floor, babe. You look like you're going to fall off that chair."

The cat picked that moment to plant a paw on the small of Danielle's back. One claw went through her sweater and dug into her skin. She jumped to her feet, hands flying. "What the hell?"

Ryan jumped up too and swatted at Barnabas. "Git, cat."

Barnabas jumped, squalled, and sprinted across the room.

Danielle and Ryan ended up facing each other about arm's length apart.

"The cat..."

"My roommate's." His gaze intent, focused, he touched her sleeve.

The room heated up, or possibly her blood was boiling from the friction between them. Her field of vision narrowed to the late-day scruff framing his mouth, and the full curve of his lower lip.

He lowered his hand to hers, interlacing their fingers.

She didn't stop him. She curled her hand around his and her eyes slid half closed.

"C'mere." Ryan tugged, and instead of backing away, she rocked forward, drawn to him by physics or hormones or old-fashioned need.

"Damned cat hates me," she said, relishing his musky scent.

His free hand reached up strong and sure to cup her jaw. "Well, I like you," he whispered.

His kiss was gentle, testing the water, giving her space to push away. He tasted malty and masculine, a flavor that could very well become an addiction. He moved closer, and then both his hands wrapped around her waist and she stretched full against him.

All of her reasons for stopping ran through her head on a continuous loop: *Maeve and age and L.A. and Cherry, Maeve and age and L.A. and Cherry*. He drew back so their lips were barely touching, and the scent of him and the warmth of his breath and the melting heat at the core of her body scattered those reasons like a flock of startled birds.

They left her sweater on a dining room chair and his sweatshirt somewhere in the living room. In the hall, he reached for the lacy hem of her cotton tank top. She gripped his wrist before he could pull it off, too.

"Wait. No." He eased back and Danielle fell against the wall. "Sorry."

"'S'all right. I've wanted to kiss Dani Jacobsen since I was a kid." He flashed a dimple. "I'm already ahead of the game."

She covered her mouth with her hands, to hide both her surprise and her ridiculous smile. "No way."

"Way." He dove in for round two, nipping and nudging her hands until she moved them and he could reach her lips.

The kiss went on until she lost track of time, but he kept hold of her arms and shoulders and there was almost a Bible's worth of space between their bodies. Her rational mind appreciated his restraint. The rest of her wanted to claw his clothes off.

"You know how good you feel, right?" she said.

He worked his way down the side of her neck, his lips and tongue tasting, teasing, drawing out a gasp that was almost a whimper.

"About as good as you do," he murmured against her skin, gruff and sexy.

She pulled him up to look him in the eye. "No, I mean it. I want…"

More than just rebound sex.

"Me too," he said. He pulled her hand close to his mouth, dragging the bristles of his five o'clock shadow across the sensitive skin of her palm. She cupped her fingers to receive his kiss.

"But we really shouldn't."

"Because of Maeve."

She tapped his chest with her index finger. "Because I'm only in town for a couple months and I'm nine years older than you and…" She grabbed a breath, then plowed on. "And I need help with my house and if we have sex and end up hating each other it'll be awkward." *There's also Maeve and Braden, but who's keeping count?*

"Last time I checked I was above the age of consent, which means the only reason you're turning me down is a house." He stretched his hands along her ribs, pulling her closer.

His math wasn't any better than hers. "I've done stupider things." She slid her fingers under his to loosen his grip. "I just can't think of any right now."

* * * *

In hindsight she recognized the cliché: couples who know they've found the right person after talking all night. They had, and she knew.

They lay on his bed side by side, her head on his shoulder, his arm around her waist. Under the covers. Mostly dressed.

She told him things she didn't usually talk about, like how her mother had gone to San Francisco in 1978 and come home with a daughter named Danielle, how her grandmother had done more to raise her than anyone else, and how jealous she'd always been of Maeve's houseful of family.

She listened to his stories too, about his certificate in construction management, his goal to learn everything he could about home remodeling, then run his own company. About how lies and game-playing drove him crazy. And about Cherry. Way too much about Cherry.

"If you don't mind my saying so." Danielle interrupted a long-winded soliloquy. "You might have ended it, but something tells me you still need to let go."

He got real quiet. He pressed his lips against the top of her head, his exhale tickling a few strands of hair across her brow.

"I'll be right back," he said.

She followed his retreat with her gaze, wondering if her flash of insight had cut too deep. Either he'd gone to the bathroom or he was heading out to his truck, but she didn't hear the front door slam.

A few minutes later he came back, laughing to himself. "Princess, my balls are so blue I'ma be walking with a limp for a week."

"Shoulda taken a cold shower while you were out there."

He stood by the bed and stared down at her, his expression gentle. "Shoulda done a lot of things different."

He crawled back under the covers and she curled up next to him. They both drifted off, only to have the persistent buzz of Ryan's cell phone wake them up about fifteen minutes later.

"Huh?" Ryan said before Danielle even had her eyes open. "Shit. What time is it?"

Danielle propped herself up on one elbow. "What's going on?"

"Shh." He placed a finger over her lips and turned back to the phone. "Shut up, Maeve. None of your business if there's someone here."

After another short pause, he swiped the cell to disconnect the call, mumbling a variety of very dirty words. "Cherry got pretty hammered last night, and now she's on her way over to..." The groove between his brows undermined his weak smile. "I don't know what."

Panic shook off the muzzy sleepiness in Danielle's head. She scuttled around and got her knees under her, wishing she had something more substantial on than a flimsy cotton tee shirt. "Why? It's like six in the morning."

"Make that nine." He brushed her cheek with the back of his hand. "Guess we fell asleep."

The front door banged open, and footsteps pounded up the stairs.

"Christ." He swung his legs over the side of the bed.

"Ryan?" The voice was halfway between a screech and a yelp. "What the fuck? Whose Mini Cooper is parked out front?"

Danielle's only moving part was the heart slamming blood through her veins. She was about to meet the semi-ex-girlfriend in the most awkward way imaginable. Her muscles locked in a war between diving under the covers and diving out the window.

"Ryan!" Cherry was way too close to the bedroom.

Ryan jumped out of bed, tearing through the room in about two steps and slamming the door behind him.

"Get out of my house." Rage laced his tone like flames licking the surface of a dry pine branch. "Give me my fucking key and get out."

"You *do* have company." One of them hit the bedroom door. "Come on out, honey. Ryan's girlfriend wants to meet ya."

"Give me her sweater and leave, Cherry. I mean it."

"This sweater? What is it...Anthropologie? Good choice."

"Cherry." That one word was so dense, so heavy with anger, it dragged Danielle out of bed. He'd loaded Cherry's name with the impact of a blow, and for a crazy second Danielle was scared he'd follow it up with his fist.

"Fuck you, Ryan O'Connor."

Danielle gripped the doorjamb, white-tipped fingers digging into the wood.

"Just gimme the key and go."

Footsteps moved off, steady at first, then a stumble and a body thumping against the wall. "Ow, shit."

"Wait a minute." His voice blasted through the bedroom door and the handle turned.

"This is *not* over." Footsteps on the stairs. Sobbing. The front door banged shut.

Danielle backed up until her calves hit the bed and she sat down hard. What could you say after something like that? She didn't know whether to be embarrassed or relieved. A window escape started looking like the better alternative.

"Damn it. She's too drunk to drive." Heavy, rapid footsteps pounded down the stairs. "I'll be back, Dani."

The front door slammed shut a second time. Danielle stepped out of the bedroom. Her sweater lay on the carpet in a heap, alongside a house key.

More yelling came from the front yard. A car door slammed. An engine started, echoed by the heavier rumble of a Ford F250 truck.

It took about two minutes for Danielle to gather her things and get out the door. It took a lot longer than that for the shock to wear off.

Chapter Three

The weather finally caught up with the calendar, and Tuesday afternoon Ryan drove across town in a steady downpour. It was almost dark when he pulled his truck into Danielle's driveway. Under the glow of his headlights, her little car all but waggled its fingers at him. Sporty and flirty and fun, a Mini Cooper's driver would never be accused of taking themselves too seriously.

He slammed the truck's door. Chasing after Cherry hadn't given Dani much reason to take him seriously either. At least she still wanted him to work on the house. The light was on so Ryan knocked once, then let himself in.

The house smelled smoky and the hearth was all wet, ringed with a rolled up log of soggy towels. Dani sat at the big cherry wood dining table, wearing her parka and a pair of gloves, arms crossed, chin down, gaze directed at a diagram on her laptop screen. File folders and paper, pens, and an oversized calculator surrounded her.

"We just got the paging operators on board with the new language. We can't change it." A woman's voice came from the computer in a very cultured version of pissed off.

"But if the pediatricians can't figure out what you want them to do," a man said with a subtle Southern drawl, "they'll keep on missing deliveries."

The combination of a sharp exhale and a tiny shake of Dani's head pretty much defined frustration. Ryan rounded the other side of the table, catching her eye as he passed behind the laptop.

"Conference call," she mouthed.

Ryan jerked a thumb at the living room."What the hell happened here?" he said, barely above a whisper.

"Don't ask." She murmured in response.

"Did you have something to add, Danielle?"

Whoever the woman was, she sure had her bitch voice on, and Danielle straightened up like she'd been caught napping. "No, Sharon, I'm sorry, my ... uh ... contractor just came in."

"Oh good. Are you making progress, then?" Like flipping a switch, the woman came across as friendly and warm.

"So far so good. The electrician started this morning and the plumber comes next week."

Ryan traced the laptop's cord to a power strip, and from there to a ground adaptor connecting the power strip to the wall socket. Not a perfect set-up, but with a bit of luck, his buddy Dan would keep the electrical panel from catching fire.

"I'll be in the kitchen," he said.

She gave him a half-hearted wave and started writing on the clipboard in her lap.

In the kitchen, Ryan dumped his toolbox on the floor, pausing to watch Dani through the door. The floor lamp sent streaks of red-gold down her thick braid. The disembodied voices continued arguing about pediatricians and pagers, then moved on to an arcane discussion about a problem drawing blood from babies, a problem that was Dani's to fix.

She hunched over the laptop, jaw tight, tapping the pencil on the clipboard and scrawling notes. The discussion turned into a complicated negotiation around how much she was willing to do from Seattle. She had an obvious commitment to her job, and made it plain her stay in Seattle would be limited. Ryan inhaled deeply and rocked his shoulders back and forth to loosen them. Her calm, professional tone did more than anything else to highlight their differences. Why would a woman who argued with doctors date a guy who hammered nails for a living? More importantly, why would a woman who was in town for a limited time get involved with someone who was too stupid to untwist himself from his ex-girlfriend?

No reason in the world.

If ever a man needed to kick his own ass... He pulled a small spiral notebook out of his jacket pocket, along with a stubby, flat, carpenter's pencil and headed upstairs to look for leaks in the roof. It was better than bellyaching about what he couldn't have.

* * * *

"I promise, Sharon. I'll hit up the NICU here at UW and the one at Seattle Children's, and I'll get the girls' feedback on their poster presentation by early next week."

With that, Danielle finally shut down the conference call from hell. *Jesus.* The endless dickering over minutiae made her want to crawl out of her own skin. Setting up Wi-Fi might have been a tactical error.

A set of heavy footsteps crossed the floor above her and the ceiling whined in protest. "Shit. Ryan. " Sharon and Dr. Guidry had her wound so tight she'd forgotten he was there. Tossing the clipboard on a pile of papers, she headed upstairs.

He was stretched out tall, tugging at a corner of a ceiling tile marbled with brown stains. A couple of leather-wrapped tools hung from the belt around his waist, nicely framing the fit of his jeans over his...

No I am not *checking out his ass.*

The tile gave way in a shower of dusty gray yuck. "That's disgusting," she said.

He squinted at her over his shoulder. "Sorry, Princess. You should stay downstairs." Flecks of gray had landed in his sideburn, giving his smile an evil tilt. "It's gonna get dirty up here."

She stuck her fists on her hips and gave him a stern look to cover her embarrassment. Despite the drama of the other morning, she still wanted to get all kinds of dirty with him. "You have to reassemble anything you tear apart."

"Sure." He brushed himself off and scratched something on a small spiral notebook. "But first you need to talk to some roofers." He shoved the notebook back in his pocket. "There's no point in doing a bunch of work if we're just going to end up re-doing it because the roof's not solid."

Some of the starch melted out of her arms. "So much for slapping on a new coat of paint and calling it good." She stifled a sigh.

He didn't seem to know whether she was joking or not. "At any rate, I'm done up here, and I think I've got a pretty good idea about how things should go."

He brushed past her, a move that sent little burrs of excitement down to the palms of her hands.

"Are you coming?" he asked from halfway down the stairs.

"Pushy much?" She jogged down after him.

He grabbed one of the dining chairs and straddled it, a masculine move that sent the little burrs deeper into the core of her being. Good thing she still had her jacket on and she could stuff her hands in the pockets. Otherwise she might just snatch him up for some less constructive conversation.

"What's with the water all over the floor?" He nodded in the direction of the living room.

She plunked her butt on the edge of the table. "The oil tank and I had a slight difference of opinion, and I was cold so I bought one of those Presto-Logs, and the whole place filled up with smoke, so I dumped water on the log to put the fire out,"— she threw both hands in the air — "and that's how I figured out the chimney is blocked."

He clamped his lips together.

"Don't you dare laugh at me." She covered her mouth, not quite fast enough to hide the smirk.

He fake-coughed into his fist.

"I'm such a dork," she said.

"Nah." He got up, crouched down in front of the fireplace, and peered up into the chimney. "Can't see anything without my flashlight."

"Don't worry about it. I've got a chimney guy coming out Thursday, along with a furnace guy to clear out the vents." Danielle slid back down behind her laptop and brought up her schedule. "The oil truck will deliver in the morning, and by this time tomorrow I should be able to take my coat off."

"Awesome." He straightened up slowly. "You're an administrative genius."

She bit down hard on her lower lip to keep from kissing away his teasing smirk. She'd been sure they'd made a connection, at least until Cherry showed up. Since then, Danielle and Ryan had been careful, clinking off each other like crystal glasses in a paper bag. They might have relaxed enough to flirt, but nothing had changed. He still had to deal with Cherry, and she was still leaving, which was exactly why she should have kept her hands to herself in the first place. Wrong time. Wrong place. Wrong man.

"I was going to finish the patch on the floor tonight," he said.

Reluctantly, Danielle brought her focus back to the house. "That'd be great." She went into the kitchen to admire his work from the night before. "Can I run out and grab you some dinner?"

"Nah, I had a late lunch." He filled the dining room doorway, gripping the doorposts at shoulder level. His tee shirt stretched tight across his chest. "You don't have to stay. I'll finish patching the floor and knock off. Go keep my sister out of trouble."

"Yeah, she's already been after me about going out to dinner."

"Bet you'll be doing that a lot." His smile said he knew as much about his sister as Danielle did.

"But she's letting me stay at her apartment, so it's all good." Hanging with Maeve might keep her up late at night, but then, her life had turned sideways anyway. Braden gone, L.A. on hold, and Ryan...

What was a little sleep deprivation between friends?

* * * *

The next morning, Danielle left Maeve's apartment after the worst of the morning rush hour. Swaths of grey clouds hung over the trees on Perkins Lane, with only the occasional streak of silver or black to give them definition. The house seemed to be sulking behind its laurel hedge, although Danielle couldn't tell if it was the sodden weather or something else bothering it. She let herself in the front door, loaded down with a fresh stock of cleaning supplies. A steady drip-drip-drip greeted her before she hit the living room.

Shit.

She dumped her bags on the dining room table. The wall between the dining room and the kitchen was darker than normal, though it took a moment for her to understand why. The two inches of water covering the kitchen floor was a more obvious clue, along with the beads of moisture making a line across the ceiling before splashing down. She stalled, barely aware of the puddle of water spreading out across the dining room floor. A chunk of plaster from the kitchen ceiling let loose, plunking right in front of her feet.

She grabbed her cell phone and sent Maeve a text.
Help! Need towels!!!

Taking another couple steps into the kitchen, she tried to grasp the scope of the situation. This was bad, but not life-threatening. The part of her brain that managed patients in the N.I.C.U. kicked in and the request for towels became a footnote. Time to triage. Grab the broom, open the back door, and encourage the water to go someplace else. The broom was in the mudroom, the closet-sized space between the kitchen and the back deck.

Oh. Wait. Start by finding the source of the leak. Must be upstairs.

As she squelched back through the living room, her soaking wet feet plus the cold, raw weather and no heat in the house created a new problem. The shivering started just as her phone buzzed.

Emergency towels? WTH?

Maeve's voice came straight through the text, and Danielle paused halfway up the stairs to message her back, hysterical giggles forcing their way through the shivers.

Plumbing crisis. Water everywhere.

At the top of the stairs, she got a reply.

Work is lame. B rght thr.

Either Maeve's graphic design skills were legendary or her boss was easygoing. Didn't really matter. Danielle grinned, her teeth chattering, her lips stiff with cold.

Thanks. Dry clothes 2. N sox. Plz n thnx.

The stairs to the second floor started in the foyer and ended at a broad landing leading to three bedrooms and a bathroom. The bathroom sat across from the top stair, right above the kitchen. Squishing with every step, Danielle crossed the landing and opened the bathroom door.

Everything looked fine. Only when she got down on her knees could she see water surrounding the base of the toilet like a thin layer of clear caulk. It was an old-fashioned set-up, with pipes running behind the stool along the wall. Matching handles interrupted the pipes several inches above the floor.

"Righty tighty, lefty loosey," Danielle muttered, twisting both handles to the right. From below another chunk of ceiling splashed down on the floor.

"Dammit."

Shivers came from the pit of her stomach and rattled their way out. If she kept moving, it wasn't too bad, although she had to blink back tears when Maeve's car pulled into her driveway. By then, most of the dripping had stopped and she'd swept much of the water out the back door.

"What the hell happened?" Maeve blew through the door, her arms loaded with paper shopping bags.

Danielle met her in the living room. "There must be a broken pipe upstairs."

The O'Connors all looked alike, and Maeve had the lighter, feminine versions of Ryan's blue eyes, snub nose, and smile. Her hair was darker, straighter, and cut short, framing her face in angles and spikes and playing up her baby blues. She dropped her packages in the general vicinity of the wing chair and wrapped her arms around Danielle. "Oh my gosh, girlfriend. You're freezing."

A hug from Maeve was more of an angular squeeze than a comforting cuddle, but right then anything felt good. "The heater won't come on. I don't think there's oil."

"There are dry clothes in here." Maeve shoved one of the paper bags into Danielle's arms and grabbed the broom. "You go change, and I'll … um … go see what…"

Danielle didn't wait for her to finish. Maeve didn't have the D-I-Y gene, and likely wouldn't do much until Danielle got back. If Maeve had really planned on helping, she'd have changed out of the tall heels, borderline-too-short skirt, and silk blouse she'd worn to work.

Danielle was in much better shape when she headed back downstairs, happy her friend had packed jeans, a sweater, thick wool socks, and a pair of rubber boots. She found Maeve in the dining room, tapping away on her smart phone.

"I appreciate this," Danielle said.

"Eh, my boss didn't want me at this afternoon's meeting any more than I wanted to be there." Maeve winked. "I always manage to stir up trouble." Her bright eyes were more like the sky in August than the current grey November shroud. "Did you call my brother?"

Danielle looked away, hoping Maeve wouldn't notice if she blushed. "Ryan? Yeah, um, he came over and patched the floor."

"No, I mean this morning."

"Why?"

"To help you with," — Maeve stood and waved her arms around — "this." Another wet splat came from the kitchen. She lifted up one foot, displaying the red sole. "These shoes weren't built for clean-up."

Maeve stalked into the living room, the heels in question snapping on the hard-woods. She tapped a number on her cell phone before Danielle could protest.

"How's things, bro?" She spun back toward Danielle with a smirk on her face. "Yeah, well, I'm at Danielle's house, and there's a bit of a plumbing disaster going on. Can you help?"

Maeve paused to listen, then held the phone out. "He wants to talk to the princess."

Danielle took a deep breath as she put the phone to her ear, wincing as Maeve's scathing echo turned the word into a question.

"'S'up?" Ryan's easy baritone took the edge off her chill.

"The patch you put in the kitchen floor is clean." *Sort of.*

Ryan snorted into the phone. "Worse things could happen."

"Actually, I think there's something broken under the toilet upstairs. I've shut the water off, and swept most of the standing water out back, but the kitchen ceiling is toast, and some of the walls are … lumpy."

"Lumpy," he echoed. "Awesome."

"And shit's falling from the ceiling." Maeve's comment was accompanied by another splash from the kitchen.

Ryan laughed as if he'd heard her. "Well, the rules say you can't do a remodel without at least one plumbing blow-up."

"I can check it off the list, then." Danielle sighed, using her free hand to scrape the hair away from her face.

"I'm thinking I'll clean up what I can and pull down the soggiest bits, and if you can come over after work—"

"Tell you what. I'll jet over on my lunch break. I'll have a better idea of what I'll need to fix if I see it first."

"You will? Thanks." Somehow that warmed her up almost as much as the wool socks Maeve brought.

"No worries, Dani. I'll see you in a while."

Danielle passed Maeve her phone, carefully keeping her face blank.

"Princess?" Maeve said, her expression flopping between surprise and confusion, her eyebrows bunching together under her spiked bangs. "You two must have really bonded."

"Yeah, he's the little brother I never had." Danielle shrugged and headed back into the kitchen, hoping her tone was sarcastic enough, the rough edges of a rock and a hard place hemming her in.

* * * *

On Friday, Danielle met Maeve at Cutters, the restaurant next door to her office building. Maeve had big plans for the evening, and Danielle figured prominently as the designated driver. Since she'd be claiming Maeve's car keys, Danielle took the bus downtown. She blew into Cutters on a blast of November wind, soggy, chilled, and cranky. Maeve was tucked into a table near the gas fireplace, her tailored wool dress cut short enough to show off a pair of glossy riding boots.

Rain coated the windows, limiting the view of Lake Union. "Thank you for respecting my L.A. constitution." Danielle dropped into a chair, happy to be sitting close to the fire. She'd chosen one of her warmest outfits, a pair of wool slacks and a cashmere sweater, with a sage pashmina scarf draped around her shoulders. In addition to an added layer of warmth, the scarf played up the dark hazel color of her eyes.

"Hope you still thank me after you have a sip of the cocktail I ordered for you."Maeve tapped a long-stemmed Cosmo glass brim-full of a shimmering clear liquid with a single dollop of pink in the bottom.

Danielle twisted the scarf closer around her neck and stared out into the cold, wet, dark. "This is the Angel's Tears thing you texted me about?"

"Yep."

"It better be good, because I'm not having seconds."

They clinked their glasses, each sending a small wave of liquid over the edge.

"You didn't used to be such a lightweight," Maeve said.

"Braden didn't drink." Danielle took a tiny sip. "I got out of the habit." She hadn't thought much about Braden all week, and his name was like an awkward and half-remembered word she hadn't used since high school French class. She poked at the dead spot a little, but it stayed dead. "I just need some practice."

"That's what I like about you, Dani. Always ready to take one for the team."

They toasted again, the crisp liquor making its giddy way through Danielle's head.

"So is that how you did it?" Maeve asked.

Danielle hesitated to answer Maeve's left-field question. "What?"

"I swear you wear the same size you did in high school." Maeve grinned over the top of her Cosmo glass. "All those years of good behavior kept you skinny."

Danielle snorted into her cocktail. "Sweetie, my bra's a bit smaller and my jeans are the next size up." As if gravity had redistributed things according to some contorted plan. Her body wasn't bad, but she was definitely on the plus side of thirty. She'd been tortured with anxiety in her teens and twenties, but at thirty-three, she finally felt good about herself.

But would a twenty-four year old notice the whole gravity thing? Danielle swallowed enough vodka to drive the question – and any other thoughts about a certain twenty-four year old – right out of her mind. Tonight was about Maeve and girl talk and catching up.

Not Ryan.

"Well, you look pretty hot to me, but Cherry's meeting us later, and she's the professional," Maeve said.

Danielle's belly lurched like the floor had dropped several inches. "What?"

"I told you she works at Nordstrom's, so she always knows what looks good." Maeve flicked a strand of Danielle's hair away from her face. "We hang out together a lot."

Danielle must not have been paying attention when Maeve mentioned Cherry during one of their long-distance catch-up phone calls. "Really?" *Because that won't be at all awkward.*

"Well, she was always around. She and Ryan dated for, like, ten years, you know? We've been hanging out since everyone my age got married and started having babies." Maeve gave her a wide-eyed grin, obviously expecting her to agree. "She's going to be my sister-in-law one day, but oh my God, is she ever furious at Ryan."

The conversation left Danielle floundering. *Sister-in-law?* "He isn't too happy with her, either."

"Oh, and you're the expert on all things Ryan now, right *Princess*?" Maeve asked.

"Hello? I left him at my grandmother's house pulling down the picture-rail molding." Danielle took another sip of her cocktail, scrambling away from the thin ice they'd slid onto. "I didn't ask, exactly, but the subject came up."

Maeve's eyes fired up with curiosity. "Did he tell you the woman's name?"

Caught up in a visual of Ryan stripped down to a thin tee shirt and jeans, it took Danielle a moment to respond.

Maeve waved her hand in front of Danielle's face. "Do you know who she is?"

Danielle blinked and brushed Maeve's hand away, guilt washing heat through her cheeks. "Who?"

"The woman he slept with last weekend."

"Um…" Danielle grabbed her cocktail and gulped some down, sending herself into a fit of wheezy coughing. "Don't know." She prayed Maeve would fall her for performance. *Thank God Cherry never opened the bedroom door.*

"I mean," Maeve said, paying more attention to the liquor in her glass than to Danielle, "a guy's gonna do what a guy's gonna do, you know? But he and Cherry are *so* perfect together."

"Didn't he break up with her?"

Maeve downed the rest of her drink and waved at the waiter. "My brother's a nice guy, but he wouldn't know a good thing if it bit him in the ass."

Danielle choked back a laugh at the disconnect between the man she'd been working with and his sister's description of him. "I'm sure they'll work it out."

"Yeah, he just needs to do the wild thing a couple times and then he'll settle down." Maeve grinned in a spot-on imitation of the Cheshire Cat. "Anyway, they were supposed to get together to try to work things out last night. I wonder how it went."

Really? A cell phone's buzz distracted both of them from the conversation. It was Cherry calling, which gave Danielle another moment to wonder why a guy she'd known for a week had her in such a swivet, when apparently all his talk was just bubbles and wishful thinking.

Braden might have left her with a dead spot, but Ryan was starting to piss her off.

Chapter Four

Ryan parked his big truck in front of 24 Hour Fitness ten minutes earlier than he promised to meet Chubb. He turned the engine off, keeping the key cocked to listen to the stereo. Stevie Ray Vaughn's guitar cried like the sky, which just about fit his mood.

The parking lot was nearly half full. Pretty good for a Saturday morning. A woman in a pink sweatshirt and grey leggings got out of the Prius next to him. She walked past the front of his truck, talking on her cell phone. Chubb would probably think she was cute. Ryan didn't like her. Didn't dislike her, either. He followed her progress as she cut through the parked cars, his truck's engine ticking as it cooled off. He didn't shake off his stupor until she disappeared into the gym. He'd put off checking his phone messages as long as possible.

They were all from the same number.

Cherry's.

If he played back her messages now, he'd have an hour in the weight room to burn off frustration. He swiped the phone, tapping the voicemail button.

Hey, babe, it's me. I'm headed out with your big sis and her friend. Come find us.

He erased the message.

Ry-an. You're avoiding me. I totally get that, I do. I just think if we sat down and talked things through, we could work it out. We're headed for the Pig. Call me.

"We could talk for a week and not work things out, Cherry. Sorry."

Hey, you know I'm really sorry I got crazy at your house the other day. Call me.

By now her vowels were stretching, her consonants getting softer.

Drunk.

He listened to the rest of the messages, each one more rambling, the words slurring into incoherence. His morning coffee curdled under a surge of disgust, pity, and pain, and he had to work hard to keep the whole thing from building into rage.

Everyone thought he'd broken up with her on a whim. In truth, he'd done his homework. He'd read books about alcoholism, and talked with a guy at Al-Anon. He and Cherry had been together since high school, and he'd been up close and personal for her slide into chaos. Sometimes he wondered how long it had been since they'd been in love, rather than bonded by guilt, desire, and manipulation. In the past he'd tried to just walk away, but she'd always dragged him back. This time he'd been very clear: get help or I'm gone.

She refused.

He left.

Tough love, for both of them. Taking care of Cherry Kinney was a damned hard habit to break. As a reward for his trouble, she was the one who got to spend the evening with Dani. God had a sick sense of humor.

With a deliberate effort, he found something else to focus on. He pictured Dani – or Danielle, as Maeve called her – lying in his bed, her silky red hair spread across the pillow and his beat-up old quilt not quite covering her breasts. *Damn, she was hot.* The quick visual sent a different kind of energy surging through him, giving him another helping of frustration to work off in the weight room.

Several sharp taps on his driver's side window brought him back to reality. Chubb stood outside, his eyes puffed with sleep and his dreads pulled up in a messy topknot. Tony Saunders, nicknamed Chubb for no good reason, had a pretty heavy World of Warcraft addiction, and from the look of him, he'd been up most the night, glued to a computer screen.

Either that or some girl was about to have her heart broken.

Ryan popped the lock and got out. "Dude."

"Dude."

"Barnabas missed you." Ryan only allowed the cat to move in because he and Chubb were already friends before they became roommates.

"Jeremy and I went out for a few beers and got stuck in his play room."

Ryan hid a snicker behind his fist. "Good thing I know you both or I might get ideas."

"Fuck you." Chubb headed into the lobby, with Ryan right behind him. Standing side-by-side at the front counter, Chubb elbowed Ryan. "Heard from Cherry?"

Ryan slapped the pen down on the clipboard, clenching his teeth to keep from saying something rude. "She left messages."

"Ran into her at the Pig last night. She was pretty wasted."

Ryan walked away, headed for the locker room. Not his problem. He hadn't forced her to drink, and he couldn't make her stop. Some days he had to repeat that to himself many, many times.

Chubb caught up to him and put a hand on his shoulder. "I'm pretty sure some friend of Maeve's drove her home."

Awesome. She sucked Dani into her shit. He tossed his leather jacket and shower kit in the locker and flipped the door shut, sorry the gym didn't have a punching bag. "I'm going to hit the treadmill for a while."

"Yeah, man, I'll see you out there."

* * * *

It was almost five on Tuesday afternoon and Danielle had reached the Pinterest stage. Despite having oil for the heater, Gram's living room held a chill from the raw November wind, and the sun had been down for a good half hour. All day long she'd had to balance working on NICU crap with periodic rewards in the form of sandpaper and elbow grease. The living room wainscoting needed the help, and she got to indulge her remodeling urges. Now, curled up in the wing chair with a fleece blanket around her knees, she didn't feel guilty about fishing for a little inspiration.

Surrounded by salt sea air and the soft slurp of the waves down on the beach, she was deep in an online dream when a pair of headlights swung across her front lawn. Ryan. Her belly quaked from the swift kick of adrenaline.

Danielle wasn't stupid enough to claim she hadn't been waiting for him. Her scientific side correctly identified her rapid heartbeat, fluttery stomach, and dry mouth as visceral responses, outside of her control. The only thing she could control was her behavior.

Memories of a Friday night spent listening to Cherry ramble on about a big reunion did little to squash the excitement frothing under Danielle's ribs. Even though she suspected Cherry was mostly kidding herself, Danielle could almost sympathize. After all, she'd spent a ton of energy convincing herself things with Braden were fine, right up until the moment he left. He'd wiped her so flat she still hadn't caught up. She looked toward the door for a moment, then back at the laptop. Ryan had the spare key. He could let himself in.

Right about the time she started to wonder what was keeping him, a clattering crash followed by muffled curses broke up the evening peace. She jumped up and popped out the front door. Ryan was on the porch, bent at the waist and clutching his right shoulder. The porch light had burned out, and the only light came through the living room window. A stack of two by six sticks of lumber were fanned out across the front steps like a deck of cards spread for someone to cut.

"Are you okay?" *Stupid question, Danielle.* "I mean, what happened?"

Ryan tipped his face up, one eyebrow raised. "Missed my step."

"Come in the house." She went to his good side and helped him straighten up. He shook her off and strode through the door, holding his right arm close to his body.

"I just wrenched it good. It'll be okay," he said, flexing and extending the fingers on his right hand.

"Let me help you take your jacket off." Danielle kept her voice low and calm, without leaving room for argument. If he could move his arm, nothing was broken, though the tension in his brow and the set of his jaw suggested he was in a fair amount of pain. She flipped the fleece blanket off the wing chair. "Sit." She eased him out of his coat. "Let's put some ice on it."

He tried to lift his arm. It reached shoulder height when a muttered "shit" ended the attempt. "There's a cold pack in the first aid kit in the truck," he said. "Here are the keys."

By the time she got back with the ice pack, Ryan had pulled off his sweatshirt and was down to a faded blue tee with a Mariner's logo on the back. He stood facing the fireplace, tugging the neckline down and turning his head as far as possible so he could look over his shoulder at the injury.

"Take your shirt off," she said. "I want to make sure you're not bleeding." *And that's the only reason.* She gestured at him to return to the chair and helped him ease the tee over his head, rolling her eyes to the ceiling when she couldn't keep from staring at the definition in his deltoids. A deep pink, fist-sized scuff marked the downhill side of his shoulder, with tiny beads of blood forming along the far edge and a deep purple blotch at the center.

He tried to lift his arm again and cursed, though this time he raised it above his ear. "Give me the cold pack."

She passed it to him and he slapped it over the bruise, hissing when it hit his skin. His combination of physical beauty and vulnerability tagged her like a punch to the gut. She popped her palm against her thigh, as if the gesture could absorb his pain or shake loose her guilt for letting the stupid porch light burn out, or diffuse her regret for not getting up off her ass to open the door.

"You didn't have to set a trap to get me to take my shirt off," he said, with the hint of a chuckle in his voice.

"What?"

"Don't deny it." He shifted the cold pack a little, his grin turning sly.

Must be feeling better if he's teasing me. She crossed her arms, covering her internal kerfuffle with an apologetic smile, doing her best to conceal how the naughty tone of his voice made her mouth water. "I need to get that porch light fixed."

"Tell your contractor."

"Um…" She accidently let her eyes drift across his chest. *Trouble.* She half-lifted her hand to run her fingertips through his scattering of dark chest hair, nearly giving in to an impulse that hit her quicker than thought.

Broad and buffed, his abdominal muscles formed perfect bricks, and his biceps swelled dangerously. A quick glance at his eyes showed her he knew exactly what was going on in her head. That quick glance lengthened.

Don't do this.

Every thought in her head had to be running across her face, and there was no way she could afford to let him see. She ducked, covered her mouth with a palm, and cleared her throat. "You should put your shirt back on. It's cold in here."

His gaze traveled over her slow and easy, like he could have stood there all night. "That's right, Princess. Show's over."

She should have been annoyed that he'd aimed his words in the direction of her breasts, but she really wanted to help him. *Don't lie.* Really, she wanted to rub up on him until she coated his body like a sugar glaze. She didn't trust herself to get close, so she planted her feet and gazed at the ratty upholstery covering the wing chair.

"Gimme a hand here?" He pinned the corner of the ice pack in place with his chin and tried to shake out his shirt.

"Oh. Yeah." Her mouth spasmed into a hyper-wide grin. She crossed the room, and he rocked his head in the direction of the icepack, wordlessly asking her to hold it in place.He worked his injured arm through the sleeve and when he reached up to claim the pack, his hand covered hers.

For a moment she couldn't move, held in place by the buzz of electricity where they touched. Instead of snatching her hand back to safety, she slowly slid farther up, resting her fingertips along his hairline. He smelled a little like sawdust, a little like smoke, a little like a guy who'd been working hard, and a lot like raw masculinity.

Tension buzzed, hummed, and sizzled around them. Her mouth opened, as if she'd be able to taste him despite the distance from her tongue to his skin. The tendons running up the back of his neck were tough as rawhide. This was where her rational mind should evaluate the facts and say, "*Don't, Danielle. Don't.*"

The rest of her wasn't much listening to rationality.

She dropped into work mode because it was safer than relationship mode. Like a good nurse, she pressed her thumbs along the bands of stress, careful to avoid the injured shoulder. He slouched forward with a soft sigh, giving her better access. "Tight," she muttered.

"Been a long couple days."

"Want to talk about it?"

"The usual."

She bent her elbows to get more force behind her knuckles as she ran them up and into his dark curls. He felt so good it brought a flash of tears to her eyes. "I hope this job isn't adding to it."

"This job," he said, letting his head hang propped against the palms of his hands, his voice a sexy rumble, "is the only thing keeping me sane right now."

All kinds of responses skittered through her mind, but instead of choosing one, she scooped up a handful of curls at the nape of his neck, intending to focus on the cords of muscle running along the tops of his shoulders. He had a tattoo right under his hairline, behind his ear.

A bunch of cherries tied with a black ribbon.

Danielle touched it, running her fingertip along the ribbon. Ryan rocked forward, hard, and shook his head, covering the mark. *What the hell?* She stifled a burst of semi-hysterical giggles, rubbing her cheeks and pressing her mouth shut. At least he didn't have Cherry's name on his ass. She hoped.

Before either of them found the right words to break through the awkwardness, they heard someone stumble on the front porch. She backed away, mumbling about the door.

She opened it to find Uncle Jonathan standing with his feet placed carefully between the two-by-six boards still spread across the steps. He was about sixty and nearly as tall as Ryan, with a broad-boned face and a fringe of graying ginger hair. An unbuttoned black wool overcoat covered his pin-striped business suit. "You need to replace your porch lightbulb, Dani, especially if you're going to leave booby-traps like this."

"Oh my God, I'm so sorry." She held out her hand to help her uncle step over the lumber. "Ryan hurt himself carrying the boards in, and I forgot the mess out here."

Ryan was up and stretching out his injured shoulder when she turned back to him. He had pretty good range of motion, but would likely have a fabulous bruise very soon. Crisis averted … or at least deferred.

Uncle Jonathan came in farther, his heavy coat draped casually over his forearm. "Looks like you dove right in," he said, nodding his approval as he looked around. "This is tremendous."

"Well, you gave me the key." Danielle laughed. Uncle Jonathan was the good uncle, the only one from her mother's family who smiled as if he liked her. Uncle Eric had last been seen in Vegas dropping bills on a blackjack table. In Danielle's childish memory, he was loud and rude and made her cry.

Her mother was the easiest to get along with. They just didn't speak. Danielle had always wanted a warm, tough, loving presence like Maeve's mom. In contrast, her mother had eased the crushing burden of childrearing by traveling to Europe.

Alone.

Not that Danielle was bitter or anything.

If not for her grandmother, her rock of stability, Danielle would have been a very lonely girl.

"Did you want something to drink?" Danielle asked. "I've got a bottle of lemon-lime seltzer."

"And beer," Ryan said, making her uncle laugh.

"You are definitely Patricia's daughter." Uncle Jonathan put his free arm around Danielle's shoulders, drawing her in with his unusual cologne. "I'm good. Just here for the tour."

"Ryan's been doing most of the heavy lifting." Danielle slipped away from him and clasped her hands behind her back, holding onto a tactile sense of Ryan's skin.

"Literally," Ryan said, still gently shaking out his right arm.

"Well, show me around," Uncle Jonathan said, his coat folded over his arm. "I want to hear all about your plans for Mother's house."

The tour didn't take long. Her uncle inspected the patch on the kitchen floor. He liked Danielle's dream appliances and her idea to redo the bathroom using white subway tile. He thoroughly approved of the plan to refinish all the wood trim so it matched. The combination of speaking her dreams aloud and her uncle's enthusiastic support hit Danielle like champagne on an empty stomach — light, bubbly, and a bit giddy. Despite her effervescent state, she caught a deeper hum. Her emotional connection to the house was stronger than she'd ever realized.

Throughout the tour, Ryan followed behind, his arms crossed and his mouth shut except for a couple times when her uncle's questions got more technical than Danielle could answer. Twice their eyes met, held,

Ryan's expression a perfect balance of desire and restraint. She couldn't imagine what her face gave away.

When they returned to the living room, Uncle Jonathan offered Ryan his hand.

"This is a great house, and I'm real happy to have the chance to work on it," Ryan said. They shook, two men taking each other's measure through a clasp of hands.

"I'm just glad to see Danielle has someone helping her who cares about the place as much as she does." Uncle Jonathan looked Ryan right in the eye as he spoke. "You're not the kind of mealy-mouthed shyster she usually goes for. I like that."

"Uncle Jonathan." Danielle's cheeks blazed and she waved her hands, batting away his implication. "He's working here. We're not dating."

"Oh, right." Uncle Jonathan winked broadly, including both of them in the joke. "Well in case you ever change your mind, I approve."

Danielle dove behind her SoCal Barbie persona and opened the door, her real self swallowing a huge gulp of embarrassment. "Thanks for coming by. I'm glad you like the progress we're making."

"Oh, wait, I almost forgot the reason I came over in the first place." Jonathan shifted his shoulders to settle the overcoat in place. "Your mother called. She didn't realize you were in Seattle."

Oh shit. "I was going to surprise her."

"Oh, she was surprised all right." Her uncle paused in the doorway, his affable expression shading into something more critical. "Remember, kiddo, Patricia was pretty annoyed Mother left you the house," he said, tapping the air in her general direction. "Avoiding her is a ticket to hostility."

But talking to her made hostility inevitable.
Danielle funneled her anxiety into laughter and patted her uncle's shoulder. "Well for sure I don't want her any more irate than necessary."

"Call her." He brushed a kiss on Danielle's forehead and, after one more sharp look, headed out.

Closing the door on her uncle, Danielle turned to find Ryan standing much closer than he had been before.

"Dude." She put a hand on his chest, shifting him back a couple inches. Not because she wanted to, but because the cherries tattooed behind his ear said she had to, and she'd promised herself she'd do the right thing. Even if it sucked. "Let me help you bring those boards in."

"Right." He flipped the ice pack from one hand to the other. "Why'd your grandmother leave you the house?"

"Because I'm cute." She scraped back a stray hank of hair, her smile as blank as she could make it. Danielle suspected her grandmother had left her the house because it had always been her safe place, but Ryan didn't need a rehash of her poor-little-rich-girl saga.

His eyes still held a question, but after a moment he nodded and stepped farther back. "Let's get those boards."

"Cool."

They carried in the two-by-sixes, silence buffering their actions. Over the weekend, Ryan had widened the doorways on either end of the dining room, though the rough edges needed to be enclosed in trim. Once they carried in all the supplies, Ryan stroked the molding she'd sanded. "Nice work with these." A half grin showed off his dimples. "This place is going to be sweet when we get it done."

"I'll take your word for it." She went over to the kitchen sink, looking out over the old wooden porch to the Sound. A single light moved across the blackness. "Was it hard to open up the doorways?"

"Just had to work around the king studs."

I bet I could work around your king stud just fine. "The what?" Danielle broke out a super-plastic smile, hoping Ryan couldn't guess what was on her mind.

"The extra support beams framing the doors and windows." He glanced at her, doing a quick double-take. "What?"

She dredged up willpower from some deep internal source, in need of every shred to keep pretending he was just a remodeling buddy. "Nothing."

"The homeowner's always right." He chuckled and headed back into the living room. "If you're happy with my work, next summer you can hire me to rebuild that nasty old porch out back."

Danielle's feet stuck as she got a sudden visual of Ryan, shirtless and sweaty, working in her backyard under the sun. By the time she could move again, he had his jacket on and was headed for the front door.

"Well, thanks for dropping stuff off," she said.

"Need more ice on my shoulder." He paused with his hand on the doorframe, assessing her with that perfectly controlled heat, an expression way too grown up for only twenty-four. "I'll swing by tomorrow and work on the trim."

Her fluttery response demonstrated all the maturity of a teenager.

"Oh, and while I'm thinking about it, Mom said to make sure you know you're welcome to join us for Thanksgiving dinner," he said.

Since she couldn't hug Ryan, Danielle hugged herself. "Really? That'd be awesome."

"Maeve didn't mention it, did she?"

"No, but it's not the night before." She laughed, because Maeve had always sucked at planning things in advance. Her laugh made Ryan laugh, and then things were better.

Almost.

Chapter Five

"Question … are they paying you for all the work you're doing?" Maeve rocked back in her chair, eyes sleepy, last night's mascara making a shadow under her lower lids.

Danielle sat at the cute Ikea table in Maeve's tiny dining room, actually a corner of her slightly-bigger living room. Maeve had talked her into doing the designated driver thing for what turned into a late night at the Pig, and Danielle felt stale; leftover instead of hung-over. To fight it, she'd made a wake-up run to Starbucks for breakfast treats, unaware they'd booby-trapped the scones with evil fruit. She picked currants out of hers, ignoring Maeve. Her only defensive hope lay in offense. "Are you taking today off?"

"You didn't answer my question." Maeve scooped up the growing pile of currants from the woven placemat in front of Danielle.

Damn. Maeve wasn't going to give it up. "You didn't answer mine."

"Yes I'm going to work, but most of my clients already took off for Thanksgiving." Maeve's smile morphed into something between cockiness and victory. "There's no rush." She mashed the currants into her scone. "Your turn."

Danielle broke off another bit of scone and examined it carefully for the little squishy mini-raisins she hated. The silence got long enough that she started to feel silly for dodging. "I'm salaried."

Maeve snorted through her bite of scone. "Is this a paid leave?"

"The work needs to get done." Danielle sipped some coffee, still looking for a way to get out of the conversation. "I can pay my half of the rent, if that's what you're worried about."

That earned Danielle an indignant scowl. "Yeah, ya freeloader. That's totally what I'm worried about." Maeve picked up some crumbs from her woven placemat with long, taupe-painted fingernails. "If it's an unpaid leave, where do they get off loading all this work on you?"

Danielle scratched her hairline at the back of her neck. If she excused herself to take a shower, she could totally get out of this. "It's not that much really."

"Bullshit." Maeve tapped the table like an egg timer, turning up the tension. "You didn't have to come up here. You could have hired someone to work on the house, which tells me you wanted to leave." Maeve's gaze nailed her good. "Which makes me wonder why you're working for free."

Trust a true friend to ask the million-dollar question. Danielle fooled with her placemat's fringy edges for another minute, while Maeve smiled and tapped and layered on the pressure. If Danielle was a true friend, she'd answer honestly, even if it meant picking at the dead spot where Braden had once been. "It's a combination of professional responsibility, brownnosing, and..." *Nut up, girl. You can do this.* "I couldn't stay one more night in the condo."

"Why?"

"Braden's such a dick." Tears slipped through the words. The dead spot cracked, setting off a blast of sorrow and loss.

"Ah..." Maeve steepled her long nails. "I wondered when we'd get around to the 'B' word."

Maeve's restrained sympathy gave Danielle a buoy to hold onto, stabilizing her. She rubbed her knuckles along the corners of her eyes, wiping away the tears. "It's not like I'm feeling sorry for myself or anything. I mean, women get dumped every day."

"Still sucks." Maeve said.

"It's okay." Danielle used the physical act of clearing her throat to drag the cover of the dead spot back into place. "He's down there, I'm up here and I've got some time to figure out what it is I want to do." Her words pinged against a layer of denial. "About the condo, I mean."

"I know what I want to do." Maeve wrinkled her nose, as if her memory of Braden smelled bad. "I want to cut off his balls for the trophy case."

Danielle had to laugh at that. "You and me both."

"So what did he do, exactly?"

Danielle shrugged behind a shield of straight red hair. Maeve stood up, leaned over the table, and blew hard, clearing the way to Danielle's eyes. "No hiding."

Danielle exhaled like her soul might escape and blinked away tears. "I tried to call him at work one day, and his assistant said he'd taken the day off, which was weird because he hadn't mentioned it. About three minutes later, he called me to say he'd moved all his stuff out of the condo. We were done."

Maeve sat down hard. "Da-yum."

Danielle's chuckle held six months' worth of bitter confusion. "That's what I said."

"Was there someone else?"

"That's the thing. I don't know." Danielle threaded both hands through her hair, massaging the back of her skull. "And it was months ago. I should be over him already, but it's going to be a while before I believe any guy won't just disappear off the face of the earth." She shook her hair out, sending Braden back to the depths of her consciousness. "Anyway, Ryan says I should be able to move back into the house by around

Christmas." She straightened her shoulders, adjusted her sweater, and cleared her head.

"Geez, if I'da known I was going to be stuck with you for a whole month…"

Danielle blinked away the few remaining tears. Just saying Ryan's name shouldn't have sidetracked her – too far, anyway. "You know you love me. Besides, it gives you an automatic designated driver."

"Well there is that." Maeve raked a hand through her hair, making the spikes stand out farther. "Last night was wild." Her grin deepened as if she was flirting with the memory. "What did you think of that Christopher guy?"

"He was nice."

"That's it? Nice?" Maeve made a show of taking a deep breath and puffing out her cheeks as she exhaled. "You are hopeless."

Christopher, the guy in question, had gone to the Denzel Washington School of Incredibly Handsome Men. "Okay, he was *nice* nice." Danielle put an extra spin on the first one, giving her friend a better idea of her thoughts on Christopher.

"I've seen him at the Pig before. Did you give him your number?"

"Yeah." As pathetic as it sounded, she half hoped Christopher would distract her from both Braden and Ryan.

"His friend Jason's pretty cute, too. We can double date." Maeve rested her forearms on the table. She was eager. Way too eager.

"Sure."

"Thanks for the breakfast, sugar buns. I'm off to the shower." She rose and patted Danielle's head.

"Do you think your mom needs any help with dinner? I could do a pie or something."

"Call her and ask."

While Maeve was in the shower, Danielle sat down and made a to-do list. She put down calling Maeve's mother, Vickie. She put down a Home Depot stop and sanding trim. She did not put down reviving memories of L.A and Braden. And she definitely did not put down daydreaming about Ryan.

* * * *

Ryan hit his key fob twice, the sharp beep from the truck confirming he'd set the alarm. All the boxwood shrubs edging his parents' front walkway looked like little green meatballs. Mom must have hired a landscape crew, which was awesome because it meant she wouldn't be after him to do any pruning. He shook his head, half smiling as he took the cement steps to the front porch two at a time. She'd just come up with something else for him to do.

The smell of roasting turkey leaked out from around the front door. *Oh yeah.* Mom made the best damned turkey. He knocked once, then turned his key in the lock to let himself in. A few angel statues dotted the living room, the scout team from the small army that would take over in the weeks between Thanksgiving and Christmas. Classical piano music took the edge off the silence. "Mom?"

"In here." His mother's voice came from the back of the house.

Ryan shucked his jacket and headed for the kitchen, sticking his head in the family room on the way by. "Yo, Niall," he said to his older brother, who was already planted on the overstuffed sofa watching football. "No angels in here yet."

"Soon though." Niall got up, greeting Ryan with a half-hug, half handshake. "Be careful out there. She's got a list for you."

"Why doesn't she ask you to do shit?" Ryan tried to sound mad, but he was mostly proud of the way his mother always came to him first. She'd hated all the little rooms on the main floor, and right after Ryan graduated from high school, she'd hired a contractor to turn three of them into one large room. Ryan talked his way into a job as a laborer, and ended up knowing what he wanted to do with his life. "By the way, nice buzz cut, dude," Ryan said, rubbing his brother's freshly shaved head.

"Less for the bad guys to grab."

"Works for me." Ryan reached around his brother and waved at his wife Rhonda. "Happy Thanksgiving."

She waved back, her smile as frosty as the silver bullet beer can she held in her perfectly manicured grip. In the five years since they'd been married, Ryan had tried like hell to warm up to his sister-in-law, without much success. He counted the smile as a win, and cuffed his brother's shoulder. "You have to work tonight?"

Niall still worked the night shift after over ten years on the police force. Ryan figured it was a survival strategy for being married to Rhonda.

"Nope. Somehow I scored the weekend off." Niall punched him back, his fist carrying a 'don't fuck with me' message. Ryan was taller and broader than his brother, but Niall was older and meaner.

You win. "I'm going to go find Mom," Ryan said, bouncing on the balls of his feet, his stomach yapping as pumpkin spice drifted over the roast turkey smell. Good food, family, and hopefully some time with Dani were going to rock his Thanksgiving day.

"One of the danglies has a burned out bulb," his mother said from her position at the center island that divided the kitchen from the dining room. She gestured at the fist-sized gold and blue speckled glass pendant lights hanging over the sink. "The halogen bulbs are in the pantry closet."

Ryan crossed the room, wrapped an arm around his mother's shoulders, and kissed the top of her head. "Happy Thanksgiving, Mom. Good to see you." He got an elbow in the ribs when he reached over her, pinching a bit of the cheesy crust off the top of the potato casserole resting on the blue granite countertop in front of her. The shortest one in the family, Vickie barely reached his shoulder, but he had a healthy respect for her fire and energy.

"The snacks are in the TV room. Go fix the bulb please." She stretched some tin foil over the casserole and tugged open a drawer near his hip, pausing to reach up and give him a kiss on the way by.

Ryan gave up on snitching food and did as she asked, rooting around in the pantry cupboard until he found a replacement. The old bulb was stubborn about giving up, taking enough of his attention that he didn't hear the front door open. He didn't pay attention to the swell of voices and the shout of laughter. He barely noticed when Maeve came through the door.

But when Dani followed her in, he damned near snapped the bulb off at the base.

She carried a pie-sized plastic container, and her hair was tied back in a loose braid. Her forest green turtleneck clung to her form and made her skin glow. The bulb chose that moment to cooperate, giving him something to do so he didn't try to wrap her up in a hug. His mother met her halfway across the room, her hands open to take the pie.

"You remember Danielle, don't you?" Maeve said to her mother on her way to the food.

"Of course I do," Vickie said, giving Dani a hug. "I'm happy you're here." Without turning around, she scolded her only daughter. "No scavenging, Maeve. Snacks are in the other room."

Maeve turned on her spike heels and braced her knuckles on the center island. "Yo, bro," she said.

"What's up?" Ryan snapped the bulb into place and stuffed his hands in his pockets, still itching to unwind Dani's braid. He could tell himself all day long that hooking up with Dani while Cherry could still mess with him wasn't fair to her. But when she stood close enough for him to smell her faint vanilla floral perfume, to see her broad smile and the way her slim waist flared out into the perfect curve of her butt, all he could think about was what was underneath those classy trousers and how good her lips would taste.

Shee-it.

Danielle came over to the island, nearly close enough for Ryan to touch, and Maeve sauntered out into the dining room, the geometric pattern of her sweater working with the spikes in her hair to make her even more angular than normal. "I see our bitchier-in-law is honoring us with her presence."

"Maeve." Vickie O'Connor scowled at her daughter.

Maeve raised an eyebrow as if daring her mother to shut her up. Rhonda stalked into the room.

"Niall wants another beer," Rhonda said, her smile dropping into the frigid zone.

"I'll grab one," Vickie said, her blue eyes extra wide, as if the rest of them weren't snorting with laughter at the awkward timing. Ryan had once bet Joey how long it would take Maeve and Rhonda to get into a full-on hair-tearing screamfest. So far the women had avoided outright war, though Ryan figured they'd get into it one holiday or another.

After sending Rhonda on her way with two more cans of Coors, Vickie turned on her daughter, fists cocked on her hips. "I hope when you get married, we all get to vote beforehand, because God forbid you end up with someone who doesn't win the majority."

"As if," Maeve said, arms crossed on her chest. Ryan and Dani exchanged sideways glances, sending a surge of heat south, to parts of his anatomy that shouldn't act up in his mother's kitchen. It was hard – literally – to be around her without getting closer than he should. He'd been dumb to think his biggest problem at Thanksgiving dinner would be the chores his mother asked him to do.

"Someday you'll meet the right guy, Maeve Mary," Vickie said, "and paybacks are a problem. Now could you girls set the table?"

Ryan volunteered to hang up their coats, and when he came back into the kitchen, Dani and Maeve had spread a white linen cloth over the big dining room table and were setting out plates and silverware.

"Why only seven plates?" Maeve asked.

"Well, Joey's still in Indiana, and Eamon's having dinner with friends." Vickie peered into the oven, releasing a wave of roast turkey smell. "Dad'll be back any minute with the wine, and dinner should be on the table in an hour."

Great. An hour spent knocking off chores from Mom's Honey-do list, of filling up on cheese and crackers in the den, of pretending to like football, of watching Maeve and Rhonda take shots at each other.

An hour spent keeping his hands off of Dani Jacobsen.

* * * *

After dinner, Danielle helped Maeve and Ryan clean up. Rhonda took off to see her family, while Niall went back to his football game. When the dishes were done, Maeve curled up next to Niall on the couch, lying on her side and tucking her toes under his bum. Within a few minutes, she fell asleep. Danielle sat cross-legged on the rug, resting her back against a chair and staring at the television. Her belly was so full she couldn't find a comfortable position.

"Hey, anybody want to go for a walk? It's not raining." Ryan stood in the doorway between the kitchen and the living room.

"Fourth quarter, dude," Niall said, keeping his eyes on the television. Maeve snored softly beside him.

Danielle straightened up, glancing toward the big front windows. A walk sounded intriguing, despite the overcast and the fading afternoon light. *Right.* After sitting across a table from Ryan, making casual conversation and pretending he was just a guy who did some work at her house, her self-discipline was frazzled. "Yeah, I'll go." She reached up to wake Maeve, but Ryan caught her with a single, long glance. The reach turned into a grasp, a simple move using the edge of the cushion to leverage herself to a standing position.

Maeve shifted, snuffed, and slept on.

Danielle's dressy leather mules weren't meant for winter walking, though the problem was easily solved. In minutes, she and Ryan were tromping along the sidewalk in the direction of Green Lake Park. Vickie O'Connor's hiking boots fit Danielle fairly well, as did her puffy down jacket, which was light-years warmer than Danielle's leather coat.

The air was cold and the dampness made it feel colder. Two blocks in, Danielle's cheeks tingled, then her nose started to numb. She had to pay attention to where she put her feet because the sidewalk was cracked and uneven in places. Of course, she could always grab onto Ryan for support. The way he'd watched her at dinner made it pretty clear he'd be open to any grabbing she wanted to do. She just needed to decide when and how much.

Huge rhododendrons sprawled around the houses, providing a note of continuity in the otherwise mixed bag of architectural styles. Doing her best to match Ryan's longer stride, Danielle kept her hands stuffed deep in her pockets as she walked, stifling any urges to touch him, fishing for something clever to say.

"You guys are just as … rambunctious as I remembered." It wasn't the most original thing she'd ever come up with, but it was honest.

Ryan snorted a laugh, showing a puff of frosty breath. "Wait'll Joey's around. He makes Maeve look like Mother Theresa."

Maeve was one of the best pot-stirrers Danielle knew. "Yeah, he was like six years old the last time I saw him."

They reached an intersection and stopped, waiting for the light to change. Very few cars were on the road, but people in Seattle waited for the walk signal regardless of traffic. Ryan knocked into Danielle's shoulder with his own.

"What?" she said.

"Nothing." He did it again.

"What?" She used more emphasis, laughing at the way his grin showed both dimples, loving the way his blue eyes shone in the misty air.

"Just checking."

They headed for the three-mile trail that circled the lake. As fast as the light was fading, it would be dark by the time they got back to his parents' house. Ryan put a hand on Danielle's lower back as they started across Green Lake Way. She liked the feel of it, the weight of it. She liked the sound of his voice, resonant and laced with humor. She even liked the icy numbness of her nose and the way little needles of cold prickled her face. His hand slid away and she missed it, feeling a cool spot on her back where it had been.

Neither had much to say. Ryan walked and Danielle more-or-less floated, drifting along in the current of his presence. Being near him warmed her, and she found herself shooting glances in his direction, memorizing the way his hair curled around his face under his black watch cap, the way his sideburns faded into his five o'clock shadow, the way the cold reddened the tip of his nose.

They passed a tiny box of a house and Ryan pointed at the big front window. "I'm not sure it's historically accurate to have a flat-screen TV covering one wall of your 1940s home."

"Must be time-travelers." Danielle smiled with stiff lips, nerves fluttering under her breastbone when he smiled back. She loosened up enough to deal with something that had been bugging her all afternoon. "So … can I ask you a question and you promise you won't get mad?" *Because I'm apparently thinking like a thirteen year old right now.*

He tilted his head and gave her an affable smile. "Maybe."

Danielle's cheeks flamed up. "I mean, this is kind of embarrassing, but I want to know what's up with you and Cherry."

The space between them grew by several inches and Ryan's grin tightened up. Despite the risk of ruining the day, Danielle pushed him for an answer. "Maeve said the two of you got together to try to work things out, right?"

He stopped, rubbed his mouth with the palm of his hand, and laughed with just enough bitterness to make Danielle feel bad.

"I'm sorry." She tried to sidestep her apparent social gaffe. "I was just curious." Her voice trailed away. She'd expected either a flustered explanation or some kind of Rico Suave cover up, not frank frustration verging on anger.

He stuffed his hands deeper in his pockets and walked along. "I told you when we first met. I'm done with her," he said, tossing the words over his shoulder like saying them made him tired.

In that exhaustion, she heard the truth. "Hey, Ryan."

He stopped. "What?"

"I said I was sorry." She took a step toward him, the rushing in her head louder than the random traffic noise. "I didn't mean to make you mad."

She reached his side.

He nudged her with an elbow, the tension fading from his body. "Okay."

A couple ducks paddled along the edge of the lake and a lone jogger whipped past them. They walked quietly, the cool air and shifting water settling them both down.

"I got another question for you," Danielle said.

His laugh held a touch of concern. "Now what?"

Danielle giggled into the evening gloom. "What were you like in high school?"

"What do you think?"

"I think you were the bad boy."

Some memory or other flashed through Ryan's eyes and he snorted a laugh. "Yep. I was the rowdy one."

He bumped her with his shoulder again. "Mostly fighting, a little pot, getting drunk before class. You know, nothing too serious."

"You're so mellow. I can't imagine you fighting."

"Dad got me into boxing because he wanted me to put my fists to good use." He gave her upper arm a couple demonstration punches. "Guess I did my cutting loose when I was young."

"Younger." She emphasized the second syllable. "I mean, you're still young." She smirked at him and he shook his head.

When it was nearly dark, they left the path around the lake and cut up to the street because the light was better. Most of the stores and restaurants were lit up for the holiday, with fairytale white lights and fat colored bulbs wrapped around just about anything that didn't move.

The cold had worked its way in, first hitting her fingertips, then sliding down her neck. When she gave an involuntary shiver, Ryan put his arm around her.

"Closer is warmer," he said.

He was right.

Danielle looped an arm around his waist, trying not to think too hard about how natural it felt.

They were a couple blocks from his parents' house when a red light stopped them. Ryan rubbed his cheek against her forehead. "Better?"

Her lips were numb enough that she didn't want to talk. "Mm." They hadn't been this physically close since the first night they met, and she had to swallow hard against the twittery feeling in her chest. The bulk of his muscles cuddling her shoulders carried through the padding of their winter coats and made her want more.

And more.

Her hand slid into the back pocket of his jeans, molding around the curve of his ass. *Damn.* The feel of his breath on her cheek both calmed and excited her. She did an internal run-through of all the reasons they shouldn't get involved, a litany she practiced daily. This time, she ran straight into Braden. His imaginary incarnation kissed her casually, then jogged off toward the Saab parked next to her Honda in their condo's garage. Like every other morning of every other L.A. day, except on this day he hadn't gone to work.

He'd moved out.

Instead of cupping Ryan's ass, Danielle's hand loosened and fell down to her side.

Instead of snuggling under his arm, she shifted. Taking one step away, then two.

"What?" he asked, mostly puzzled, a little wary.

What? Danielle wanted to crawl under the safety of the sidewalk. She'd been so focused on Ryan's ex-issues, it never occurred to her she might have some of her own.

Shouldn't have been a surprise, since she'd basically shoveled her emotional dirty laundry into a pit the day Braden left, covering it with the hope it would just go away. If any of her friends had tried something similar, she totally would have called them on their stupidity.

The light changed and they stepped off into the crosswalk. Traffic was minimal, only the occasional pair of headlights passed them in the dark. Danielle's foot hit an icy patch and skidded forward, forcing Ryan to change his grip to keep her from falling on her butt.

"Watch out there." Ryan's hands circled her waist, the question still plain in his tone.

They paused in the middle of the crosswalk and Danielle rested her hands on his chest, balancing against him, balancing on the edge of a decision. "Thanks."

He nodded, his silence giving her space. Either he was the most mature twenty-four year old in the history of ever, or her back-and-forth frightened him.

And if he was frightened, then at least she had good company.

"We should go," she said, easing away. "Your parents will be wondering about us."

A car pulled toward them and tapped its horn, and they scrambled up onto the sidewalk. Danielle took a couple steps, but Ryan pulled her close. She tipped her head up to ask him a question and almost ran into his mouth.

She gasped, startled by his proximity, startled by his warmth, startled by how desperately she wanted to close that distance. Kissing him seemed like the best idea she'd had in a long time.

"Do me a favor," he whispered, his lips so, so close to hers.

"'Kay."

"Don't listen to the shit my sister says."

"'Kay." *Oh crap we can't do this.* Imagining Maeve's quirky grin froze over any enthusiasm Braden had left standing. Danielle jerked to the side, nearly skidding again. She caught herself and picked up the pace, ready to get back to the safety of the O'Connors' house.

Ryan let her go for a few steps, then caught up. They walked side-by-side the rest of the way, trapped in a cold and painful silence.

Chapter Six

Saturday morning, Danielle was at her grandmother's house, painting the dining room molding with stripper to remove the mustard-colored paint. *What the hell, Gram?* Danielle's fingernails were trashed from all the sanding and scraping. Little sacrifices, worth her time, though the more she worked on the house, the more memories she unearthed.

Danielle smiled at her eight-year-old self, running full-tilt down the stairs and out the front door, then leaping off the porch like she could fly over the lawn. Or her sixteen-year-old self, kneeling on the old couch that used to sit in the front window so she'd see Maeve's car pass the laurel hedge. Or standing in the kitchen with Gram watching rain squalls roll in off the ocean, each one fiercer than the last. She'd tucked those memories away like they were nubby woolen sweaters.

Danielle had no use for sweaters in L.A., but this was home.

Where did that *come from?*

She'd been sanding for about an hour when Christopher called. Once they established that she remembered meeting him the night before Thanksgiving, he got down to business.

"So … next weekend," he said, letting his words trail off, teasing her with their promise.

She let the pause settle before prompting him, halfway dreading what he would say. "Next weekend."

"I've got a couple tickets to see the UW men play basketball Saturday."

"That's cool." *Sort of.* She plopped down in the wing chair. She leaned back, stretched her legs out, and then curled them under, tipping forward and planting her elbows on her knees.

"My buddy Jason's got a pair, too, for him and Maeve."

A double date would be perfect. Christopher wasn't Braden, wasn't under thirty, and wasn't related to Maeve. As a bonus, he had a nice voice, a blend of warmth and confidence she couldn't help but like. Going out with him might actually be fun.

Except it felt a little like eating vegetables or getting enough exercise.

"That sounds great. Who are they playing?" she said, the artificial enthusiasm adding vibrato to her sound.

"Oregon. We can grab some dinner over at University Village before the game."

University Village was a trendy outdoor shopping area where the young and beautiful accessorized the high-end stores and pretty restaurants. It would be just like the dinners she used to have with Braden and their friends, except everyone would be paler and wearing more layers, their faces mirrored in the rain-splattered windows.

Christopher offered to pick her up about five-thirty. She agreed before giving herself any time to think, because thinking would give her a chance to come up with excuses not to go.

She hung up the phone, proud of herself for taking a stand. Her goal was still to get the house sold and get back to L.A. Christopher would be a divertissement; fun, entertaining, someone she could walk away from without causing any pain.

Unlike her best friend's younger brother, who was an addiction in the making.

A key jiggled in the front door. She wasn't expecting Ryan, but it had to be him. Danielle's breath got tight and her pulse hit double-time. She jerked to her feet, convinced he'd overheard her phone call.

Not like just seeing him would cause so much excitement, would it?

He came through the door, smiling like his dimple was a peace offering after the awkward end to their Thanksgiving walk. His eyes were sleepy and his hair looked like he'd combed it with his fingers, and Danielle had to squash the image of Bedroom-Ryan before she could talk. "You don't need to work today."

"Chubb's coming over in an hour to help me haul your antique appliances to the dump."

He hung his leather coat on the arm of the wing chair, and for a moment they both shifted their weight forward, like magnets pulling together. Danielle stopped first. "You're starting the kitchen for real?"

Ryan took a step toward the stairs, his dimples fading a little. "We'll pull out the appliances, then you and I can figure out where you want the new boxes for your cabinets."

"I'll have to make a sketch to visualize how things'll work," she said.

"Sure." Ryan headed for the kitchen. "It'll be easy enough to take some measurements for you."

Danielle followed at his heels, doing her best to keep her mind on the remodel and not Ryan's butt or the way his muscular shoulders moved under his waffle-weave shirt. The cuffs were frayed, and her eyes tracked him as one at a time he shoved them up over his elbows.

"I'm thinking stainless steel appliances." She waved into the vintage kitchen, trying to focus, trying to ignore the fizzing energy between them. Trying to act like an adult.

She hated being the grown-up.

While she scrambled to remember the things on her to-do list, his gaze traveled from the top of her sloppy up-do down to her worn-out Keds. He spent an extra moment on the Chili Peppers logo across her chest, and his raised eyebrows made it plain he liked the gap between the hem of her tee shirt and the waistband of her jeans.

Enough already. She planted her knuckles on her hips and tried to scowl him down. His smirk made it plain he enjoyed needling her, which turned her cheeks from pink to blush to girl-is-on-fire.

"And where's a good place to buy flooring?" she asked, shading her tone with enough annoyance to keep them both on-task. Even without the plywood patch in front of the sink, the existing floor needed a replacement, since the scuffed and faded olive geometry vinyl came straight out of 1970.

Ryan leaned against the chipped Formica counter. "There are a couple places we can check out." He braced himself with his palms, making his shoulders look around six miles wide. "Might be kind of fun."

Humor tempered her annoyance. "Home Depot on a Saturday. Yee-haw."

"We could get lunch later, you know, grab a beer somewhere."

"Like on a date?"

His gaze dropped back to the gap between her tee shirt and jeans, heating her core, melting her resistance.

"If you want."

"Ryan!" Despite solid, rational, reasons for staying away, her body resented the short distance from his side of the kitchen to hers. "Dude, you're, like, nine years younger than me." The age difference was her most obvious and least inflammatory excuse.

"So?"

"I feel like I should wear leopard print and growl like a jungle cat when I'm with you."*See? This is why we shouldn't mix sex and sheet rock.*

He chuckled, but his eyes weren't happy.

Before he could speak, she went on, doing what was necessary for her own peace of mind. "Listen, I'm thrilled with the work you're doing, but let's just focus on the remodel for now, okay?"

"This is about Maeve, isn't it?"

"No, it's about me, and going back to L.A. in two months, and being a lot older than you, and…" *Please don't leave me alone with all of this.*

A short, angry laugh interrupted her comment. "Sure, Dani. We can focus on the remodel." He made a half-assed attempt at finger-coming his unruly curls. "I'll get the appliances out today, then we can talk about the cabinets."

"Right." She rubbed her palms on her thighs so she'd have something to do.

"And when the kitchen's done, I'll finish trimming out the dining room, then move upstairs." Anger deadened his voice.

Danielle countered with sweetness, a plastic smile, and a softer tone. "The built-ins around the fireplace could use some work."

"I'll do that, too."

"And the bathrooms?"

He rubbed his mouth with the palm of his hand and nodded. "Yeah."

"The tub downstairs here looks pretty trashed. Do you know someone who can re-do the enamel?"

"Geez, I hate…" He looked off to the side and snorted. "I should take a sledgehammer to it and get rid of the thing. The cracks in the tile and grout make me think we'll find some kind of weird science experiment underneath it, but…"

"I'd have to buy a new tub, then." With the focus strictly on the remodel, she felt more secure – and tremendously relieved.

"That'd be best. You could get one that's deeper, the kind with some jets."

She didn't like the look in his eyes, a mix of anger, frustration, and pain. She really didn't like knowing she put it there. "Sure."

"You'll need a new roof at some point, too, and windows. Then I'll paint, and you can get someone in here to refinish the floors."

A new roof would cost over ten thousand dollars, and would wipe out her savings. She couldn't even think about the windows. Just more stress for her to swallow down. "I'll have to talk to Uncle Jonathan."

"Sure."

"And you're keeping track of your hours, right?" *Because reminding him he's an employee is the perfect wedge.* "I'm going to pay you for this."

He started to say something, then stopped. "Yeah."

"Good, I mean, just give me an invoice or something." She drove the wedge in farther, then clamped her teeth together to keep anything else from leaking out.

"Yeah."

They stared at each other, Danielle trying to apologize with her eyes. She didn't know what she was apologizing for, exactly.

Except she did.

* * * *

Danielle flipped the strips of bacon, each one sending up a fresh wave of crackles. She'd left her grandmother's house early Monday to get back to Maeve's apartment in time to cook dinner, and possibly also to avoid Ryan. She hadn't seen him since their little talk on Saturday. Just as well, given the garbled mess she'd made of their non-relationship.

"Food," Maeve said as soon as she came through the door. She dropped her oversized purse on the dining room table and kicked off her pumps.

"Cob salad." Danielle couldn't disguise her happiness at having someone uncomplicated to talk to. As long as she didn't mention Ryan, she and Maeve should get along just fine. "Christopher called the other day."

"Yeah, Jason told me." Maeve's short skirt was wrinkled after sitting at her desk all day but gel still held her cropped hair in a precise part with stylized spikes along the edge of her face. "We'll all go see the Dogs play on Saturday night."

Pressing her palms into the countertop, Maeve arched her back, rotating her ankles and groaning into the crackle and pop. For just a second the façade shifted, giving Danielle a glimpse of the tired woman behind the aggressive veneer.

"There's some white wine in the fridge," Danielle said.

"Cool." Maeve didn't immediately grab a glass. She surveyed the array of bowls on the tiny countertop, each holding a different chopped vegetable. A mound of sliced ham sat on the cutting board next to a pile of crumbled goat cheese, and fresh greens almost overflowed the salad spinner in the sink. "Cherry and I talked about grabbing dinner somewhere, but this is better."

"There's enough for her, too." Danielle lifted the greens out of the sink and upended them into a large pottery bowl.

Maeve tilted her head with a get-real grin. "Won't that be a little weird?"

Danielle willed her face into cool neutrality. "I like Cherry."

"You like Ryan, too."

Grease from the bacon spattered up and Danielle grabbed the pan, moving it off the heat. "I don't want this to burn." She used a fork to lift the strips onto a plate covered with a paper towel.

"I know I'm not the most observant person," — Maeve paused to snag a crumble of goat cheese from the bowl and pop it in her mouth — "but I'm not stupid. You two tried so hard to ignore each other on Thanksgiving it was almost embarrassing."

Danielle's first impulse was to play with her hair, to cover her face, to dodge the inevitable. "I'm not sure what you mean."

Maeve's bleat of surprise turned into a laugh, not nasty but not happy either. "Right." Her laughter dwindled to an exasperated chuckle. "I'd get grossed out if you dated Niall, because my brother? Eeuw." The ick-factor resonated through her voice. "But, at least he's older than us. My God, Danielle. Ryan's a kid!"

Something sizzled in Danielle's gut, and it wasn't the bacon. Anger, frustration, and a bellyful of repressed desire piled on top of each other like a full-on emotional rugby scrum. "If he's such a kid, why do you keep talking about him getting married?"

"Because Cherry's a kid, too. They're perfect together." Maeve pranced to the fridge and dug out the bottle of wine.

There was no good answer to that. Danielle gaped at her best friend's back, jaw slung wide enough to catch flies. She didn't intend to date Ryan, so arguing about whether he should marry Cherry was an exercise in pointlessness. Instead, she dumped the greens from the spinner into a bowl and tossed the plastic colander into the sink, a little – no, a lot – harder than necessary. Immediately she felt like an idiot for showing her internal disarray.

The silence between them stretched to the point of discomfort, but Danielle kept her mouth shut. If she couldn't explain Ryan to herself, she sure as hell couldn't explain him to anyone else. Finally Maeve passed her a glass of wine and Danielle took a deep swallow.

Truce declared.

"At any rate," Maeve said, sounding satisfied that she'd made her point. "We'll have fun on Saturday night."

Sure. "What about Where's Waldo? Won't he mind if you go out with someone else?"

Maeve snickered. "He'll *hate* it. Jason could have the personality of toenail clippings and he'd rate over Waldo Beamer."

"Someday I totally have to meet him."

"Waldo? Nah. It's probably not safe. You might be his type."

Danielle had no clue if that was a compliment or not.

"You don't want to mess around with him, anyway," Maeve said and drained about half her glass of wine. "Christopher's so damned handsome."

Danielle dumped piles of chopped vegetables on the salad greens, creating wedge-shaped sections of tomato, avocado, and mushrooms. Which was a lot harder than it should have been, because she really

93

wanted to throw those bowls of food at the wall, like some kind of modern art exhibit. *Hey, kids. This is what crazy looks like.*

Maeve poured them both more wine and took a deep sniff of her glass. "This is pretty good," she said.

Danielle set the salad bowl on the table and sat down, taking a sip from her own glass. The blend of fruit and mineral notes worked okay with the fresh veggies in the salad. In the end, talking about wine–or just about anything else–was easier than talking about men. Though when Maeve smiled just right, dimples framing her feminine version of Ryan's grin, a shot of pain hit Danielle somewhere under her sternum.

Right next to her heart.

What a mess.

* * * *

The Friday Happy Hour crowd at the Pig N' Whistle had started to move out, opening up seats for the more serious drinkers. Ryan and Chubb were camped at their favorite table in the front corner near the window. They had a view of the room and the street outside, which prevented random ex-girlfriends from launching sneak attacks.

Chubb had his bangs pulled back in a ponytail. It made his nose and chin look longer than normal, as if a sculptor had stretched them both while the clay was still soft. He wore a beat-up UMass sweatshirt, though he'd never been to Massachusetts, and Ryan figured he probably pulled it out of the lost and found box at the gym. A couple of girls sat at a table nearby, taking turns eyeing Chubb like he was a pair of spike heels on the sale rack. Something about his ratty hair and scruffy goatee drove women crazy, and Ryan was used to being the benchwarmer on their team.

"You still doing double shifts?" Chubb asked after taking a measured sip of his beer.

Ryan really didn't want to talk about Dani, but if he didn't answer, Chubb would work it to death. "Not this week. She's, um … I've been pulling long hours at the day job, you know?"

"Ah ... the day job." Chubb punctuated his comment with a snort that amplified his disbelief.

"Shut up."

Chubb tipped his pint glass and swirled the beer with a grin on his face. Ryan went back to watching the girls watch Chubb and trying not to think about Dani. Every time he made any progress with her, something happened to slow things down. It pissed him off.

He'd been with Cherry for long enough that he'd lost the habit of looking at other women, though the redhead on the left looked pretty. Then she tucked a strand of her long straight hair behind one ear, something he'd seen Dani do. *Shit.* He gulped the rest of his beer in one swallow.

"You're a mess, dude." Chubb toasted him with a half-full glass, as if getting twisted up by a woman was some kind of accomplishment. "I've never seen you this bad before."

"Didn't I say shut up a minute ago?" Ryan asked, keeping one hand on his beer and the other on his temper. "I think I said shut up, so maybe you should."

"Dude, you're killing me. If you want her that bad, go out with her."

Right.

The familiar neon beer signs reflected off the big mirror on the wall behind the bar. Ryan caught the waitress's eye and raised his glass. Getting hammered on a Friday night was an old-school way of dealing with his problems. Guess this was the night to tear it up.

"She's not into me."

"What?" Chubb rose halfway to his feet, his weight on his knuckles, laughing at Ryan. "Man, I know she took off right after I got there the other day, but I saw her give you a look like you were a plate of fried chicken and she was a Weight Watchers refugee." He dropped back down, still laughing. "My ass she's not into you."

"I'm never going to look at chicken the same way again," Ryan said into his empty mug. He'd spent almost a week telling himself all the reasons he and Dani would never work out. He knew they were bullshit, but it helped his pride. Hearing the opposite message from Chubb just about killed him. The waitress came by to drop a fresh one, and he managed to trade glasses and thank her without taking his eyes off the table.

Chubb interrupted his pity party. "When I was hanging out here the other night, Maeve was up at the bar going on and on about Dani's ex."

Ryan nailed him with a glare. "What?" Dani hadn't ever said much about her past, and he needed every bit of information he could gather.

"Geez, touchy much?"

"Tell me."

Chubb grinned a little more sympathetically. "Actually – and I'm not just saying this because you're my friend – he sounds like a douche." He hunched forward, like he had a bunch of dirt to share. "He's like, a partner in an architectural firm down in L.A."

"I hate architects."

"He drives a four-year-old Saab, owns a condo with a view of the Mulholland canyon, and I guess," — Chubb took a swallow of beer and scuffed the foam off his mouth with the back of this hand — "his personal grooming expenses are, like, large. *Way* large."

Ryan could almost see the guy — blond hair, expensive loafers but no socks, perfectly manicured five o'clock shadow. David Beckham without the tatts. "So unlikely she'd be interested in me, then?"

"Lemme remind you of my fried chicken analogy." Chubb raised his beer like he was proud of himself. "Maybe she's tired of douches."

Or maybe Ryan had gotten ahead of himself on this one. He went back to staring at the tabletop. Danielle was used to more than a guy with a pick-up truck and power tools.

Chubb's whisper dragged him back from the ledge. "Don't look out the window, man, but Cherry's coming up the sidewalk."

Ryan glanced up at his friend, who grinned like they were sharing the best joke ever.

"Is she alone?"

"Yep."

"Walking straight?"

Chubb paused. "She just tripped over a pebble."

"Awesome."

"She's seen us." Chubb's grin faded some and he turned more directly toward the window with a cool wave.

Ryan didn't have any choice. He nodded in the direction of his ex-girlfriend, who was standing outside, smiling broadly. She blew him a kiss and skipped toward the door as quickly as a drunk girl in three inch heels could manage.

There was no bouncer yet, and no one delayed her as she made her way to their table. "Hey! Have you guys seen Maeve? Some friends dropped me off here, and she's my ride home."

Ryan had some trouble finding his words, and after an awkward pause, Chubb filled in. "Nah, not yet."

She smiled down at them expectantly, and Ryan tried to find at least one good reason to talk to her. No luck.

"Um," Chubb said, giving Ryan a significant look. "Do you want to grab a chair and wait for her here?"

Her smile got wider still. There was the usual shuffle as they asked around to borrow another chair, then the waitress came over to take their orders.

Ryan switched to soda water.

The conversation lurched along, with Chubb doing the heavy lifting and Cherry finding every excuse to put her hands on Ryan. He tried to take a mental step back and look at her objectively. She'd spent a long time getting her hair to look casually messy, her silk and lace blouse cost more than he'd spend on a suit, and if he kissed her he'd taste her favorite lipstick and the chemical flavor of alcohol.

The more she relaxed, dragging both of them into the rhythm of their faded relationship, the higher his frustration rose, until finally it crossed the line into anger. When she wrapped her arm through his, laughing at a funny work story Chubb told, he lost it, wrenching his arm away and halfway rising from the table.

"What's wrong?" She gave him the same tolerant, semi-apologetic look that always used to bring him back in line.

"You're hanging all over me, Cherry, and…" *And it's fucking annoying.* Until pretty recently, his two options for dealing with anger were to leave the situation or to hit something. He still needed to work on a third option.

"C'mon, Ry-Ry." She leaned closer to him.

He pushed farther away, trying to get a handle on his anger. The guy at Al-Anon had told him to call her on her behavior. "Listen, you're drunk, and Maeve's not here."

"It's okay, I'll just hang out and wait for her." Her eyes got wide and kind of hurt.

Chubb slid his chair back a bit, meeting Ryan's glance. "I think we were just leaving," he said.

Ryan raked a hand through his hair, which was safer than punching a hole through the table. "Yeah, it's time to go."

She stood up quickly, stumbling into the table when she landed awkwardly on one heel. "I'll sit at the bar 'til Maeve gets here, then."

"You don't have your car, right?"

"No." She blinked once, slowly. "Maeve's my ride."

Let her stay, then. He was supposed to let her live with the consequences of her decisions, even the bad ones. Except Ryan couldn't do it. Taking care of Cherry was second nature. "Come on. I'll get you a cab."

Leaving Chubb to handle the tab, Ryan marched Cherry out of the bar. Luck was on his side, and a Yellow Cab cruised up Greenwood before they'd stood there for more than a minute. Ryan opened the door and aimed Cherry in, pausing only briefly when she lurched toward him. She planted both hands on his chest, her face close enough for a kiss. "Get in the cab," he said, forcing the words out through clenched teeth. He was done with happy hour, done with women, and seriously done with Cherry.

She pouted, the naughty gleam in her eyes trying hard to sway him, and if he'd been less angry, he might have caved. Instead, he pushed on her shoulders, forcing her down onto the back seat of the cab.

"We're done, Cherry. This is over." He leaned in to talk to the driver. "How much to get her to Capitol Hill?"

The cab driver looked from Cherry to Ryan and back again. "She's pretty drunk."

"That's why she's in your cab."

The cabbie nodded once. "About twelve dollars."

"Here's twenty. Don't let her talk you into driving any place else."

He backed away and the car pulled out into traffic. Chubb was standing on the sidewalk behind him. "I grabbed your jacket, man."

Ryan took the leather coat from his friend. "I owe you for the tab."

"You'll get me next time. Besides, I think those chicks bought us a round or two." Chubb reached up and loosened his ponytail, turning it into a bun on top of his head.

"Did you say thanks?"

"Nope." Chubb snickered. When it came to women his self-confidence bordered on arrogance, especially since most of the time he'd rather be playing computer games.

"You dog."

"Says the man who just stuffed his girlfriend in a cab."

"Ex." It was a sign of their friendship that Ryan didn't smack him.

"Whatever. Her Volvo's parked right over there."

Ryan sighed, letting go of some of his frustration. "I saw it, but she was too drunk to drive, anyway."

"I bet she saw your truck and stopped."

Letting the bitterness in his smile answer for him, Ryan walked off toward the parking lot, pulling the keys from his pocket on the way. She could pay for a cab ride back in the morning. When she was sober.

Chapter Seven

On Tuesday morning Danielle found an invoice from Ryan when she got to her grandmother's house, charging twenty-five dollars an hour for about forty hours of work, along with a pile of receipts for supplies. She would have paid him a lot more than that. She wrote him a check and left before he showed up.

On Wednesday morning, the check was gone.

Friday turned into a jumble of remodeling frustration, topped off by an email from Sharon, her boss, who tossed out a bunch of random ideas for Danielle to work on. These scattershot emails were part of Sharon's style, and normally they didn't bother her, but this time every bullet point ratcheted up her irritation until it passed exasperation and headed toward fury.

Sharon could take her wild ideas and blow them out her ass.

Ryan showed up around five, and instead of taking off, she stayed, hiding behind her laptop at the dining room table.

"Hey, are you okay if I make some noise in here?" Ryan dumped his toolbox on the kitchen floor.

Danielle minimized the offending email. "Sure." She was too tired to feel uncomfortable anymore, and she tried to keep the conversation going. "What are you working on?"

He gave her a guarded look. "Now that the plumber's done, I'm going to start patching some of the holes in the walls."

"Sounds good."

"Yeah."

So much for conversation. He ducked back into the kitchen, and she went back to her laptop, attempting to draft a response to her boss to the intermittent grinding buzz of his table saw. Finally she gave up. Some things were better handled by phone.

Because of the noise, she went out to the living room. She reached voicemail. Irritated, she tossed her cell phone at her purse and dropped down into the wing chair, catching her fingernail in the shredded velvet covering the arm. "Ow! Damn it!"

Ryan leaned through the doorway. "What's up?"

"Nothing." She stuck her finger in her mouth and swallowed down the sigh that wanted to blow through the word as she spoke.

Expecting him to go right back to work, she hunched in the chair, trying to figure out why this email bent her farther out of shape than most of the others. Yes, she was going back in less than two months. Yes, she'd agreed to do some work while she was gone.

Yes, time and distance were giving her a new perspective on her job.

Like, maybe Maeve had a point.

When the table saw didn't start right up again, she glanced toward the dining room. The doorway framed Ryan, his hands gripping the molding above his head and his Levis riding low on his hips. His tee shirt stopped about an inch above the waistband of his jeans, and it took effort to pull her gaze away from the gap. "What?" Her voice caught, nearly scrambling the syllable.

"Just checking." He halfway grinned, wary, cautious, the overhead fixture making shadows out of his dimples.

Something inside that had been all tight and wonky since the day she'd pushed him away started to unwind. "I'm pretty much screwed, I think," she said, tucking her hands under her thighs, afraid she might accidently make a grab for all his yummy goodness.

His expression turned naughty. "And I missed it."

"Shut up. That's not what I meant." She fell back into the chair, laughing in spite of herself.

"Stuck my head upstairs the other day." Ryan let go of the molding and crossed his arms. *Because that did nothing to make him look pumped.* "The more rain we get, the more leaks I find."

She had to work to keep her gaze on his face. "Super." Bringing up the roof reminded Danielle she needed money, which distracted her from Ryan's guns. "My mother is crazy."

He stood straighter. "You talked to your mother?"

Frustration boiled up like a geyser. "Hell no."

"So…"

"So what?"

He rubbed his chin thoughtfully. "She must have done something to upset you, or you wouldn't have mentioned her. Right?"

For a moment, she hoped silence would redirect his sympathy. It didn't. He waited, patient, allowing her to find the words.

"I can't afford a new roof, but if I ask her nicely enough, she might help me." She let him see the turmoil that had just opened up underneath her.

"That's cool."

The concern in his expression reached out to her, as if he'd offered his hand to help her walk through a stony patch.

"You should talk to her for me. She'll be nicer." Danielle got up and moved slowly to the big front window. Words churned in her gut and she kept her back to his unspoken sympathy. "This is going to sound crazy, but I don't really know what I'm doing here." She paused to sort through her real thoughts. Sleet spattered the glass, thrown by bursts of wind. "This project is a lot bigger than I expected."

"This place has been coming apart for a while." His tone was neutral, relaxed even. "How'd it get to be such a mess?"

Danielle started with a sigh and ended up on a snorting chuckle. "My uncle Eric—"

"You have an Uncle Eric?"

"Yeah." Danielle massaged her temples and kept going. "He's a dick, and unfortunately for Uncle Jonathan, he's real hard to get a hold of. Add in my mother, who disagrees with people on principle, and there wasn't much Jonathan could do."

"I don't get it," Ryan said.

"Gram suffered from just enough dementia to balk at anything Jonathan suggested. He'd hire someone to live here with her, and she'd kick them out. He couldn't get his stupid siblings to agree to make him her guardian." She had to choke back tears to get the words out. "You know, when I was a kid, my mother would take off for weeks at a time, and I'd stay here with Gram." She pulled her hair out of the ponytail holder, then scooped it up, twisting it into a knot at the nape of her neck. "Do you remember how in the summer Maeve would come over? She'd bring Kelly and Trina, and we'd go down to the beach, hang out all day, and come back up here and have massive sleepovers."

She faced him, daring to meet his gaze, near tears from the struggle for honesty. "Gram gave me a place, more than my mother ever did, and despite that, I let her die alone." She paused, swallowed. "When Uncle Jonathan finally got her into a home, he and Mom told me she wouldn't know me even if I came, and I was self-involved enough to believe them."

His continued silence made her nervous, as if he thought her confession was a load of crap. "When Uncle Jonathan called me about the house, I had the Mini headed north as fast as I could." She pivoted slowly, waving a hand to take in the whole space. "Fixing the place up … was something I could do, you know? I just didn't expect it to be this complicated."

"Because of your mother?"

"Because I grew up here, and she gave it to me."

"I get that."

They shared a long moment, until finally Ryan knocked a fist gently against the wall. "Guess I'll get back to work, then."

"Thank you." Relief spread over her like a warm blanket. He was as strong as the studs he was building around, and she was grateful.

He stepped back into the dining room, his head tipped down, his smile young and vulnerable. "Hey, um…"

The gravel in his voice tickled her most sensitive places. "What?"

"Nothing," he said, and ducked out of sight.

She might have snapped. She shouldn't have snapped. She must have scared him off.

The table saw started back up, and Danielle stayed in the living room, wrestling with all different colors of guilt.

* * * *

Ryan knew his way around guilt, a soggy blanket of feeling that could tighten like a python, wrapping around him and squeezing everything positive out of his head. Happened almost every time he thought about Cherry.

Late Saturday afternoon, it fueled his feet and kept him pounding along the treadmill, running until exhaustion took over and everything else faded.

The club's flat screen television played a music video, some gyrating blonde wailing "gimmegimmegimmemoremoremore." Damned pop music would give him a headache faster than anything. He slowed his pace for a minute, dragging his earbuds out of the pocket in his shorts and starting his playlist. The White Stripes chased away the pop-tart's wail.

He shot a glance around the room and saw a redhead working the stair stepper. She was taller and curvier than Dani, but show him some ginger and he had something to run for.

He loved working with Dani, and not just because she reminded him of Nicole Kidman or Gwyneth Paltrow, all cool polish and elegance. She made lists and did research and figured out what she needed to know. They talked about the remodel like partners.

If only they could talk about more stuff like that.

Over the weeks he'd spent working on her grandmother's house, his half-remembered schoolboy crush had grown up into a full-on Thing. A hard-on Thing, too, for that matter.

Either way it had a capital T.

He liked that her smile was too broad for her face, and that her hair never stayed in its ponytail holder, so smooth and straight it worked its way free and draped over her eyes. He liked her curves, at least from what he could see through the worn sweatshirts and jeans she wore to work on the house. He liked flirting with her, because when she blushed, it made him want to push her up against a wall and see what was under her baggy clothes.

It bugged him that he'd had her in his bed without finding out for sure.

She'd backed him off, told him to focus on the house. Rational decision. Dating his sister's friend created instant drama. Common sense said not to do it. Maeve would bitch, and he already had more relationship crap than he wanted. That's if she'd settle for dating a guy who worked with his hands. He'd do the job she'd hired him for while trying to ignore the way her eyes followed him as he worked.

Dani played her cards pretty close, but her body talk said a lot. He just had to let her work things out in her own head, and be ready if she did. When she did.

He ran himself into something close to peace and slowed to a walk for a few minutes. A quick shower and a short drive home later, he stood in his kitchen, cursing Chubb for drinking the last beer. Chubb wasn't home, but Barnabas was, making an orange tabby shackle around his ankles. He shot his roommate a text, reaming him for neglecting his cat and demanding an expensive microbrew as compensation.

Chubb promised to bring beverages, ignoring the crack about the cat.

"Your daddy's a loser," Ryan said as he dumped a can of chicken-like substance into the cat's dish, blinking at the pungent smell.

Barnabas ignored him, diving right into the food. Ryan briefly wondered how long it had been since the cat had been fed. Likely a couple of twenty-something guys were too irresponsible to be pet owners.

Instead of beer, Ryan found a bottle of wine in the cupboard and poured himself a glass. Chubb's laptop was on the table, and Ryan idly booted it up and logged into Facebook, managing to connect after only a couple do-overs on his password. He wasn't much for the whole social networking thing, but at one point Cherry had signed him up for a page he rarely used.

He scrolled through the feed, seeing half-remembered names from high school and baby pictures from one of the guys at work.

And pictures of Cherry. Making out with a guy. Posted the night before, by someone he didn't know. Three pictures of them on a couch. In one, they toasted the photographer with raised cocktail glasses. In one, the guy had his arms around her shoulders while her head was tucked under his chin. In one, they were mashed together, tickling each other's tonsils while she held up her hand in the universal 'stop' sign, aiming at the photographer, not at the guy with the tongue.

He closed the browser and downed his wine in one swallow. Barnabas jumped up onto his lap and started to knead, piercing his thigh with tiny claws. Ryan tossed him off. The cat landed on the kitchen floor in a scramble of scratching and one firm yowl, then stalked away.

She was probably drunk when it happened.

She had every right to go out with other guys.

Whatever.

He really, really wanted to hit something.

* * * *

At Maeve's insistence, Danielle agreed to go shopping before their big double date. "You dress like an old lady!" This became Maeve's rallying cry, a phrase Danielle heard every time she picked up a hanger. The compromise outfit involved a pair of black leggings, a loose silk top in a soft dusty rose, and a big fur vest. They'd argued for ten minutes over whether or not Danielle could wear her black Ugg boots, until finally she gave in and agreed to borrow a pair of riding boots from Maeve's closet.

Since Danielle was a minimalist, she was ready to go well ahead of Maeve.

Her memory of Christopher had faded into a vague impression of dark-skinned sophistication. In her imagination, he was a jungle cat, just like Braden. One of them a jaguar, the other a golden lion. Both sleek. Both dangerous.

Compared with them, Ryan was a wolf: rough, shaggy, but no less dangerous.

Sometimes her head went in such unexpected directions.

"I can't believe I let you talk me into the vest." Danielle patted down the front like it was a dog giving her a hug. Maeve had mixed cocktails while they were getting ready, vodka and pomegranate with lime wedges and corn chips on the side. Danielle's glass was still half full, and she was doing her best to keep her hands off the chips.

Maeve poked her head out of the bathroom, a tube of mascara in one hand, the fluorescent lights behind her making a halo. "Shut up. It looks cute on you."

"Humph." Danielle straddled a dining chair, her chin on her hands, watching the elaborate process involved in getting Maeve ready to go out. Hair products and make-up covered the gold-specked Formica countertop and half a dozen hangers dangled from the shower curtain rod. For all that Maeve had clear ideas of what Danielle should wear, it had been hard for her to decide on her own outfit. The winning look combined super-skinny jeans and a vintage blouse with a brocade corset worn on the outside.

For a while Danielle entertained herself by trying to walk in the sky-high heels Maeve intended to wear. After a stumble sent her shin smacking into the chair, she gave up. She pulled on her borrowed boots and grabbed her phone, bringing up the Facebook app. Almost immediately, she saw pictures of Cherry French-kissing some guy.

Surprise made her tentative. "Um … Maeve?" She'd have to tread lightly or things could start exploding.

Mascara tube in hand, Maeve made eye contact with Danielle's reflection in the bathroom mirror. "Yeah?"

"Have you been on Facebook today?" Danielle tried to keep her tone casual, though from the pinch in Maeve's lips, she wasn't entirely successful.

"This morning."

"Did you see these pictures of Cherry?" Danielle held up her cell phone like she was presenting evidence in court.

"What?" Maeve grabbed the doorposts to rock backward and look over her shoulder. "Well damn, girlfriend, way to go."

Danielle dropped her hand, but Maeve grabbed it, bringing the phone back to eye level.

Maeve's sarcastic chuckle crawled right up under Danielle's skin. "Ryan's going to see these, right?"

"Like, next month when he checks his Facebook page." Maeve flicked the screen, changing the picture. "What do you care, anyway?"

Bristling at the suspicion in Maeve's voice, Danielle's response had some snap to it. "Because he's a nice guy and this will hurt his feelings."

Maeve tipped her head down to glare at Danielle from under her eyebrows, then flipped around to the bathroom mirror.

The small apartment shrank around Danielle, its old damp wood smell choking her. She shuffled through mature thoughts about how any two people living in such close quarters and spending too much time together were bound to get on each other's nerves. Then she snapped again.

"He is your brother. Why aren't you on his side?"

Maeve stepped out of the bathroom, her chin raised as if she was looking to take a punch. "You'd just love to make this all Cherry's fault."

"What are you talking about?" The floor did one of those shifting things that meant either they'd had an earthquake or Danielle was really, really mad. "It's no one's fault."

The words came out in a hollow squawk, relatively benign compared with the tirade in her head. In the kitchen, the old plastic portable phone rang, which meant someone was downstairs buzzing the doorbell. With lips so thin they were almost invisible, Maeve crossed the room and answered it. "Okay, we'll be right down."

Without a word, she flicked off the bathroom light and grabbed her purse. Danielle hesitated, almost giving in to the temptation to pull off the stupid vest and tight boots and settle down to finish the rest of her cocktail. Maeve was out of sight by the time Danielle closed and locked the front door, which was a relief. She wouldn't have to get into the elevator.

With her best friend.

Who had apparently gone crazy in her old age.

Chapter Eight

Husky basketball fans took their games seriously. Out of the crowd of fifteen thousand, half wore purple and gold UW gear. Everyone else dressed for Saturday night, and the date clothes Maeve insisted on fit right in. Danielle stayed close to Christopher, who looked fantastic in skinny jeans, a dark grey turtleneck, and a long black leather coat. He offered to buy her a beer and she turned him down, hesitant to mix alcohol with the witches' brew of leftover anger and nervousness agitating her gut.

Focusing on Christopher allowed Danielle to pretty much ignore Maeve. Although she couldn't quite focus on Christopher, because her internal monologue was too loud. She'd pissed Maeve off by standing up for Ryan, and she'd pissed Ryan off, in part because of Maeve. Despite all kinds of gymnastics, she'd landed in the exact situation she'd tried to avoid.

Damn.

Christopher shot her a quizzical glance. "You okay over there?"

"Oh, yeah. Yeah. I'm sorry. I've got a lot on my mind." Danielle straightened up and rubbed her palms on her thighs. *One problem at a time.* Playing along with Christopher would help her salvage things with Maeve. She'd just have to deal with Ryan later.

She gave Christopher a smile that had its roots in the warm Southern Californian sun, as pretty and superficial as possible. He held her elbow loosely and guided her to their seats.

For the first half, Christopher sat with his elbows on his knees, dividing his attention between the game and Danielle. She divided her time between chatting with him and noticing details: the slight gap between his two front teeth and the light sprinkling of salt in the dark curls at his temples. When he smiled broadly enough, creases formed around the corners of his mouth, setting it off like quotation marks. The effect was more distinguished than Ryan's boyish dimples.

Not that she was going to spend all night comparing Christopher to Ryan.

The second half Christopher leaned back, draping an arm along her chair, almost but not quite resting his hand on her shoulder. She responded by canting forward, resting her elbows on her knees and her chin on her knuckles, as if the back and forth action on the court required her absolute attention. Then Maeve asked if she wanted a soda, giving Danielle the most normal smile in the world. The 'be nice to Christopher' strategy appeared to be working. Danielle relaxed into her seat, brushing his shoulder on the way by.

The score was basically tied, though Christopher seemed fairly confident the Huskies would win. "They're getting all the rebounds," he said after a particularly bad miss by one of the UW players. His delivery was intimate, humming against the sensitive skin below her ear, even though the subject was basketball and they were sitting in a crowd of thousands.

"Wouldn't it be better if they just scored more points?" Basketball had always been a mysteriously frenetic activity, and while Danielle hated showing off her ignorance, she had to ask. It would give him a chance to be the expert.

He smiled big enough to show off his quotation creases. "Eventually their shots will start falling. As long as they keep the score close, they'll be okay."

"If you say so."

"You watch."

He gave a cocky chuckle, and she could feel his eyes on her. "What?" she asked.

"Just checking you out." His eyes were dark, almost black, rimmed with the kind of long lashes most women would kill for. For a second, she pictured the two of them in bed together, tangled in sheets, cocoa-colored limbs wrapped around strawberries and eggshell skin.

She didn't want a jaguar, she wanted a wolf.

But the wolf was off-limits. At least she had some experience taming a jungle cat. "The game'll be over soon."Her smile might have been a touch plastic, but she layered on as much invitation as possible.

"There's five minutes left on the clock, but it'll take most of a half an hour for them to finish." He tightened his arm around her. "I was thinking we could go out for drinks later."

She shoots; she scores. "That'd be great."

By the final buzzer, his arm lay more heavily across her shoulders and his fingers teased through the ends of her hair. He helped her with her coat, running his thumbs along the edge of her collar as he adjusted it. For half a second she thought he might try and kiss her, then Maeve tossed a wadded-up napkin at them.

"Watch out for that guy," she said, standing at the end of their row of seats arm-in-arm with Jason. "He's a tricky one."

"Watch out yourself," Christopher said, laughing. "And be good to my friend."

"I'm always good," Maeve said, tossing her head back, her lip curled in half a sneer while Jason nuzzled at her neck. There was some general discussion about where they should go next. Maeve and Jason wanted a dance club, while Christopher and Danielle were hoping for something quieter.

Quiet won, mainly because Danielle pointed out that Maeve and Jason could grope each other anywhere, while she and Christopher wouldn't be able to talk in a dance club. She couldn't help but notice the way every woman they passed on their way out of the stadium checked Christopher out. Some tagged her with snotty looks, too, and she rebuffed them by standing straighter and holding Christopher's arm more securely.

Deal with it, ladies.

Once they were tucked into a corner table at Delphina's, she and Christopher talked real estate while Maeve and Jason stepped outside to smoke cigarettes and make out. The wall sconces weren't any brighter than candlelight, the table was covered with white linen, and the red wine was a much better quality than what she and Maeve usually drank. Wine lubricated the conversation and when Christopher made a point by patting her hand, then wrapping his fingers through hers, Danielle knew they were headed for a goodnight kiss.

She was right.

Maeve and Jason gave up on the quiet atmosphere and grabbed a cab, leaving Christopher and Danielle tucked in their cozy booth.

She liked the rumble of his voice and the spicy scent of his aftershave, similar to something Braden would have worn. When he draped an arm around her shoulders, she relaxed into it, and when he brushed her lips with his, she kissed him back, tasting red wine and seduction.

Wrong.

The word was as clear as if someone had said it aloud. She broke the kiss and pushed away, covering her mouth with her hand and fixing her gaze on the table after catching a glimpse of the surprise on his face.

"I'm sorry," she whispered.

He didn't respond for so long Danielle was forced to meet his gaze. Surprise had been replaced by amusement, with an underlying note of calculation.

"I mean, I like you and … it's just…" She lurched through an undertow of embarrassment and gave herself a solid mental smack for using one guy to deal with another. He didn't look resentful, which was a relief, because he had more reason to be angry with her than either Ryan or Maeve.

"There's someone back in L.A.?" he said, filling in the blank.

Braden's cocky smirk flashed through her mind. "No."

"Someone here, then."

She could lie and make up some lame excuse, or she could tell him the truth. "Yeah, kind of."

"Interesting." He shifted away, still letting his arm rest against her shoulders. "It can't be too serious, or you wouldn't have gone out with me."

"I feel like an idiot."

"It's all right." He reached over and petted the shoulder of her fur vest. "I'm up for the competition."

Her answering grin felt forced, like her big front teeth were trying to bust out through her lips.

His eyes tracked the movement of her mouth. "Go out with both of us until you decide which one you like better."

"The thing is, though, I'm not even really dating him," she said, then swallowed hard when she realized how lame she sounded. The whole story came out, in bursts of words punctuated by awkward giggles. Christopher listened, prompting her occasionally. By the end, his arm had shifted until he was barely touching her.

"You got it bad for this guy," he said.

"Yeah." She reached over and patted his hand. "I just can't do anything about it."

"Well, I can't help you there. I mean, I'm pretty sure I've met him before. He goes out with Drunk Girl – at least he used to go out with her, from what you're telling me."

"Oh my God, you gave Cherry that nickname?"

"Yeah, she's Drunk Girl. Jase and I see her and Maeve out in the clubs all the time. Usually by the end of the night, Maeve's hooked up with some dude and Drunk Girl's on the phone sobbing, waiting for your boyfriend to come haul her home." He didn't look angry, more bemused by how crazy people could be. "I talked to him a couple times, because it was better than listening to Jason whine about how he didn't hook up with Maeve again."

"That sounds bad in many, many ways."

Christopher chuckled and ran a knuckle down her cheek. "Well, you let me know how things go. I'm not the pushy type, but I'm not going to give up, either."

She pulled his hand away from her face. "You're a good guy, Christopher."

He smiled, showing her the full force of his handsome charm. "You're all right too, Danielle. For a cougar."

She choked on a laugh, and he scooted to the end of the booth.

"You know I'm only here until February, right? The least you could do is let me pick up the tab," she said.

"Oh hell no. You might be a client someday. I'll expense it."

He was a smart man, too. When the house was ready to put on the market, he'd be her first call.

* * * *

"Did you kiss him?" Maeve pounced before Danielle even woke up.

Danielle still wore her new black leggings, though she'd changed her fur vest and silk top for an old tee shirt. Blinking back sleep, she sat up, crossing her legs Indian style and pulling the comforter tight across her lap. "Did *you* kiss him?"

"I asked you first."

Danielle's bed was the futon couch and she shifted over slightly, inviting Maeve to sit. "Maybe."

"Maybe?" Maeve squeaked. "Yes? No? Tongue?" Maeve's tongue waggled as she dropped onto the futon and tucked some of the comforter around her feet.

"No," Danielle giggled, determined to keep the details to herself. "We didn't get very far."

Maeve ran the knuckles of her index fingers under her lashes to wipe away yesterday's mascara. "Why? Wasn't he hot enough for you? Because girlfriend, that's about as good as it gets."

"Oh yeah. I just like to take my time." *Because at thirty-three, I've got all the time in the world.*

Maeve huffed. "Didn't used to be a tease."

"Didn't used to be a lightweight, either. People change." Danielle nudged Maeve's foot with her own. "What about you? Is Jason a good kisser?" The easiest way to sidestep a discussion was to make it all about Maeve. "He looked pretty interested."

"Interested in himself. I swear, he would have been better off kissing a mirror."

They both laughed, flopping back against the pillows, upper arms touching. "Hey, I'm sorry I got angry last night," Danielle said.

Maeve was quiet for a long while. "Me too. It's just that, if Ryan and Cherry break up, I'm going to lose a friend."

Dude, they broke up a month ago and you're still friends. Because Danielle didn't want to fight again, she kept her snark to herself. Maeve didn't want friends and brothers mixing, and Danielle knew from personal experience how hard it was to control feelings. They did what they wanted to do, and if Maeve was scared or unreasonable or just plain crazy, telling her to change would do very little good.

"Those pictures are kind of hurtful, don't you think?" Danielle said.

Maeve paused even longer. "Yeah, I guess. He's had it coming, though."

Danielle sunk lower, her head resting on Maeve's shoulder and her hand on her friend's thigh. There were many responses she could make. "*Don't be stupid*" led her list of possibilities. Maeve's cell phone chirped before she chose one.

"Who the hell's calling me already?" Maeve asked herself, rolling off the couch. By the time she dug the phone up, the call had gone to voicemail.

Danielle rested her head back, eyes closed, while Maeve fussed with the phone. Sleep swelled up around her, sucking her down until Maeve's squeal sprung her from her doze. "Oh my God, will you listen to this?"

"What?"

Maeve pressed the phone to Danielle's ear. The message was from a man. *Hey, babe, remember me? I'm the guy from last night. You know, the one with the magic tongue. Wanna do it again?*

"Wow. That's … icky." Danielle could barely get the words out without laughing.

"But he was pretty."

"Somehow I can only picture him with finger pistols."

Maeve doubled over and came up firing, making guns with her hands and aiming them at Danielle. She tripped over the hardwoods and threw herself down on the futon couch. "What. A. Loser."

The women slumped together, their equilibrium restored. "Your friend Waldo's not that bad," Danielle said after a while, her eyes sliding shut as she pulled the quilt up to her chin.

"Totally brilliant. I'll fix Waldo up with Jason." Maeve crawled off the couch, moving with the agility of a born predator. "Except, I have to go out with Jason at least one more time."

Danielle propped an eye open in a display of tired skepticism. "You do?"

"Yeah, so we can double date at the New Year's Eve party."

Maeve's enthusiasm forced both of Danielle's eyes open. "New Year's... What?"

"Party. Every year Cherry and I host a party, and this year you can host with us."

"Sure. In a month or so." Sleep curled around Danielle, gently tugging her down. "It'll be fabulous."

Danielle slept until the smell of bacon got too strong to ignore.

* * * *

When Ryan let himself into the house Wednesday night, Danielle popped out of the dining room with a smile brighter than the overhead light.

"Guess what!" She'd taken off her sweatshirt and he got an eyeful of all kinds of bouncing under her lace-trimmed tee shirt.

"What?"

She made it across the room in about four steps, then grabbed his arm, dragging him toward the dining room. "You gotta see this."

She dropped into a chair and tilted the laptop screen, giving him a look at a stainless steel range.

Just because he wanted to, he put a hand on her shoulder and tilted his head closer. He took a deep breath, recognizing the spicy scent of her hair products. "Aveda."

She rocked around to stare at him. "Seriously?"

"What? Cherry went through a phase."

Something flashed in Dani's eyes, compassion or even pity, and she didn't have to say anything. She'd seen the Facebook pictures. Time to talk about something else. Anything else.

He took another step back, slipping out of his jacket and tossing it on a pile of papers. "Found something you like?" He pointed at the laptop.

"Oh, yeah." Her bright smile came back. "Can you do me a favor?"

"Sure." Anything to keep from talking about Cherry and those goddamned pictures.

"I just bought this off of Craigslist, and the guy said I can come over any time this evening and pick it up. Could I borrow your truck?"

He scratched the back of his head because pumping his fist would make him look like a dork. The opportunity was too good to pass up. "You going to lift an oven by yourself?"

She rolled her eyes. "I'm sure he'll help me."

"Or I will," he said, shrugging back into his jacket. "C'mon. We can stop at Dick's for burgers on the way back."

An hour later they were parked at Dick's Drive-Inn, burgers in their hands and a gently-used stainless steel oven in the bed of his truck. The walk-up service windows glowed with bright white light, and the orange fluorescent Dick's sign shone down from the roof. The air was heavy with grease laid over a foundation of old cigarettes and damp pavement.

Ryan played it as cool as he knew how. They worked easily together on the house, but for anything else the next move had to come from her. "This week I'll finish the cabinet boxes for the kitchen," he said, wiping his French fried fingers with a napkin. "I'll put the walls back together and clean up a couple other details. Then I'll have to take a break until you get the roof and windows taken care of."

Her smile drifted away, likely because he mentioned big-ticket items and not because he wouldn't be around until she got them done.

"What about the bathrooms?" The droop in her voice had hope pinging around in his head like a drunken Tinkerbell from the old Disney movie.

She might miss him after all.

"Yeah, you're right. I can start in on those while you figure the roof thing out," he said, gripping his cool with both hands.

"If you don't want to mess with them, I can find somebody else."

He might hate the hell out of plumbing and tile work, but no way would he let her hire it out. He willed himself to sound cheerful. "Nah, I'll do it."

"I mean, you can give me some names or something."

"I'll give you anything you want, Princess." He made it sound deliberately flirtatious.

Her eyes got big, and even in the semi-light from the drive-in's fluorescent bulbs he could see her blush. "Ryan O'Connor."

He winked at her, and after a weak attempt at looking stern, she smiled back. "You are trouble, young man."

"Guess I need an older woman to keep me in line."

He got a peek at her grin before she covered it with her hand. *God she was fun to flirt with.* He let her stew for a minute, then turned the key in the ignition. "Let's get your new prize home."

She carefully folded up her burger wrapper and put it in the empty Dick's bag. When she spoke, her voice was almost too quiet to hear. "What am I going to do with you?"

Anything you want. Maeve can go to hell.

Chapter Nine

Friday sucked. Danielle got a call from a familiar number, one with a 3-2-3 area code. L.A. Braden. She let it go to voicemail. Then two different roofers came out to give her bids, and both wanted well beyond what her savings could handle, which meant talking to Uncle Jonathan. Which would be hard, but way easier than asking her mother for money.

Ryan called to say he wouldn't be over and Maeve invited her out for dinner and cocktails, but Danielle wasn't in the mood to party. Instead, she sat at the big cherry wood table, listening to music and searching eBay for some vintage pottery for the fireplace mantle.She was supposed to be putting together a Power Point for work, and the irony of spending money on decorations for a place she'd never live in gave each bid a dollop of desperation, as if someone — her boss, her mother, her guardian angel — would walk in, see the mismatched Red Wing vases, and say, 'Of course, Danielle. It was meant to be'.

If what *was meant to be?*

A pair of headlights streaked across the front window, interrupting her bid war. A minute later, heavy footsteps crossed the porch. Then someone knocked hard on the door.

She jerked out of the chair, her confusion exacerbated by the heavy pounding of her heart. No one should be here. The door rattled like someone was messing with the lock. She made a sound halfway between a bleat and a scream when the door opened.

Ryan came in. "Hey, you're here," he said, dimples flaring.

"What are you doing? You scared the shit out of me." She braced herself on the table, pulling in a deep lungful of air.

He just stood grinning at her, hands in his pockets, curls gelled into something close to order. The laptop streamed soft music that all of a sudden sounded romantic, and she panicked, hoping he wouldn't get the wrong idea.

"Glad you think this is funny," she said.

"I thought you'd be out with Maeve." He held up his hands, calming her, placating her. She really wanted those hands touching her.

Down girl.

"I just had to finish up a couple things." She straightened up and rested her knuckles on her hips. Instead of his usual worn jeans and tee shirt, he was dressed in black pants and a light blue button-down shirt that looked like silk and made his eyes crazy bright. His tie was navy and he'd changed out his usual UW hoodie for a black leather jacket. "You look … um…"

"Company Christmas party." He spoke too quickly, like there was something going on under the surface.

"You should be out hanging with your crew." *And not here torturing me.*

"I need to take the clamps off those cabinets I glued up."

The expression on his face had nothing to do with carpentry. He took a couple steps toward the dining room, then veered over to where she stood, moving fast. She fell back, carried by his wave of energy, and in seconds he had her up against the wall, his hands bracketing her head, his hips pressed tight to hers.

"Ryan, no. What are you…"

He covered her mouth with his fingers. "Sh. Just let me be close to you for a minute."

She tipped her chin up and his fingers slid down her neck, stopping when his thumb hit the hollow at the base of her throat and his strong hand cradled her shoulder. He rocked forward, resting his mouth against her forehead.

She stood still, caught up in the heat of his breath on her skin and the soft woodsy smell of his aftershave.

"I know I'm not supposed to do this, Dani."

The scratch of lips against skin made her mouth water. "It's … okay. Just … we shouldn't."

His head turned and lowered. He meant to kiss her. If he succeeded, there was no way she'd stop. She wanted him so, so bad. He cupped her face with both hands, pinning her.

Crap.

His mouth closed over hers like the final piece of a puzzle dropping into place. She stilled, time stopped, the universe paused. She didn't push him away.

Sometimes not choosing becomes its own choice.

Instead, she reached up and grabbed the collar of his silk shirt and hauled him closer. This was what she wanted. To hell with all the arguments against it.

He shoved a thigh between her legs, and his hands grew rougher, grabbing her hair to change the angle of her head. He tasted of mint and gum and beer. The heat rose between them, and oh my God she wanted it. Wanted him. He pulled back, flicked her lips with his tongue. The sound she made was nearly a sob. She drove her hands under his leather coat and pulled his shirt free. When her fingertips reached the warm, velvety skin of his lower back she almost sobbed again.

His kiss got harder, rugged, more demanding, and his hands dragged her ass closer still. Her body lit up, her core turning to liquid flame. He got under her sweatshirt, kneading her breasts. Her head rocked back against the wall and her laughter swirled out under the exquisite torture of his hands on her nipples. His lips and tongue mauled her ear and down her neck, and she keened a victory sound, tiny and high-pitched, her hips rocking slowly against the growing bulge in his groin.

She went to work on the buttons down the front of his shirt, ready to indulge in exploring his muscular chest, but he wrapped her hands in his and shifted his weight away from her.

When he spoke, his voice was rough, heavy. "I'm sorry." He turned slowly, moving like a man three times his age. "Jesus, I know you don't want ... I'm sorry, Dani."

She let the wall support most of her weight, breathing hard, all that warm liquidy goodness turning to ice. Her sweatshirt rode up around her ribs and her bra was off kilter. She tugged everything back into place, embarrassment verging on mortification washing over her. *Why the hell did he stop?* He'd acted on an impulse she felt just as surely as he did. Then he tipped forward a little, unsteady, almost losing his balance, and she put the pieces together. "How much did you have to drink tonight?"

He scrubbed his face with his hands. "A bit."

"A bit too much." She punched his shoulder. He reached out like he would gather her in for a hug, but she sidestepped him. "None of that, now. Let me get my stuff together then I'm going to drive you home."

"Nah, I'm fine."

"Um, right. Give me your keys."

After a brief staring match, he flipped his car keys in her direction. She'd seen pain in his eyes, hiding behind a whole boatload of frustration.

All emotions she could relate to.

"I'm going to go lock the back door." Dodging the kitchen construction zone, she headed into the mud room. She'd just thrown the deadbolt when she heard a sharp crack, along with an indecipherable curse.

Looking back through the dining room, she could see most of Ryan framed in the doorway. He stood with his head bowed, flexing the fingers of his right hand. When she reached the living room, she saw a fist-sized crater in the wall. Without a word, she went back to the kitchen, to the first aid kit she'd stashed in one of the new cabinet boxes. Bringing an ice pack back into the living room, she took his hand in hers.

He didn't look up, letting her hold the ice pack over the raw skin on his knuckles. His shoulders seemed to fold forward, wrapping around her protectively even though he kept his arms at his sides. "I'm trying, Dani," he whispered, raising his head enough to meet her gaze.

That did it.

Her world tightened down to the curve of his upper lip, the faint depressions left by his dimples when he wasn't smiling, the shadow of his beard. "Me too."

The knuckles of his good hand brushed her cheek. She turned into the caress, pressing her lips into his palm. He shifted his weight, resting his forehead on hers. Calm. Quiet.

They stood that way for a long time, until the icepack dropped to the floor and he gathered her in. She arched up, stretching out against the length of his body. The relief from finally being close to him made her dizzy.

Still, when he turned his head to kiss her, she eased out of his grasp, a move requiring more inner grit than she knew she possessed. *Maeve and age and L.A. and Cherry.* "Let's not press our luck."

The humor was undercut by the tremor in her voice, but he got the message. He picked up one of her hands for a kiss, his lips gentle against her skin. "Right."

It took her a minute, but she pulled her hand away. "Let's go."

He laughed, sounding as shaky as she felt. "I'll patch the wall."

"At least," she said, doing her best to look stern. He smiled, then she laughed, and in the time it took her to pack up her laptop, things started to feel more normal. They might have stood closer together, and when Ryan held the front door open, Danielle could have skimmed his body with hers as she passed. She didn't. The brush of his heat against her skin barely satisfied her. She refused to return his keys, and after some halfhearted protests, they both got in her car.

His presence in the passenger seat was like a magnet, pulling all the little fibers in her being toward him. She had to use all her concentration to keep the car on the road.

She had to use all her willpower to drop him off alone.

* * * *

Danielle was up and out of the apartment early Saturday morning, making it as far as the Magnolia Coffee Company for a latte and borrowed Wi-Fi. Camped out in one of the overstuffed chairs in front of the gas fireplace, laptop open, she searched for self-help articles on how to date a friend's brother. She needed to get a handle on the transition, because the whole "keep away from Ryan" thing was very close to going down in flames.

Basing a strategy adjustment on one kiss might be an overcall, but it never hurt to be prepared. Besides, it had been a flaming, sparks-flying, blow-up-the-fuse-box kind of kiss. Her adult mind could list the reasons to stay away from Ryan from now until next Tuesday, but as Gram told her more than once, "the heart wants what it wants."

Some of the webpages were surprisingly helpful. Don't diss your boyfriend to his sister. Made sense. Limit the PDA aspect. Made even more sense. Make sure to spend time with your friend so she doesn't feel left out.

Danielle would make a point of it, providing they were on speaking terms.

After caving in and buying herself a second latte, she headed over to the house, cutting through a neighborhood of huge old homes hidden behind fat rhododendrons and dense green lawns. Closer to the water, the number of Madrona trees increased, their twisted branches and peeling cinnamon bark adding an interesting texture to the fusty grey sky.

She'd never been one to act rashly. She'd done the school thing, working her way to a Master's degree. She'd done the work thing, moving from staff nurse to charge nurse to assistant manager. She met a man who fit her lifestyle, they got serious, and things moved along according to her plan.

Then Braden left, and Danielle-Red-Riding-Hood had come straight to Grandma's house.

And found a wolf.

Leaving L.A. was the most reckless thing she'd ever done. Until she met Ryan. Now, she'd apparently made 'reckless' her middle name.

She drove up Perkins Lane, surprised to find Ryan's truck in the yard. Literally *in* the yard. He'd backed up across the grass, aiming the bed of the truck at the front porch. The truck's gate was down, ready to be loaded.

Edging past it, she heard noise before she even reached the door. A heavy thud, followed by the sound of something shattering. The front door was open, the floor lamp in the living room was on, and one of Ryan's sweatshirts was draped over the wing chair.

She found him in the bathroom. He wore a pair of wrecked jeans, shabby even by his casual standards. One sleeve of his old tee shirt hung crooked because of a huge rip in the shoulder seam, which was okay because the gap showed off his muscular shoulder. Sweat pasted down curls at the edge of his hairline and his shadowy beard suggested it had been over twenty-four hours since he'd shaved. Chunks of the bathtub spread across the bathroom floor, and the smell of mold gagged her.

"What the hell are you doing?" Surprise added a bitchy tang to the words. She hadn't been 100% set on replacing the old bathtub.

Oh well.

"Penance." Shoulders rounded as if exhaustion weighed him down, he turned back to the ruined tub. Sections of the tile had given way, revealing a moldering black mass underneath it.

"Ooh," she whispered. "That's ugly."

Using the sledgehammer, he tapped the wall, knocking off another chunk of the yellow 4x4 tile. "I'll get all this out of here today, then pick up some new cement board to replace the rotten stuff."

It was only nine in the morning, and God only knew how long he'd been working. Sweaty and filthy dirty, he was the sexiest thing she'd ever seen. She set her latte cup in the sink, fighting hard to keep from grabbing the closest part of Ryan she could reach. "You got drunk last night and now you feel bad."

He stared down at her, keeping a wall between them with his gaze. "About some of it, yeah."

Despite all the warm fuzzy reading she'd done, the grown-up part of her mind refused to give in without a fight, so instead of flirting, even a little, she kept on-task. "All right, well, is there anything I can do in here to help?"

"Nah." He tapped the hammer on the floor and chuffed a laugh. "This room's too small for both of us. I might not be able to keep my hands to myself."

Apparently his adult mind didn't get the memo. "Listen, about that. We should probably talk—"

"I'm in the middle of disemboweling Jabba the Hut over here and now you want to talk?" he snapped, rubbing his forehead with the back of his hand.

She wasn't used to him using anger to keep her away. "Later then." An idea hit her head and made it out of her mouth before she could consider the consequences. "We could grab dinner after we're done working."

The sledgehammer thumped against a piece of the broken tub. "Did you just ask me out?"

"Not exactly." She raked a hand through her hair. "I guess. Maybe?"

He didn't smile at her weak attempt at humor.

"It's not like a date-date, but we do need to figure things out," she said, scrambling to find a way to make it all better.

He still didn't smile.

"Don't worry about it, then. I'm being silly." She ran out of words.

He gave the demolished bathtub a long, considering look. "I'm just hung over, Princess." Meeting her gaze, some of the tension left him. "You're right, we should talk. Dinner sounds great."

"Really? Like, pizza or something?"

133

His smile showed the ghost of a dimple. "That'll work."

For the next few hours Danielle searched online for bathroom fixtures and tried to find the cheapest price for white subway tile. Then she sanded some sheetrock and applied a layer of stain to the molding she'd stripped.

In response to her multiple offers, Ryan said the one thing he needed her help with had nothing to do with a bathroom remodel.

The only hitch in the otherwise quiet morning was a phone call from her mother. She almost picked it up, paused, and then let it go to voicemail. She could listen to the message later, after she'd had some time for strategizing.

If she was really brave, she'd listen to the message from Braden at the same time.

* * * *

Ryan spent more hours than he cared to think about clearing the broken tub and tile and hauling the mildewed lathe and plaster wall from the main bathroom. His hangover faded by lunch, helped along by the teriyaki take-out Dani brought him. The only awkward moment happened right before he took his filthy butt home to clean up.

He chucked the last armload of tub debris into the bed of the truck, and Dani met him in the doorway with a towel. He wiped sweat off his face and rubbed down the back of his neck. When he opened his eyes, she was staring straight at his right ear.

The damned tattoo.

Her face got a tight look, like the reminder of Cherry discouraged her. She came right up into his personal space, her hand reaching for him.

"Don't," he said, jerking away. "I smell worse than I look." He was still steamed that he'd let himself get talked into the tatt in the first place.

"At least it's not as obvious as some." Her hand dropped, her expression tightening farther. "That your only tattoo?"

"Yep."

She made a soft, satisfied noise, like she'd been afraid to get any closer in case Cherry's face peered out from between his shoulder blades or something.

"So?" He phrased it as a question, giving her one more chance to change her mind. It would kill him, but if she meant to back away, now was the time to do it.

She fluttered her hands in the direction of his driver's side door. "So … go take a shower. You're all gross."

He reached for his keys, taking one last swipe at his face with the towel. She crossed her arms under her breasts, her semi-flirtatious smile tagging him with a heady surge of heat. His eyes dropped to her chest, obvious enough to make her laugh. He gave her a half-assed wave, and, acting like he couldn't stop looking, got into the truck.

He didn't have to act that hard.

Twenty minutes to get from Perkins Lane to his North Seattle house. Almost an hour to shower and shave. Closer to thirty minutes to wrestle the surface-street traffic to Maeve's apartment. Three times around the block to score a parking spot on the street.

Several lifetimes waiting for her to come out.

He sent her a text, letting her know he was outside. No response. The brake lights came on in the car ahead of him, splashing his dashboard with red. He scanned his phone. Nothing. He locked his eyes back on the main entrance to her apartment.

What if she'd gotten into it with Maeve?

What if someone made her a better offer?

He never wasted much time with doubt, but in reality, he was a carpenter. Why would someone like Dani —older, more educated, and professional — want to go out with him? His house didn't have anything close to a view of the Mulholland Canyon.

His own insecurity threatened to turn the heat in his belly from anticipation into anger.

Then she pushed the door open, looking around eagerly, her smile huge when she saw him. Yeah, there was no good answer for why.It only mattered that she was headed for his truck and they were going to get dinner. She'd talk, he'd listen, and then they'd see what they'd see.

* * * *

They had dinner at a funky pizzeria surrounded by college kids and Sounders fans. Danielle had hoped she and Ryan would share enough of themselves to come to a decision. Either they were going to act on their impulses or they were going to focus on the remodel. Instead, they ate pizza and talked about random stuff, apparently content to continue in a netherworld of unsatisfied desire.

Afterward, Danielle huddled in her jacket, waiting for the truck's heater, shivering from a combination of nerves, excitement, and a full belly.

"I'm thinking we should head over to Gassworks," Ryan said. He started up the engine and put the truck in gear.

"I haven't been there in years."

"It's close." He eased the truck out of their parking spot. "It's dark." He paused at the edge of the lot before pulling into traffic. "And it's pretty."

"Pretty."

"Like you."

Danielle let her twisted lips rebut his opinion, but Ryan's laugh both squashed her denial and layered on another compliment. His proximity sharpened her need to touch, creating a raw prickling in the palms of her hands, and the steady pulse of an old Rolling Stones tune on the stereo only reinforced her instincts.

They made the trip to Gassworks Park in about fifteen minutes and ended up surrounded on all sides by city lights. Downtown was ahead of them, Capitol Hill on their left, and Queen Ann on the right. Ryan found a parking spot, shut everything down, and opened his door.

"We're getting out?" Danielle's voice squeaked. The cab of the truck had warmed up nicely, but outside it was somewhere in the thirty-degree range, and intermittently spitting rain.

"I thought we could walk down to the water."

Scrambling out of the truck, Danielle stuffed her hands in her pockets and wished for either a heavier coat or a stronger cocktail, something that would take the edge off the chill. "We're the only people here."

"I know we're the only people here." Ryan took a loose hold of her hand and led her through the darkness in the general direction of the water. "That's the idea."

He tugged her along, keeping more or less to the path circling the old industrial plant that gave the park its name, a hulking Steampunk fantasy of metal pipes and silos that made a dark black silhouette against the night sky.

The third time Danielle stumbled, she whipped out her cell phone and turned on the flashlight. Walking — and her proximity to Ryan — had warmed her up enough to be curious about what he was up to. "The park is probably closed."

"Yeah, so you should turn that flashlight off before someone sees it." He goosed her ribs.

"Hey now." She scooted away from him. "Don't mess with me."

His grasp non-negotiable, he drew her against his body. "But I want to mess with you."

This. This closeness, this gentle embrace eased the tension tying up her breath since they'd kissed the night before. She tucked her head under his chin, his aftershave a warm, spicy top-note to the cold earth smell from the field of grass under their feet. The city lights surrounded them, as if they were standing at the bottom of a bowl full of stars.

"You're not even going to try to stop me?" he asked.

"Don't want to."

So they'd made a decision after all.

Their bodies were separated by bulky jackets and gloves so Danielle couldn't give him a true demonstration of what was on her mind. She cupped his chin with her hands and stood up on tiptoe to kiss him.

He went off like a bottle rocket, all heat and raw hunger. He clasped her head, claimed her mouth, and used his lips and tongue to give her a lesson in need.

Danielle met him with a flare of her own. She opened up and drew him deeper. His growl rumbled against her chest and she clutched the collar of his coat, clinging to the only source of heat in the frigid night. He tasted malty from the beer they'd shared over dinner, though that observation was filtered through the prism of bruising kisses and the thrust of his swelling cock against her thigh.

He folded over her, licking and nipping and sucking a fevered trail down her neck.

She gasped, giggled, and gasped again. "Are we going to do it in the dark in the park?"

"With a guy named Clark," Ryan murmured, his warm breath teasing her ear.

"Shut up." She laced her fingers through his hair, getting enough of a grip to pull him up so they could talk. Her nose was numb and her toes were colder. "Seriously. What are your intentions, young man?"

"The best." He pulled her tighter against his body. "Let's go back to my house."

Reservations snuck through, despite the fever heat between them, his clean soap smell, and the generous strength in his arms. "Wait a minute. What kind of woman do you think I am?"

Stepping back, he held her cheeks with his palms and rocked his head gently from side to side. "Dani, Dani, Dani," he said, his voice just louder than a whisper. "Why we gotta make things so hard?"

Irritation pinged her like glass shattering on concrete. She brought her hands up hard between his, to fling herself out of his grasp. "Because it is hard, you condescending little twerp."

At his shocked expression, she covered her mouth with her hands to stifle the laughter, but it didn't work. Soon they were both laughing, then Ryan's hands were on her shoulders, and then she folded back into him. "Let's go back to the truck, at least," she said through a wave of shivers.

Without giving him time to argue, she pivoted and headed back up the path. After a second, he strode up beside her and put his arm around her. They fell in step, the streetlights lining the parking lot giving them enough light to go on.

Ryan barely let her get her car door shut before he cupped her jaw with one hand and leaned close. Their lips brushed together, once, twice in light touches, as if there was still an invisible barrier they needed to tear down. Then his grip on her tightened and his lips closed in, hungry, demanding a response. She wove her fingers through his damp curls, shifting her weight so she was on the edge of her seat and her knees dug into his thigh.

He reached around, sliding his hand up under her jacket, gripping her thigh, the tips of his fingers hitting the crease between leg and butt. Desire and restraint went to war, and a shiver that had nothing to do with cold started in her chest and coalesced a lot lower down. If he tugged at all she'd end up straddling him, her back smashed against the steering wheel and her lady parts…

There wasn't a lot of space between the wheel and his lap.

Their kisses made a rhythmic wave, light grazing flutters alternating with deep, soul-shearing strokes. She opened herself to him, setting free her own wild energy, bringing a groan from the depths of his chest. She reached out and found the bulge in his groin, its heat matching the lava pooling between her legs. She massaged him through his jeans, frustrated by the layers of heavy clothes and the distance between them.

Suddenly that space between his lap and the steering wheel didn't look so narrow.

She nuzzled the rough whiskers under his chin. He thumbed her nipple through her velvet shirt, his other hand cupping her ass. With every slight shift of her body against his, he brought his fingertips closer to her sweet center, and she stroked him more firmly.

He left her mouth, running the tip of his tongue along the line of her jaw and settling behind her ear. The shivering started again and this time she rocked forward, severely tempted to straddle him. The fire in her veins burned away most of her reservations. When she accidentally on purpose popped open one of the buttons in his fly, he froze.

"You seriously want to do this in the truck?" He hissed, a sharp intake of breath.

"Oh crap." She fumbled with the button, doing it back up. "No. I'm sorry. I'm losing my mind."

"Be better in a bed." He reached for her hand, bringing her fingers to his lips and kissing each one.

The burn inside faded, dampened by their predicament and by the icy rain crackling against the windshield, echoing the static energy between them. Instead of responding, she found one of his hands and brought it to her own mouth, taking care to give each of his blunt and calloused fingertips individual attention, teasing with the tip of her tongue, sucking gently on his thumb until he moaned.

"Shit. We're going back to my house."

The reality of it dumped over her like ice water. "We can't."

"Why not?" Surprise rattled through his words. "We just turn the engine on and drive."

Telling him she didn't want to sleep with him *now* because someday she'd turn forty and he'd only be thirty-one was dumb. Reminding him she had to be in L.A. in six weeks wouldn't help much, either. Danielle massaged her temples, wondering how much of her reluctance was valid and how much was based in fear because her ex was an asshole.

In the end, she played the Maeve card. "Let me talk to your sister first." She met his disbelieving gaze as squarely as she could. "I feel weird sleeping with you until I do."

Ryan had the engine running before she was all the way back in her seat, and when he spoke his words were clipped, tight."Seems like you felt fine about it ten minutes ago."

"I'm a flake. I know." She put a hand on the side of his face, forcing him to look at her. "A flake. A horny flake, and you make me do crazy things." She bit her bottom lip, wondering what she needed to say to make things okay. "I want you so bad I'm seeing sideways, but my gut's telling me to wait."

"Your gut, huh?" He bounced his head against the seat a couple times. "Sideways, huh?" His mouth softened.

"I'll make it up to you."

He reached down and grasped himself. "You will, too."

"Promise."

By the time he dropped her off at Maeve's apartment, his smile was almost normal. Good thing, too, because mixing sex into the house project was a huge gamble. More importantly, she knew from as deep as her bones and her blood that with Ryan, it wouldn't be just sex.

Chapter Ten

Danielle leaned against one of the only blank stretches of wall, tucked between a pair of antique display cabinets loaded with lacy lingerie. "Why would a man who tossed me out like yesterday's tuna suddenly call and wish me a merry Christmas?"

Maeve stopped pawing through a rack of velvet shirts and swirling silky skirts. "He called because he wants something." She raised both eyebrows, adding an eloquent *duh* to her comment, before holding the sleeve of a deep green blouse against her chest. "He's a guy, right?"

"Oh yeah." Danielle scooted a pair of pink panties into line with its mates. "Right."

It had taken her a while, but Danielle finally listened to the voicemail Braden left. And listened to it. Three times. Each replay fed her growing sense of *"WTF?!"* He'd told her how much he missed her, and how he hoped she was having a fantastic time in Seattle.

'Fantastic' was one of his three favorite words.

"Don't ask stupid questions if you don't want obvious answers." Maeve stuck the shirt back on the rack and grabbed a long black skirt, whirling it around until the fabric fluttered in a circle. "Why am I even looking at this hippie shit? I'd go mental trying to wear this much fabric."

"You're the one who wanted to stop here," Danielle said. She didn't want to spend money on new, expensive clothes, the kind found in hip little boutiques in funky shopping districts. They'd gone that route for her date with Christopher, and she had a fur vest to show for it, a trophy she'd likely never wear again.

"Cherry said I should check it out." Maeve moved from the pool of light over the freestanding rack of clothes to a second pool of light over a rack against the far wall.

Danielle drew a couple quick breaths, steadying herself. Talking about Cherry was only a couple steps from talking about Ryan, and Danielle needed to bring him up, to let Maeve know that things were changing. Things had changed. The cat was on its way out and wanted to toss the bag. "Nordstrom's let her shop in a place like this?"

"She has to bury the receipts in her back yard." Maeve shifted her weight, easing back into the shadow. "C'mon. Let's get out of here." She moved toward the front of the store.

Danielle followed as far as one of the overhead spotlights. "Wait, I mean, has she said anything about Ryan?"

Possibly the least-graceful segue ever.

The glare from overhead made it hard to read Maeve's expression, but Danielle was determined to keep going until they'd sorted things out. Or until she'd laid some groundwork, at least. Right now Maeve was a cornerstone in her sense of security, and Danielle needed her support for the idea of letting Ryan in on the ground floor.

"Why?" Maeve's pinched-lip expression made it clear she really, really didn't want to talk about Ryan.

"Nothing." Danielle wrapped her pashmina scarf tighter. *Your brother and I...*

Maeve shifted her weight from one foot to the other, arms crossed, shields up, waiting.

Danielle's lips locked. She mashed her thumbs into her temples, frustration spinning tight little circles in her head.

"Let's get the hell out of here," Maeve said.

Deep breath. Not giving up. "Next door looked interesting," Danielle said, referring to a place with the kind of Christmas presents you could give a guy, where she could pick up a pair of nice leather gloves or a sleek new wallet and when Maeve asked if it was for Christopher, Danielle could say, *no it's for Ryan.*

Maeve batted at the nearest rack of clothes and stepped out under a spotlight. "Eh, I think it's time for a cocktail."

Danielle squeezed the heck out of her inner chicken. "I'd like to pick up a couple Christmas presents first."

Maeve paused halfway to the front door, giving her a sneer that dared Danielle to say Ryan's name. "For who?"

"Well, there's Uncle Jonathan," and Ryan, "and my cousin," and Ryan, "and I thought I'd bring something to your mother for inviting me over." And Ryan.

"What about Christopher? I bet he'd like a nice bottle of wine or something." Maeve's comment was as much of a dare as anything else, a test to see if Danielle would really go there.

Fail. "Yeah."

"Come on," Maeve said, her tone infused with relief. "There's a wine bar across the street that sells bottles. Two birds with one swoop, and all."

Following Maeve out into the rain, Danielle gritted her teeth. If she could handle an ornery attending physician and talk a staff nurse off the ledge, she ought to be able to handle Maeve. *Say something.* She avoided a huge puddle by an inch. *Now.* Her smile stretched out. *Do it.*

She did something, all right. She followed Maeve to the wine bar. Unfortunately — or not — she couldn't find a bottle for Christopher.

* * * *

The O'Connor family tradition called for a party on Christmas Eve, an event attended by relatives and friends and people off the street, judging by the size of the crowd squashed into Vickie O'Connor's living room. Danielle wore a black jersey wrap top and a green satin skirt she'd brought out special for the holiday. Leftover from L.A., it was shorter and tighter than most of her Seattle clothes. Maeve almost approved.

Her new shoes deserved no one's approval. They were sky high, with toes pointed as sharp as the heels. They felt like guilt and deserved a quick trip to the Salvation Army donation box — if she survived wearing them.

Ryan liked them just fine.

In fact, he intercepted Danielle almost as soon as she came through his mother's front door. Maeve sailed on ahead, a gust of rowdy wind aiming for a back bedroom to drop off her coat, open to stirring up trouble along the way.

"Hey, boss," Ryan said, giving Danielle a once-over that started and stopped with her shoes and left a wash of heat all over her body.

"Boss?" She tried to reign in her smile, afraid of blinding him with her big front teeth.

"I'm working for you, aren't I? And you are seriously working that outfit." He said the last bit just loud enough for her to hear.

She fought the impulse to drape herself against him and hang on. Instead, she laughed and batted at his arm, the way a grade school kid would sneak a touch without being obvious about it. The house smelled appropriately Christmas-y, all warm pine trees, roasting meat, and spiced cider.

Vickie elbowed her son out of the way and wrapped Danielle in a hug. Her silver hair curled around her face and her manicure was a bright Christmas red, as warm and cheerful as the angel statues decorating every flat surface in the room. "I'm so glad you're here," she said. "Merry Christmas."

Danielle hugged her back just as hard. "Thanks, Mrs. O."

"Let me take your coat. The beer's in the cooler out back, there are snacks on the counter, and we'll sing some Christmas carols if the crazed fans ever get tired of watching football."

"Come on, Ma. It's the Whipped Cream Bowl," Ryan said, winking at Danielle.

"Really? That's a strange name for a football game," Vickie said. Then she caught Ryan's look. "You brat. You shouldn't pick on your mother like that."

"Yeah, Ryan, don't mess with Mom," Maeve said, coming back into the living room. She threaded her arm though Danielle's. "And go watch your dumb game. The girls are going to go have a drink in the kitchen."

Danielle let herself be pulled away. The smile on Ryan's face faded the farther she got. Danielle gave him a sheepish grin, then stifled it when his mother looked quickly from one of them to the other.

Vickie O'Connor didn't miss much when it came to her kids.

"Did I see Joey camped in front of the TV?" Maeve hollered as she dragged Danielle into the kitchen. The dining table had been thoroughly poinsettiaed, at least the parts not covered by trays of appetizers. More people crowded around it.

"Not anymore," Joe said, appearing behind them. "Aren't you going to give your baby brother a hug?"

Maeve kept a tight hold on Danielle and wrapped her other arm around her brother. It forced Danielle into awkward contact with a young man she hadn't seen since he was a kid. Taller than Niall but wiry where the others were solid, his variation on the O'Connor smile had less dimples and more irony. His hair was cropped short on the sides, lifting to a solid wave off his forehead. All he needed was a bolo string tie to complete the retro Western look.

Danielle's nose mashed awkwardly into his shoulder when Maeve squeezed, but he grabbed her hand, limiting her ability to scoot away. "C'mere stranger. Everybody loves a hug."

Maeve tipped into them with her full weight, arms around their shoulders. Her move knocked Danielle off her heels and sent her staggering into a cluster of people. She landed with an inarticulate squawk and a mostly humorous round of applause.

A familiar pair of hands circled her ribs from behind, setting her back on her feet. "Careful," Ryan said, close enough to her ear to send shivers down the back of her neck.

"Now look what you've done, Maeve," Joey said. "Good catch, bro."

"You okay, Boss?" Ryan asked, this time speaking up for the benefit of his siblings.

"Fine." She drew back, tugging gently at his wrists. The worst part about the whole thing was letting go of him. His hands were big and warm, and they wrapped around her ribs like a corset of happiness. She gave him a meaningful squeeze, wondering how they were going to get through Christmas Eve without making fools of themselves.

That was if he didn't lose it completely when he found out she hadn't talked to Maeve.

I'm an idiot.

The siblings hung out in the kitchen area, the only space not crowded with guests. Eamon followed Maeve and Joey in, propping himself on a corner of the center island with his back to the dining room. He was the family hippie, with shoulder-length hair, a five o'clock shadow that was nearly a beard, and a faded button-down shirt worn tie-less and untucked.

Maeve shoved Joey out the back door, demanding he grab a couple beers from the cooler.

"Then you dorks can go watch football," she said to her brothers. "Is Niall here yet?"

"Nope," Eamon said, his hands stuffed deep in his pockets and his unfocused gaze forming a patch of discomfort in the middle of his family. He took three of the long-neck bottles from Joey and passed them around the room.

Ryan waved him off. "Already got one."

Vickie came out of the crowd. "If you guys are going to loiter, you're in charge of keeping up with the appetizers."

"What about the wait staff?" Joey said.

His mother gave him a look. "Um, I've got a spare black vest you could use."

Joey struck a mock pose, one hand on his hip, the other with the palm raised. "May I take your order?"

"I'll give you an order," Vickie said, aiming a fake slap at her youngest son. "When the timer beeps, take the cheese puffs out of the oven and put a tray of the mini-quiches in."

"We're on it," Danielle said. Maeve rewarded her with a kick in the shins.

"Where is Niall, anyway?" Maeve flipped the cap off her beer with a bottle opener that started playing *Santa Claus Is Coming To Town*. Startled, she dropped the opener on the floor, very nearly spilling her beer. "Mother!"

Vickie dove back into the party, her laughter quickly drowned out by the noise of the crowd.

"This is cool," Ryan said, scooping up the bottle opener and looking from it to Danielle, teasing her before handing it over.

Their fingers might have brushed.

Accidentally.

Danielle mumbled an apology and hoped her cheeks weren't bright red. Ryan caught her with a dimple that drew her to his side by the center island. Trying to act casual, she made an attempt at keeping an equal distance between her and Ryan and Eamon. Maeve claimed a relatively clear stretch between appliances, and Joey stood nearest the back door, apparently used to being the group beer runner. Being youngest had its disadvantages.

The circle of O'Connors turned the kitchen into a private place, despite the rumbling throng jockeying for a spot at the buffet table. The kitchen was where the In Crowd hung out, and Danielle had envied this particular group since high school.

Frequent sneaky glances at Ryan kept her equal parts engaged and distracted. He wore new-ish Levis that fit him the way women dream about, a black crewneck sweater, and Dr. Martens boots. His energy sizzled against her, tightening her smile until she could have struck a match against her teeth.

Every other time she looked at him, she swore Maeve busted her.

"What have you been doing since you got home?" Eamon asked Joey, his heavy eyelids and slow drawl hinting he'd smoked a bowl of something before coming in to face the family.

"Not much. Callahan had a party last night," Joey said.

"Ooh, was Katie DiJulio there?" Maeve grinned like a kid who'd just found the biggest chocolate in the box.

Joey crossed his arms the way Ryan always did, but without the muscular definition to back it up. He was still smiling, but it had more sneer in it. "Shut up, Maeve."

Good. Let Joey distract her.

Maeve tipped back her beer with enough of a smirk to suggest she was just getting up for another round. "What'd you ever do to her, anyway?"

Danielle rolled her lips to fight a grin. Ryan bumped her with his elbow, a light touch charged with way too much heat. She glanced at him, and the laughter in his eyes made it necessary to tip her head forward and hide behind a drape of hair.

"Shut up, Maeve." Joey's tone took an ominous turn.

"No, seriously. I see her down in the Market sometimes." Maeve set her beer on the counter and crossed her arms, a mirror of her younger brother. "She'll go into Nordstrom's and talk to Cherry, but she won't speak to me. You must have dogged her good."

Joey's smile was stuck in place, but his eyes were really, really unhappy. "Shut up, Maeve."

Danielle scrambled for something to say, anything to change the topic, to break the tension. She blinked a couple times in Ryan's direction, but he had a fist covering his mouth, as if it was all he could do not to laugh out loud. Even Mr. Hippie Eamon seemed to be fighting a smile. Business as usual for the O'Connor Kids.

Maeve gave them all a glittering smile, satisfied by the job she'd done ruffling Joey's feathers. "And that reminds me. This is the first time Cherry hasn't been here for Christmas Eve in what? Five years?"

Ryan didn't say it, but the look he gave her said *Shut up, Maeve* louder than any words.

"Who's Katie DiJulio?" Danielle asked. Of the two, Joey made a better target than Ryan. Danielle wanted them talking about Cherry about as much as she wanted to step outside for a root canal.

"The only woman Joey'll ever love," Eamon said. His willingness to deflect attention from Ryan made him Danielle's second-favorite brother. After Ryan, of course.

"Jesus, can we leave it alone already?" Joey shook his head and laughed, conceding defeat. "Where is Cherry, anyway? She finally wise up and dump you, bro?"

Shut up, Joey.

Maeve's glitter turned brittle, and Ryan lost any trace of a smile. Joey looked around the circle, a sliver of realization shifting the tease in his eyes to something more sympathetic.

They all paused when the oldest brother, Niall, came out of the crowd.

"Dude, you're late," Ryan said, visibly relieved at the subject change.

"Where ya been?" Maeve draped an arm around Niall, laughing and possessive at once. "And where's your bitchy wife?"

Niall ducked underneath her arm. "Rhonda's not here." His tone said there was more going on than Maeve's needling. Danielle was relieved to be talking about anything besides Ryan and Cherry, then was ashamed of her relief when she registered the stress in his words.

Maeve missed the subtext, though. She tripped backwards, laughing and catching herself on the counter. "Well where is she?"

"Don't know."

His two words cut straight through the cheery bluster. Maeve reached out for him again, this time radiating concern. They all waited to see what he'd say next.

He pulled off his black watch cap and shrugged out of his coat. He laid them both on the center island, his blue button-down shirt almost the same color as his eyes. "You still have that house, right?" he asked with a nod in Ryan's direction.

"Yeah, man."

"I'm going to be moving out. Can I crash in your spare bedroom?"

"Sure." Ryan was half a head taller, but his eyes echoed his brother's pain in a way that rarely came out in words. "I mean, Barnabas thinks it's his, but he'll get over it."

Maeve picked up the coat, stopping to give Niall a kiss on the cheek before carrying it out of the room. Without a word, Joey ducked outside and grabbed another beer, handing it to his oldest brother.

"Thanks," Niall said with a gesture aiming at all of them, his posture straight, his expression cordially neutral. "I'm going to go catch the game." He faded back into the crowd.

"Guess Rhonda's history," Joey said, closing the back door.

Eamon straightened up. "To everything there is a reason."

He might have been joking. It was hard to tell. Joey pointed at Eamon and opened his mouth. No words came out. After a second, he shrugged and held out a couple more bottles he'd collected from the cooler. "Either of you two want another beer?"

Ryan reached for one, chuckling as if the family crazy had finally thrown him a curve ball. "Niall and Rhonda have been headed for this for a while."

"No shit?" Joey ran a hand through the smooth wave of his bangs, going from Rockabilly to rogue in one move. "I'm going to see about some football."

That left Danielle and Ryan alone in the kitchen. They stared at each other for a few beats, their elbows touching. She shifted toward him, almost close enough to rest her head on his shoulder. Her up-close look at the kitchen crazy would take a bit of time to process.

"Your family is never boring," she said. Her family specialized in sniping instead of support. The Jacobsen foundation was built on obligation. The O'Connors seemed to have built theirs on affection.

"My family." Ryan's words were almost a sigh. He raised his beer. "Cheers, babe."

Their bottles clinked together.

"Merry Christmas, Ryan."

The dense warmth of his arm against hers and the steady rasp of his breath calmed the pins and needles that had been dancing along the edge of her skin ever since she'd arrived at the O'Connor's.

"So, you didn't say anything to Maeve, did you," Ryan said. It wasn't a question. He didn't sound angry.

Still, a flash flood of embarrassment dragged Danielle downstream so fast she'd never get her good mood back.

She tipped her chin up, giving up her smile for the first time all night. "I'm sorry."

"I can talk to her." He spoke to the floor, as if looking at her would give too much away. "Tell her I want to go out with you. She'll be pissed, but she'll get over it."

"No, I'll say something."Danielle focused on their toes, his chunky black boots next to her pointy pumps. They matched their personalities. He was direct, up front about things. She only let a few things show, holding back most of her feelings.

She was about to describe this little revelation when he reached around, grabbing her upper arms and pulling her close. His tone carried impatience, his eyes the beginnings of anger, his mouth, hunger. "Damn it, Dani, this is real to me. I'm not playing a game."

She had her hands around his shoulders and her lips on his before he could say anything else. *There's more than one way to avoid an issue.* She got her fingers up in his hair and let down her guard, the happy party noise fading away as she flicked him with her tongue, drawing him out, swallowing him down. She pressed against him, her core softening against his strength. He wrapped an arm around her waist, drawing her closer still.

She couldn't tell who broke the kiss. She just ended up with her head tucked beneath his chin and her body draped against his the way she'd wanted to be since she'd arrived. The crowd could see them. She didn't care. The family could see them. She didn't care. Hell, Maeve could see them. She didn't care.

"And now I'm wondering how grabbing her ass helps the remodel."

155

Maeve's voice snapped them apart. Well, it snapped Danielle back, anyway, with a blast of adrenaline like the rush of a near-miss car crash.

It snapped Ryan into a much different place. He pulled Danielle close with an arm around her shoulders, turning them both and pressing her against his chest, hard, not giving her a chance to disagree. She wrapped her hands around his forearm, uncertain whether she was holding him closer or fighting her way free.

Maeve just stood with her fists on her hips, one spike heel tapping the floor. "So this is why you won't get back together with Cherry." Maeve directed her comment at Ryan, as if Danielle didn't even rate eye contact.

"No," Danielle said, anger working its way through the cloud of shock that had enveloped her.

Ryan relaxed a little, moving to the side, his arm dropping away from the choke-hold he'd had on Danielle's shoulders. He kept her close, though, interlacing his fingers with hers. "No, Maeve, this is not why I won't get back together with Cherry. I told Cherry that unless she got help for her drinking problem, we were done."

"Drinking problem? I see. It's all her fault." Maeve's heel tapped faster, as if she could outrun the implications of his statement.

"Don't be stupid." Ryan flicked a glance at Danielle. She nodded back, just as fast.

I hear you and I got your back.

"It's me you're mad at," Danielle said, shifting her weight away from Ryan but keeping hold of his hand. "You always said 'leave my brothers alone' and here I am messing with one."

"You always were the center of your own universe."

Ryan lurched toward his sister.

Danielle tugged his hand, pulling him back.

"Don't be a bitch," he said.

"Come on, you guys." Danielle put a hand on his arm to calm him, and the muscles bunched under her touch. Fear tried to lock her down tighter than the freakin' heels on her feet, but she couldn't give in. If she did, Ryan and Maeve could do each other real damage. "Maeve, you're my best friend, and I know this makes you uncomfortable."

"Uncomfortable." Maeve took a couple steps back, as if she was trying to avoid standing in something disgusting.

"I want to go out with Ryan." Danielle took a careful step toward Maeve. "And I want to be your friend."

"And I want your shit out of my apartment." Maeve spun away in an agitated jerk and stalked off into the crowd.

Chapter Eleven

Ryan hated giving his sister the last word, but the torn-up look on Dani's face kept him from chasing Maeve through the crowd. Shoving most of his anger and frustration in a back pocket, he cupped Dani's shoulders and pulled her rigid body against his own.

"Shh, Princess, it'll be okay."

The side of her fist landed on his chest, somewhere between gentle and thump, and she rocked back on her heels. "These effing shoes." She bit down on her lower lip. "Now she's all in a wad and I'm going to end up sleeping on the street."

"There's always my—"

She pressed her fingers over his lips. "If I go home with you, it'll make things worse."

Some of his anger burst out, giving him enough of a head rush to force him back a step. "Oh, it's like that?"

"Like what?" Her eyes shut down, turning her face into a mask, as distant as the classic movie stars she resembled.

Like what? He took another step back. "Like I'm fun to play with, but not if Maeve finds out."

"No." Her mask cracked and both hands grabbed his shirt. "No."

He wrapped his hands around her wrists and pulled her close, her sweet floral scent pushing back overcoming the negative shit.

"No."

Her whisper spread like lotion over the rest of his fire. It didn't cool him completely, but some. "So what's it like, then?"

She shifted away from him, keeping contact for as long as possible the way a wave pulls back from the beach, then planted both hands on the countertop and made a show of stepping out of her killer heels. Under different circumstances, he might have knelt down and helped her, and despite the shitstorm around them, he almost did.

"It's not that I don't want to sleep with you."

The rasp at the edge of her voice tightened his balls and softened his heart. Or his head. Right then he couldn't tell who was the bigger idiot.

"And it's not like I want to keep it a secret." She curled her hands into fists and shook her head until her hair dropped down, hiding her face.

He lifted the ginger strands and tucked them behind her ear. His fingers itched with the urge to grab her by the back of the neck and go for some mouth sex on the counter. "I pretty much hate guessing games."

Movement near the center island drew Ryan's attention. He dropped his hand, then frustrated, determined, he reached for Dani again. *She's going to deal with this, damn it.*

Niall came out of the dining room crowd, moving in the direction of the back door. His gaze traveled from Ryan to Danielle and back, his face settling into his professional blank look. Cop face. "Wassup?"

Dani jerked around, pulling free of Ryan's grasp. "Niall."

Ryan flexed his fingers. "Not much, bro. What's up with you?"

"Maeve came out of here with her tail feathers on fire," Niall said.

Danielle crossed her arms. Her smile held very little humor. He hadn't seen this side of her before, the plastic version. Their gazes met. He gave her a nod. *Your turn.*

Her blank stare turned his gut as brittle as her expression.

Either she recognized his reaction, or he'd been flashing back to Cherry's bullshit. At any rate, her slim fingers interlaced with his and she relaxed.

"Yeah," she said, "she's pretty annoyed with me."

Niall flicked a glance at their clasped hands then rubbed his shaved head. "She's been whacky about mixing brothers and friends ever since I went out with Nan Pierson."

"Who?" Ryan asked, unable to guess what Niall thought of a Ryan-Dani hook-up.

"Before your time. She was in Maeve's class and I went out with her. It didn't end well and Maeve almost got suspended for fighting."

"That sounds…" Dani began.

"Ugly." Niall's smile was tired.

Ryan didn't need any more details. Their eleven-year age difference meant it had only been the past year or two since they'd been able to talk like friends instead of brothers.

Maeve elbowed her way through the crowd around the buffet table, with an expression somewhere between surly and snarl, headed in their direction. When she came around the edge of the center island, Dani dropped his hand like it stung.

"Mom asked where the cheese puffs were." Maeve elbowed Niall out of the way and directed her question at Dani, as if Ryan had caught a case of the invisibles.

"Oh crap." Dani whirled toward the oven. She flung open the door and was lost in a cloud of black smoke.

Ryan grabbed a dishtowel and snatched the cookie sheet away from her, carrying it – and its cloud –

out the back door. When he came back, Dani and Maeve were in some kind of grimbitch face-off. Maeve had a height advantage. Dani had a tougher snarl. Maeve had more fire. Dani had more frost.

Maeve had a saltier vocabulary.

Dani had the last word.

"Get *over* it."

Without a glance at Ryan, she scooped up her shoes and stalked out of the kitchen, disappearing into the crowd. He almost followed, except he'd exceeded his Christmas limit for chick drama.

Instead, he went outside and got himself a cold one.

Two beers later, he gave up trying to deal with the crowd in the house. He camped out by the cooler, where it was easier to reach the next one. He was buzzed enough to be warm despite the forty degree temperature and surly enough to stay well clear of Maeve.

She'd be a spike-haired matador's cape to his charging bull.

Joey came looking for him, barely stuffing a grin behind a false front of coy reserve. "Mom wants you inside."

Ryan wasn't in the mood to play. "Whatever."

"What you all twisted about, man?" As usual, Joey aimed for painfully hip, ruining the effect when he fumbled getting a beer out of the cooler.

"Nothing." Which was a total lie, but if Ryan opened his mouth to tell the truth, Lord knows what would come out. He tossed off another deep swallow of Michelob, determined to keep his cool.

Then Maeve thrust her head out the back door. "Mom says everyone in for Christmas carols." She was back inside before Ryan could respond.

"Bitch," he said to her retreating shadow.

"Right?" Joey snickered into his beer. "She's crazy stressed about something."

Ryan tilted his beer bottle, rocking the bevel of liquid from side to side. "She's just plain crazy."

Joey poked him with glances. Ryan refused to give him the satisfaction of explaining the situation. Instead, he drank. About ten minutes later, ten long minutes of tense silence interrupted by his brother's unspoken questions, Maeve was back.

"Now."

"No." Ryan shut his eyes. His answer had been more of a bark than a word. Too much anger. No way Maeve would ignore the chance for a fight.

"Fine, Mr. The-Rules-Don't-Apply-To-Me. I'll just go tell Mom you're going to skip Christmas carols this year."

"Fine, ya damned diva."

Joey ducked back as if to make sure he was out of the line of fire.

Maeve took one step through the door, then another. "What'd you just call me?"

Ryan gripped the bottle so hard he almost snapped the glass. "You're a fucking diva, Maeve. " He stopped, clamped his jaw, and took a deep breath. "Dani and I might have something good, and you need to back the fuck off."

She crossed the back patio in three quick steps, reaching up to plant a knuckle in the middle of his chest. "Pull your head out your ass, dude."

He grabbed her wrist hard enough to make her bare her teeth.

"Let. Go." She jerked her hand.

He didn't let her pull away, anger burning through what was left of his restraint. "Priorities, Maeve. You want to be friends with Dani or not?"

"You think she's going to choose you over me?"

"I think she's smart enough to make her own damned decisions about who she spends time with." His voice rose until the words came out at a yell. He caught a glimpse of Joey covering his mouth to hide his laughter, which just irritated Ryan even more.

Maeve sneered at his heat. She planted her spike heels and pushed him. "Let go of my wrist, asshole. I mean, come on. She's dating Christopher."

Ryan laughed at her weak attempt to stir up trouble. "Either she's lying," — he towered over his sister, giving her a good dose of the anger running like flames through his bloodstream — "or you are."

"What the hell is going on out here?" Their father stomped through the back door and slammed the door shut. Mike O'Connor was an older, greyer version of Ryan, and one of the only people who could talk him down when he was this far gone. "The whole neighborhood can hear you two idiots yelling at each other."

Ryan released Maeve's wrist, splaying his fingers like she'd shocked him. "Nothing, Dad." He rubbed at the tension in the back of his neck. "It's nothing."

"Nothing." Maeve took a couple quick steps away from him, stumbling on the uneven pavers leading to the back steps. No matter how bad they hated each other, neither would squeal to their parents.

Ryan bent down to set his beer on the grass and held his hands palms out to prove he was calming himself down. "Sorry. I'll come inside in a minute."

Maeve was still breathing hard, her lips pinched together like it took physical effort to keep the words back.

"Get your act together, son." Mike O'Connor pointed a sharp finger at Ryan. "And you," he said, turning on Maeve. "From what I can tell, you need to mind your own business."

He ducked back into the house. Joey waited a couple seconds before heading toward the door, as if he was afraid of missing something fun. Maeve followed, stopped on the top step, and pressed her palms into the door frame. "You and Cherry are good together," she said.

"Says you," Ryan swallowed the nausea churning like magma at the bottom of a volcanic crater. "In some fantasy land you two have created. Like Dad said, you mind your business, and I'll take care of my own."

She snorted and stalked inside, slamming the door as a nonverbal exclamation point. Ryan made a slow fist with his right hand, squeezing tight, then releasing, relaxing, doing his best to let the anger go. He and Dani hadn't even slept together yet and she had him by the 'nads so tight he'd risked effing up his parents' Christmas party. Smooth. For a woman who was older, smarter, and leaving in two months. Real, real smooth.

* * * *

Flat-out rage blew Danielle out the front door of the O'Connor's house and down the street toward Green Lake Way. She needed every gust she could get because her horrible high heels chewed on her toes and rubbed her heel bones raw, and she could almost convince herself the tears clotting her lower lashes were there because her feet hurt.

Almost.

She collapsed onto a bench in front of the Starbucks on the corner of 71st and Green Lake Way. The store was closed, the streets were empty. She rapped her knuckles hard against the slatted seat, mad as hell that she'd let Maeve talk her into buying such stupid shoes. If Danielle's knuckles hurt, she wouldn't notice her feet, and if she got mad at Maeve over shoes, she wouldn't notice the essential stupidity of the current situation.

Ryan asked me out, Maeve. Deal with it!

Danielle rubbed the tears off her face and dug around her useless little clutch purse until she came up with her phone. Thinking about Ryan was the dumbest thing she could possibly do. She 4-1-1'ed the number for Yellow Cab but ended up on hold, grinding her teeth through a scratchy Silent Night.

When they finally answered, she gave the cab's dispatcher her location, then curled herself into as small a space as possible. The air temperature was somewhere in the thirties, and while the short skirt and filmy blouse worked nicely in a house full of people, her nose, toes, and fingertips – all the small pointy bits – were numb despite her wool coat.

It was still early. If the effing cab would show up, she could get her stuff packed and over to her Grandmother's house. She hung onto her phone because for once, she wanted to talk to someone. She couldn't talk to Maeve, couldn't even think about Ryan. Surely she had some friend, somewhere, who could listen to her rant about the worst Christmas in her life.

She came up empty. Most of her "friends" in L.A. were associates of Braden – and therefore off-limits. As an assistant manager, she couldn't be pals with the nurses at work, and while she liked the other two assistant managers, neither were girl-chat material. One was likely handcuffed to a bedframe playing hide-the-mistletoe with her husband and his best friend, and the other had a houseful of kids and a mother-in-law to entertain.

The wind blew icy grit into Danielle's face, and she ducked behind the collar of her coat. Maeve had always been her go-to phone call, even back in the day before everyone had cell phones with free long-distance. Alienating her meant Danielle was all alone on a freezing foggy northwest night.

"Damn it!" The words came out louder than she'd intended, but there was no one around to look awkwardly away from the crazy lady talking to herself in front of an empty Starbucks on Christmas Eve.

Then a car pulled up to the corner, one of those stunted looking Nissan Leaf electronic things, so quiet she wouldn't have known it was there unless she'd seen the lights. The driver idled the engine, although there were no other vehicles waiting at the five-way stop. The driver's door opened and Eamon O'Connor got out.

"What are you doing?" He faced her over the roof of the car.

"Waiting for a cab."

He nodded without changing expression. "Be warmer if you waited in here."

Another gust of wind sprayed her with ice. "Right." Danielle stood slowly, feet squealing in protest, and limped across the sidewalk. The door popped open and she sank into the passenger seat, lifting her legs one at a time into the car. "Yeah, um, thanks."

"No problem."

A car passed, barely slowing at the stop sign before driving on into the intersection. Eamon pushed a button on the dash and the seat warmed under her butt. Muscles along her spine started to unwind. The tension in her jaw and in the pit of her belly, not so much.

Eamon waited, quiet, one hand on the steering wheel, the other in his lap. Danielle didn't know quite what to say. Even when they'd been in high school, Eamon had kept her at a distance. He was the braniac, the kind of guy who took Physics for fun. He was two years younger, and they'd overlapped at school, but she'd never had an actual conversation with him.

Finally the silence stretched longer than she could handle. "Well…"

He still didn't say anything, though he reached across her to pull something out of the glove box. "You should probably call the cab back." Without meeting her gaze, he patted her knee and sat back. "I'm either going to talk you into coming back before Mom has a seizure, or I'll drive you over to Maeve's."

Damn. Vickie O'Connor was upset she left. Not cool. "That's okay. I'll just…" She lost her train of thought, more curious about what he was doing than what she was saying.

He held a small red, white, and green woven pouch, the kind that closed with a cheap metal zipper and was handmade by Indians in Guatemala or Peru and sold at Pier One Imports. From it, he brought out a small pipe and a tiny zip-locked bag of weed.

"Want a hit?"

"That's okay." She couldn't entirely suppress an uncomfortable smirk. "I'll take the contact high." She hadn't smoked pot since the one time in college when her dorm mates insisted she try some before a Red Hot Chili Peppers concert.

Eamon either didn't notice or didn't care about her awkward response. He shrugged, a small move she would have missed if she hadn't been fascinated by his actions. He pinched a dark, dry glob out of the baggie and tapped it into the bowl of the pipe. Next out of the pouch was a Bic lighter. He lit the pipe and inhaled so deep she worried he'd pop. The bowl glowed bright red while he drew on the pipe, then faded as he lowered it. A tiny thread of smoke swirled up from where he rested the pipe against his thigh. He held his breath for several seconds, eyes shut, enough of a smile to show off his version of the O'Connor dimples. Finally, he rolled the window down and blew the smoke out toward Green Lake.

"So…?" she said, trying to restart the conversation they hadn't really been having in the first place.

"Cancel the cab."

"Jesus." She reached for her cell phone. "You guys are all bossy. It's a wonder you haven't killed each other already."

He tipped his head back against the headrest, long hair falling over his shoulders, eyes closed. "Yep."

The musty sweet smell of marijuana smoke went to work on Danielle's nerves, like a wide-toothed comb easing the tangles out of her hair after a shower. Following his example, she let the seat back cradle her head and shut her eyes.

"Ryan likes you."

She laughed, though it came out more like a snort. "I like him, too."

"And Maeve's being a freak."

"Which shouldn't surprise me." They'd been friends for almost twenty years, after all. She cracked an eyelid enough to pull up the Yellow Cab number on her phone.

Eamon took another hit off the pipe. This time the cherry went completely dark by the end of his inhale. He held his breath, then opened the window again to let the smoke free. "Want a clue?" He rolled the window back up and gave her time to answer.

"Okay, I'll bite."

"Tell Maeve what she wants to hear, then do whatever the hell you want."

Danielle rubbed her face to smother a burst of laughter, because she wasn't sure why she was laughing.

"That's how we all keep from killing her."

Maybe it was her chemically-induced mellow, but his idea made sense. "You think I should tell her I'll leave Ryan alone, then keep seeing him, and he'll go along with me because he knows it's a Maeve-management strategy?" *Because that sounds like a disaster waiting to happen.*

"Yeah." He met her gaze and for the first time since she got in his car, he focused his whole attention on her, blue eyes slicing and dicing far deeper than she wanted him to see. "Now am I taking you back to Mom and Dad's, or do you want to go to Maeve's?"

"You better take me to Maeve's." She hit a button to dial the cab dispatcher. "There's no way I'll get through the party without making things worse." She was only going to be in town for another six weeks, and keeping peace among the O'Connors had to be her priority. For about two beats she wondered about Eamon's motivation, then decided he was too flakey to be up to something nefarious. If he was right, she could keep both Maeve and Ryan happy.

He put the pouch back in the glove box and started the engine.

"Thanks, Eamon."

Neither had anything else to say.

Chapter Twelve

Instead of spending Christmas Eve hanging out with Ryan in the O'Connor's kitchen and keeping the partiers supplied with mini quiches and cheese puffs hot from the oven, Danielle packed her suitcase. She drove to her grandmother's house and reclaimed her grandmother's old bedroom. The air mattress she bought in November needed air, but she had a pump. Of course, the up and down motion reminded her of another kind of pumping she could be doing if she'd played her cards differently.

Because horny helps everything. She capped the plug on the mattress and threw her sleeping bag down, disgusted. She couldn't have screwed things up any more if she'd belly-flopped naked into the Christmas tree, taking the herd of angels with her.

The house was cool and dark, and her grandmother's bedroom window faced west over Puget Sound. Once her bed was made, she leaned against the window sill and rested her head against the glass. Brightly-colored Christmas ships sailed to the soundtrack of the rolling waves along the beach, and she let go of the first couple layers of tension, sending them out over the onyx ocean. Ryan was pissed. Maeve was pissed. Hell, even Vickie O'Connor was probably irritated with her for leaving without saying goodbye.

Eamon's contact high had worn off, and she pulled some objectivity out of her ass. "Enough pity party already," she said to the waves.

She'd been made assistant manager of the NICU at the age of thirty for a reason. Dealing with people was her thing, although she apparently sucked at applying work skills to her personal life. She decided to follow Eamon's advice, to a point, and once she had a to-do list together, a list that started with "Call Vickie and apologize", she slid into Maeve's old sleeping bag and tried to turn off her brain.

Only to have her cell phone wake her up too early the next morning.

Maeve greeted her with a sputtering soliloquy about the meaning of friendship.

Danielle almost hung up.

"I'm sorry, Maeve," Danielle said, as soon as she could edge the words in. "I wanted to say something sooner. I just … didn't. But I apologize for taking you by surprise."

"You're letting yourself be used."

Danielle unwrapped from the sleeping bag, shivering as the fabric cocoon fell to her waist. "How do you figure?"

Maeve groaned like Danielle was being intentionally stupid. "If he's messing around with you, he doesn't have to deal with his issues."

His issues? Danielle extended her index finger to keep from accidentally on purpose hanging up the phone. Eamon had said to go along with Maeve, and Danielle thought about it, but the combination of worry and irritation had her breathing so fast she was lightheaded. "If I back off, it'll be good for Ryan?" *In some other universe.*

"Yes!"

She forced herself to attend to each inhale and exhale. "I like your brother, and I don't want to make trouble." *Both true statements.*

Maeve coughed into the phone, the rough edges to her voice showing how hard she'd played the night before. "Then give him some space."

Danielle's head got so light she saw spots. *Grow a pair, Jacobsen.* "We've been friends forever, Maeve, but

Ryan and I are both adults." Her tone of voice was much calmer than the free-for-all underneath. "If we want to have dinner together, or go to the movies or something, it's really none of your business."

"Oh." There was a long pause, as if Maeve couldn't believe Danielle had actually taken a stand. "What?" Another pause. "You mean it, don't you? You'd choose him over me."

"No." Danielle swallowed down enough frustration to keep from shouting. "I'm not choosing anyone. I'm just telling you how it is."

This time Maeve paused for so long Danielle worried she'd hung up. "Are you still there?"

"Yeah, I'm here," Maeve said. "I mean, I feel like kind of an asshole, but I'm here."

"I realize it's awkward."

"Awkward." Maeve ended the comment with a sour laugh. "And where the hell are you, anyway? Where's your stuff?"

"At my grandmother's house."

"Are you coming back?"

"Nah, I'm heading into crunch time, and I'll get more work done if I'm not driving across town." *And you won't be able to keep tabs on me and Ryan.*

"Fine." Maeve sighed, a soft puff of sound that might have been exhaustion. Or resignation. Either way, she'd regroup soon and come back for another round.

"Merry Christmas, by the way," Maeve said, as if she was trying to smooth everything over with two small words.

"Merry Christmas, Maeve."

They ended the call, and Danielle burrowed down into the sleeping bag. She was due at her uncle's for dinner at noon. Until then she'd hide, and stew, and wonder whether she had to add the word "former" to Maeve's BFF title.

A few hours later, her cell phone chirped. The text was from Maeve.

You're still on for the New Year's Eve party.
It wasn't a question.

* * * *

Tuesday afternoon, Danielle pulled on her rubber gloves and picked up the little wad of fine steel wool she'd been using to scrub decades of soot off the fireplace surround. Working carefully to keep from scratching the tiles, she uncovered brilliant greens and blues one inch at a time. The tiny repetitive movements made for slow work, and required just enough concentration to prevent her from thinking.

A sliver of steel wool poked through her glove, stinging her fingertip, and she flipped the pad across the floor. She hadn't heard from Maeve, and Ryan hadn't turned up. She'd had no reason to lie, and nothing to lie about. It ticked her off.

About the time her whining knees threatened anarchy, headlights swiped across the front lawn. High and wide-spaced, the glare ran down the side of what could possibly be a large black pick-up truck.

A huge blast of adrenaline hit her. She pulled off her rubber gloves, flexed her numbed fingers, and counted to ten to keep her breathing steady. A key turned in the lock and she stood, unable to keep from smiling wide enough to let all her big teeth show. "Hi."

Ryan dropped a toolbox on the floor and let loose a sigh. "Hi." He rocked his shoulders in a circle, running his gaze up and down her body. "You look good."

"Liar." She took a tentative step, pretty sure she smelled like a mix of unshowered sweat and chemical cleaners. He reached out. Their hands clasped. They each took another awkward step. "My sweatshirt has holes in it." *And a faded yellow chicken on the front.*

"And you still manage to look like a movie star." His head dipped toward hers, and his free hand went to her waist, a provisional gesture of possession. She raised her face to his, chuckling at their junior-high stumbling.

"I wasn't sure if I should call you or not." Part of her still wasn't sure she should be groping him in the living room.

"Probably good that you didn't." He curled around her in a big, safe hug, disabling her resistance.

She pressed her lips into the warm skin at the base of his throat. "You were pretty mad at me." She tasted salt, and his earthy scent made it hard to keep from dragging him down on the floor, cranky or not. She nuzzled in closer, debating the best way of saying, *I'm sorry and I'm an idiot.*

"You know, I came over to work on the cabinets." His voice grew warmer, naughtier, and he massaged her lower back, each stroke moving farther up under her sweatshirt.

"Ah yes, the infamous kitchen." She propped her cheek on his shoulder with her face angled up, making it easy for him to kiss her. If he wanted to.

He did.

His groan vibrated against her lips and Danielle went nuts, rubbing up against him like she could burn away the useless fabric separating their bodies.

Give me more.

More.

His kiss tasted of cinnamon, his late-day beard chapped her skin, and she twisted her fingers through his curls. Three days' worth of loneliness, capping nearly two months of longing and desire turned the simple press of lips into a deep and intimate connection. This was right, in a way nothing — not Braden, not the half-remembered boys from college — had ever been before.

When they eased apart, Danielle blinked her eyes, trying to fight the confusion brought on by her carbonated hormones. Breathing hard, she ran the tip of her tongue over her upper lip. "Gum?"

"Burrito for lunch," he said, his voice low and rumbly.

"Hmm." She laced her fingers with his, then lifted his hand to get a look at the dried paint and white dust edging his fingernails.

Her half-baked idea about what to do with his fingers was killed by a sharp rap on the door.

"Who is it?" Ryan whispered.

Danielle slid away from him, waiting until the very last minute to release his hand. The doorknob jiggled and the door opened just as Danielle reached it.

Maeve came in, grinning like the Cheshire Cat. Christopher was right behind her.

* * * *

Ryan had a lifetime to learn Maeve's smiles, and the one she wore as she came through the front door showed an evil blend of anger and triumph.

Maximum trouble with minimum effort.

Dani tucked a loose strand of hair behind her ear. *Nervous.*

Ryan stepped aside, but Maeve managed to nudge his shoulder on her way by. His father wasn't around to keep him from fighting with Maeve, and he let his claim on Dani show in his cold stare.

"Well hey, you guys. Looks like you're working hard." Maeve stuck her palms on her hips, spreading her black wool coat like a bat's wings.

A bitchy bat.

With a mean streak.

Dani moved to a spot midway between them. "What's up, Maeve?"

"Ryan, you know Christopher, right?" Maeve said.

Christopher reached out to shake, and Ryan responded, making a conscious effort not to snap the guy's hand like a bundle of twigs.

"Christopher's a real estate agent." Dani's eyes were too wide and her cheeks several shades too bright.

"Yeah, dude. Danielle's told me some great things about your progress." Christopher held Ryan's gaze, answering the challenge with one of his own. "I wanted to come see," — he threw a glance at Dani — "the house."

Ryan locked a smile in place, determined to keep a leash on his instincts. Maybe Maeve hadn't entirely lied when she said Dani and Christopher were dating. They obviously knew each other. "Take a look around." Ryan snapped the words. "I'll be in the kitchen if you need me." He strode off before he could say anything Dani would regret. She called after him, asking him to lead the tour.

He ignored her.

The kitchen was a mess of unfinished cabinets, patch-worked sheetrock, and exposed electrical outlet boxes. He'd left his toolbox in the living room, and instead of working, he leaned against the raw edge of the sink and stared out into the darkness. It had been a damned long day. He'd spent most of it fighting with a leaking double-paned window that somehow kept leaking no matter what he did to try to repair it.

He pulled off his sweatshirt and threw it across the room. The window topped a long list of assorted B.S. requests from a little old lady who couldn't remember from one day to the next what she'd asked him to do. His boss sent him out on the job because he was the only carpenter patient enough and smart enough to get it done. While he appreciated the vote of confidence, some days he'd rather be a dry-waller, responsible for nothing more complicated than mudding, taping, and sanding a flat wall.

He smacked his palms on the edge of the sink. Seeing Dani show a handsome man around her house was just the last fucking straw for his pissed off camel to deal with.

They squeaked up the stairs. Ryan scratched the back of his head and focused on the assorted sticks of beadboard and quarter round molding he'd left stretched across two saw-horses in the dining room. The trim had already been cut to size for the doorways he'd widened on either end of the dining room. All he had to do was tack it up and he could move on to the next project.

Reaching for the closest piece of trim, he tried not to eavesdrop. If he turned his iPod on, he wouldn't accidentally overhear anything. Instead of the iPod, he reached for the nail gun. It made noise too, and if he could find a rhythm he might be able to act like a grown-up when they got back downstairs. He and Dani only had an informal something and here he was acting like a jealous asshole over a simple home tour.

He held a section of molding over his head in the opening of the doorway. With a light squeeze of his trigger finger, the first nail shot home, the recoil vibrating down his arm. How would Mr. Rich and Sophisticated have behaved if Ryan hadn't been there? Squeeze. Shot. Squeeze. Shot. And why would a classy chick like Dani choose a fucking carpenter over some guy in a three-piece suit? Shot. Shot. Shot.

The questions flashed through his mind right about the time another one carried down through the floor.

"What should I bring to your New Year's Eve party?"

Shit.

They had to be standing right above his head for the baritone voice to make it from one floor to the next. Ryan waited for the response, but it was lost in a flutter of giggles.

With a quick jerk, he unplugged the nail gun and dumped it into the top of his toolbox. If he didn't leave now, he was going to kick the shit out of Maeve's friend, and for all the guy's pretty clothes, he looked like he'd be willing to fight back.

And Dani had apparently invited him to a New Year's Eve party.

Fuck it.

* * * *

Danielle was headed downstairs when she heard the front door slam. "Ryan?"

A car door slammed in response.

"Did he leave?" Christopher asked.

Danielle picked up her pace to the bottom of the steps then jogged across the living room. "His toolbox is gone."

Maeve trailed behind. "Could be he needed to grab some supplies." Her tapping heels were the sound of a one-handed victory clap.

Her false concern made Danielle want to land a one-handed clap right across her face.

Christopher moved just inside Danielle's comfort zone. He wore a light touch of exotic aftershave that made her feel like she should be dressed in a belly dancer's skirt and sequined bra. She took a couple steps away from him, but the light scent followed her.

"He wouldn't leave without saying goodbye." She did her best to stifle the hurt and confusion coloring her voice.

Christopher shrugged and smiled, playing up the creases that framed his mouth. "Show me the rest of the place."

"The rest of the place" turned out to be colder and darker than Danielle remembered. Ryan's abrupt departure felt wrong. Maeve was just being Maeve, and though he might not be thrilled to meet Christopher, disappearing wasn't his style.

Christopher admired her Craigslist appliances, acting more sincerely impressed by the quality of the work Ryan had done with the cabinetry and trim. They talked about her plans for the bathrooms and the library, and ended up standing in the middle of the living room. With only one semi-comfortable chair and no wine for pouring, there was no point in hanging around.

"Yeah, um, that's it," she said, trying to gently herd them toward the door.

"This is awesome, Danielle," Christopher said. "You and Ryan are doing some great work,"

Ryan. *Where the hell did he go?*

"Thanks." She smiled, dropping in a note of goodbye.

"When you're ready to sell, Chris is your man. You should be nice to him." Maeve tossed the comment over her shoulder, using the dark front window as a mirror to straighten her collar. "We should go out for drinks or something."

"I'd love to, but I smell all funky, and … I just want to hang out here." *And call Ryan.*

"Rain check then." Christopher chucked her under the chin. "See you New Year's Eve."

"Yeah. Looking forward to it."

She kept on smiling until the front door closed behind them, anxiety and confusion agitating her gut. Ryan must have overheard them talking about the stupid New Year's Eve party. The realization came with a crystalline certainty. Maeve had mentioned the party once or twice before and now Danielle was screwed.

Damn it, Maeve.

She grabbed her jacket and purse and ran for her car. The temperature had dropped ten or fifteen degrees, and she told herself her hands shook because of the cold.

Right.

The interior of the Mini was small enough the heater didn't have to work very hard. She held her hands in front of one of the vents, thawing out her fingers and drawing up the courage she'd need to call Ryan.

He didn't answer. She was too freaked out to start the engine, way too freaked out to leave a message.

She sat in her car replaying the evening and wondering if things could have gone any worse. Maeve apparently wanted to make trouble, and Ryan apparently tended to overreact. Danielle had to wonder if any of the O'Connors knew how to act like a grown-up.

She tried Ryan's phone again. Voicemail.

What now?

She could go back inside, grab a shower, and wait for the phone to ring. Or she could do what she really wanted to do.

Go over to Ryan's and wait for him to come home. They needed to talk about expectations.

And this is why you don't go out with twenty-four year olds.

Doing her best to squelch the voice of common sense, Danielle put the car in reverse. Traveling north-south in Seattle was fairly easy, but the east-west routes were all stop sign-laden surface streets that took forever to negotiate. She caught the tag end of rush hour, too, and reached his neighborhood at about three weeks past forever. She'd had more than enough time to create an organized list of concerns and a head full of frantic energy. At every stop light she checked her phone to see if he'd called.

At every stop light, disappointment heaped onto her emotional brew.

Finally, she parked in front of his house. The lights were on. His truck was in the driveway. She took a huge breath and squared her shoulders. Her hand was shaking. Her finger was numb. She rang the doorbell.

Chubb opened the door. "Hey, Dani. What's up?"

"I need to talk to Ryan."

She didn't like being rude, but she pushed past him, pausing to look back when she was halfway up the steps to the main floor. His semi-dreads were piled in a knot on the top of his head. Between that and the quizzical tilt of his chin, he reminded her of Shaggy from the old Scooby Doo cartoons.

"He's in the shower, but I bet he wouldn't mind if you joined him." He winked at her. "Go on up."

Um, right. Danielle stopped in front of the door across the hall from Ryan's bedroom. The spray of the water hissed at her, and the smell of faux-floral shampoo billowed out from the cracks.

Did she have the cojones to walk in while he was in the shower?

Chapter Thirteen

Was she brave enough to open the door?

Standing in the hall outside of Ryan's bathroom, she took a moment to bite at a stray cuticle, weighing her options, balanced on the cusp. Afraid to go forward. Afraid not to.

She reached for the doorknob, half convinced the floor would soften and suck her down. She half hoped it would.

"Use the other bathroom, dude." Ryan sounded gruff, tired, and bothered by the invasion of his privacy.

She almost backed out, except somehow the door clicked shut behind her and she was stuck. Floating steam blurred the edges of the scene, giving her an impressionistic view of a cream and rust counter and gold fixtures. "It's me."

He jerked open the curtain and poked his head out, tendrils of wet hair splayed across his forehead and down as far as the hitch in the bridge of his nose. Surprise, irritation, and something else flashed through his eyes, as quick as the changing pages of an old flip-book cartoon.

Hoping she had her big girl panties on, Danielle dropped her messenger bag on the floor. "You left without saying goodbye."

He ducked back into the shower, pulling the curtain closed. "Hang on." The handle gave a soft squeak as he turned the water off and the billows of steam started to fade. Without coming out from behind the curtain, he pointed at a worn white towel sitting on the counter. "Hand me that."

"Bossy," she said, mostly under her breath. The towel came off her hand funny and he had to reach to pick it up. *As if she needed a reason to blush harder.*

"You could wait in the living room."

She crossed her arms and let a few seconds spin out, the warm, moist air coating her skin. "Do you want me to?" She tried to sound tough, but he had to know she was faking it.

After a longer silence, his voice came out lower and gruffer than normal. "Not really."

She pressed her palms into the sharp edges of the countertop. She didn't have to wait long before he brushed open the shower curtain and, giving his head a final shake, stepped out. The towel was wrapped tight around his hips. Despite the blurring effects of the steam, she caught the curve of his biceps and the dusting of dark curls on his chest. He came at her, steady and aggressive. He backed her up until the edge of the counter creased her butt, the pressure of his hips against her so boldly sexual it made her lightheaded.

"Well, Princess, this is a nice surprise." He bent down and spoke right into her ear. His breath sent shivers down her neck. "Sorry I interrupted your date."

She gulped, working to steady her voice so she could get through her list of concerns. "Wasn't a date." Her nipples tightened, her lace bra becoming exquisitely rough.

"And New Year's Eve won't be a date either?"

She squeezed the counter. They needed to hash this out before she accidentally-on-purpose ripped the towel away. "No."

"It could be, right? You haven't made me any promises."

That jerked her chain, and she glared up at him. "You haven't made me any either."

"Should I?"

His big, powerful body almost bent her back over the vanity. The gleam in his eyes was steamier than the shower, and though he kept one hand on the towel, it wouldn't take much to get him naked.

She still had her jacket on.

She squirmed, wrestling her arms out of the quilted down coat, a move that rubbed her breasts against his chest. His fingers contracted, a tiny movement, a hint that he wanted to grab something. Hopefully her. He used his hips to pin her to the vanity and his gaze to pin her to the conversation.

She tossed the coat aside. "Better," she said, her voice reduced to a bare rasp.

He rested his hand on her shoulder, his thumb finding the pulse in her neck. "We were talking about promises." He crowded her space, letting go of the towel to cup her jaw with both hands. Only the press of their bodies kept the damp fabric from dropping to the floor.

If she reached down, she'd be able to put her hands on his naked ass, and the heat burning deep in her belly made it hard to think straight. *Keep your hands on his shoulders*. She didn't want to talk about promises. She didn't want to talk at all. *Shoulders, damn it*. "I'm only going to be here another month or six weeks." She had to clear her throat to keep talking. "And you just got out of a relationship."

His lips almost touched her forehead and his damp chest pressed against her sweatshirt. "That was done a couple years ago."

"Still, we shouldn't commit to something that isn't going to last." Her sweatshirt was damp where his chest pressed against her body and the heat lower down made thinking difficult. "But seriously, I don't want to be with anybody else."

He exhaled, low and throaty, and his shoulders relaxed. She tipped her face up, and he angled down to meet her lips.

Their kiss was light and cautious, dipping in and testing the waters. She parted her lips, flicked him with the tip of her tongue.

He growled, reaching around her with both arms and lifting her bum onto the edge of the vanity. The air was sweaty, steamy, hot. She opened her knees and he closed in, rocking his hard length against the seam of her jeans. Her sex clutched, a low smolder radiating through her belly, and what was left of her conscious mind wanted to magic away the layers of fabric separating them.

They kissed long and hard and sticky sweet, a mashup of lips and tongues and wrenching raw need. He found his way under her sweatshirt, fingers dancing over her nipples, bathing her in liquid fire.

"We're making out in the bathroom," she said, the sauna they'd created mellowing her voice to a whisper.

He hooked a finger through one of her belt loops and tugged. "Take these pants off and I'll show you something else we can do in here."

The husky edge to his voice blew right over her, causing her need to flame. He claimed her mouth again, a kiss so deep she could have drowned in it. She hitched up farther on the counter, locking her ankles at the small of his back.

The towel fell lower, pretty much hanging on his erection, the rest of him bare and buff and gorgeous. Danielle was busy exploring as much as she could reach when Ryan's stomach gurgled, making her giggle and him snuff a laugh in her ear. He scraped his teeth down her earlobe and shifted back, letting a breath of moist, cooling air come between them.

"Yeah, dinner," he said, and while he might have been referring to food, his eyes were all about dessert. He hitched the towel back up, but not before she'd had the chance to follow the line of dark curls south from his belly button.

"I guess I didn't eat either."

"Should I call out for pizza?"

Oh hell no. "You're standing there mostly naked and you want to talk about food?"

"Mom always told us never to answer a question with a question." He brought the towel higher on his hips. "But we can eat later."

"Later."

* * * *

Ryan cracked the bathroom door open and scanned the hallway. The only one around was Barnabas, sitting like an orange tabby sphinx, tail wrapped over his front paws.

"All clear." Keeping Dani close to his body, Ryan guided her across the hall to his room. He turned on his bedside lamp. Her hazel eyes were huge and dark, and even dressed in an old sweatshirt and grubby jeans, she looked elegant.

He willed himself to relax, determined to stretch this out for as long as possible.

Dani had other ideas.

She snared him with a kiss, as stunning as it was raw. Not gentle. Not delicate. All tearing heat and wrestling tongues. He needed his hands on bare skin. He dropped the towel and reached for her sweatshirt. She was already sliding out of her jeans.

The cooler bedroom air raised gooseflesh down his arms. Well, either cool air or nerves. This wasn't

Cherry and he wasn't drunk. This was Dani and he was sober; and he wanted her with a raging ache in his balls and a sharp desire in his soul.

He caught a passing glance at a rose-colored bra. She tossed it aside and they faced each other. Naked. He yanked on the band holding her ponytail, just this side of rough. Her hair fell loose around her face and he brought a few of the ginger strands to his lips. The silky vanilla scent made his dick throb.

"No more waiting," she whispered, and stepped into him, capturing his length between their bellies.

Breathing hard, he wrapped a hand around her neck, gently running a thumb along the soft skin of her throat. He'd held out until desire almost tore a hole in him. She gripped his ass with both hands, rubbing herself against him, smearing his leaking tip against her skin.

"No more waiting." This time she spoke louder, more assertive. He thought about saying something about how he felt, telling her some deep, personal thing. Then the tip of her tongue ran along his bottom lip.

Shit.

"You know what, Princess?" He wrapped his arms around her thighs and lifted. "I'm the boss in here."

Her gorgeous rosy nipples were at the level of his mouth. He latched onto one, laving, sucking, and tasting. She tugged on his hair, shrieked when he bit down. He pivoted and tossed her on the bed, feeling his caveman roots hard.

Leaning back on her elbows, she gave him the full view, her dark eyes begging him to make a move. He knelt between her legs and let himself enjoy the show: full breasts, creamy flat belly, neatly trimmed strip of pubic hair, and long, long legs.

He was pretty damned sure he'd never be this hard again.

Dani grasped his wrists and pulled. He resisted her, wanting to draw out the anticipation.

"I said, no more waiting." Her naughty grin hammered at his self-control.

"And I said I'm the boss."

"You aren't the boss of me," she said, all throaty and sexy. Damn, she was going to have him shooting his wad in about ten seconds.

He ran his hands up her calves, spreading her knees that much wider. She blushed but didn't fight him. "Oh yeah? When I'm working on your house, you tell me what to do, but in here, I tell you what to do."

She giggled and arched her back. "Wait a minute. At the house you tell me what needs to be done, then I say to do it. It's not like I'm really in charge."

"Well if we're lucky that's how it'll be in here, too. Now don't move." He crawled across Dani's body to the nightstand for a condom and had it stretched over his shaft by the time he got back between her knees. He loved that she was so strong, so confident, as if time had taught her to reach directly for what she wanted. Sleeping with Cherry had made him feel like a servant being allowed a roll in the royal hay. This quivering, yearning demand was something entirely new.

She half sat, wrapped her arms around his shoulders, and dropped, pulling him down over top of her. With a grin, he trapped her wrists over her head. He was poised at her entrance, his ass and thighs shaking. He worked her neck with his lips and tongue, tasting salty skin, drowning in her warm rose scent. She wrapped her thighs around his hips, drawing him farther in.

"For a classy chick, you're kinda dirty in bed," he said.

She rocked her hips against him. His body shook with the effort it took to hold back. He wanted to ease into her, slide deep into her warmth, and make every stroke last in case he never found his way there again.

"Now."

The word was a brush of air against his skin. They were forehead to forehead, their hands clasped overhead, fingers interlaced, pressed against the mattress. He thrust and held still until he could control the burning load building in his balls.

She nipped the end of his nose. "Let's go."

He did.

He pounded into her, setting a pace so fast he'd never be able to sustain it. Her soft murmured "yes, yes, yes" could have sounded like a porno movie.

It only drove him faster.

"You're so good, Dani. So sweet." He had to slow down or he'd explode. He rose up on his knees, sitting on his heels and lifting her ass in his palms, changing the angle, making it shorter, tighter, deeper. He found her bud with his thumb and rubbed small circles. He kept going until she wailed.

Her body tensed and she tossed her head back, hair spread like a ginger corona. She clawed at his arms, her spasms milking him until he could barely hold it together.

Sweat ran down the side of his face, the small of his back, and her body softened, relaxed. He lowered her hips, stretched out over her, caged her body with his arms. Her legs wrapped around him so tight he was pretty sure she was ruining him for anyone else. He buried his face in the hollow of her throat and picked up his rhythm.

"Oh my God." Dani sighed, and the sweetness in her voice sent him over the edge. He gave in to the tightening in his balls and tensed for the surge that ripped through him in an endless pulsing loop.

The universe paused for one blinding second.

He landed heavily on her, breathing hard, lips pressed against her forehead. "Do me a favor." He had trouble forcing the words out, still lost in the Neverland that only the best sex gets to.

"What?"

"Promise me we can do this again." He stroked along her side, grinning at the shivers radiating from his touch. "You are the most gorgeous woman ever."

She stared up at the ceiling, her tiny smile telling him the compliment scored a hit. "I think I need a shower, a decent haircut, and pedicure."

"Straight up, babe, I don't think you could look any better than you do right now."

One eyebrow lifted. "Easy to say when you're balls deep."

"Don't be like that, Princess." He patted her cheek. "Stay here. I'll be right back."

He rocked onto his heels, keeping a hand on the condom. His knees wobbled on the two steps it took to get to the trashcan. Landing beside her in the bed felt warm and good, and he laid a palm flat on her belly. "Now you have to believe me." He nuzzled the tender skin behind her ear. "You are beautiful."

Her only response was a long, slow kiss.

"Hey, Dani," he said, the words sneaking out while his guard was down. "Remember this in the morning, okay?"

She raised herself up and met his gaze, her expression puzzled. "Um, since I think you just gave me the mother of all hickeys, I'm betting I will."

He tried to smile, feeling like an idiot for letting his insecurity show. At the light brush of his fingertips on her cheek, she closed her eyes and settled back down against him, the thrum of her heart pulsing against his ribs.

"I won't forget you, Ryan O'Connor. Not ever."

"Good."

Chapter Fourteen

The week between Christmas and New Year, Danielle and Ryan spent as much time together as possible. Danielle didn't call Maeve, and Maeve didn't call Danielle, and Danielle tried hard not poke at it too much.

On Thursday morning Danielle was down in the basement doing laundry. Her phone vibrated in her pocket. The text was from Maeve.

Meet us at the Pig tonight. Party planning.

She assumed "us" meant Maeve and Cherry. A trip to the dentist had more appeal, shots of Novocain and all. She jogged up the stairs to the kitchen where Ryan was squatted in front of some cabinet boxes hanging the doors.

"So, tonight." Danielle took a second to figure out how to frame things. She knew she ought to go meet Maeve, but 'ought to' and 'want to' were very different things.

Ryan sat back on his heels and set the drill on the floor. "Tonight." He nodded as if feeding her the words.

"Maeve wants me to come down to the Pig to figure things out for her New Year's Eve party."

Ryan scratched the top of his head, looking up at her with a smile that managed not to show any dimple at all. "Yeah?"

"And I feel like I should go." Danielle squinted at the floor, hoping it would organize her thoughts. "The more I avoid her, the longer she'll stay mad."

Ryan stayed quiet for a minute, then shrugged. "Well, if you want to go, you should."

"You won't be mad?"

He snorted, shrugged again, and picked up the drill. "Was hoping we could spend New Year's Eve together."

"Well we can go to the party together."

Ryan's expression underlined the stupidity of that idea. Despite a laundry list of misgivings, Danielle persisted. "It'll be okay. We'll make it work."

"Sure, Dani. Whatever." Ryan eased his weight forward, turning his back to her.

Danielle fought through a wave of *oh my God if I don't do what he wants he'll leave just like Braden* and headed back to the basement. Some clothes needed to be folded, and the brainless, repetitive motion promised to be therapeutic.

Maeve's text followed her around the house like a big fat elephant all afternoon, until Danielle had the sense she was poised at the top of Class IV rapids in a rubber ducky raft. As an act of self-preservation, she booked a flight to L.A. for February 2nd so she'd know there was an end-point. She didn't let herself think about whether it would be the endpoint for her relationship with Ryan.

The Pig was crowded when Danielle arrived, full of wool-wrapped revelers with nothing better to do on a December 30th evening. Maeve had grabbed a booth, and there was no sign of Cherry. Danielle clutched her inner ducky and dove in, striding across the room like she was happy to be spending time with an old friend.

She tossed her purse across the bench seat. Maeve's crystalline smile froze Danielle's hand in mid-air. *So much for faking it.* "Um ... hi."

"Hi," Maeve said to her cocktail. She'd come straight from work, and her slim, black mini-dress with skyscraper heels made her legs look a mile long.

Danielle was just glad her jeans were clean and there wasn't too much paint under her fingernails. "I thought Cherry was going to be here."

"She's late."

Danielle perched on the edge of the seat, wondering how long she'd be able to force her way through such stilted conversation.

"Thank you for coming." Maeve sounded like she was talking to her boss or her Mom or her priest, not her best friend since freshman year of high school.

"No problem. I—"

"You went over to Ryan's after we left, didn't you?" Maeve asked, the highball class clutched tightly in her hand.

Eamon's advice – just tell her what she wants to hear – came close to spilling out of Danielle's mouth. Instead, she went for the truth. "Yeah, I did."

Maeve took a hard swallow of her drink. "So I just need to get over myself then."

Those rapids opened up under Danielle, anxiety doing loop-de-loops in her gut.

"I mean it's not like this kind of thing hasn't happened before." Maeve drained the rest of her cocktail. "It's just, you've been my friend forever." Maeve clasped Danielle's wrist, her cold fingers holding tight. "But Cherry's my friend, too."

"I'm sorry if it puts you in a tough spot."

Maeve held on tighter. "Promise me you won't tell her."

"I won't. I'm going to be gone in February, anyway." Danielle had to clear her throat to keep her voice from wobbling. "Then Ryan will do what he's going to do, and Cherry will do what she's going to do, and we can go back to being best friends by phone."

Maeve's answer was cut off when Cherry tossed her tweed cape across the table and looped her purse over her shoulder, her plum-colored tunic over chartreuse leggings and ankle boots saying *why yes, I do have more style than you* without even making a sound.

"I want one of those gin thingies," Maeve said before Cherry could sit down.

"The tall one?"

"With three limes." Maeve loosed her grip on Danielle's wrist. "What do you want?"

"I'll have a glass of white wine."

Cherry wound her way through the crowd to the bar. The brittle silence between Danielle and Maeve got heavier and harder for Danielle to hold on to. Finally Maeve tapped the table like she was calling them both to order.

"Are you still working too much?" she asked.

"What's in a gin thingy?" Danielle spoke over top of Maeve's question.

They both laughed, glanced at each other and away. Awkward. Ashamed.

"A bunch of gin and some other stuff." Maeve nudged Danielle with her knuckle, her wry half-smile offering a temporary moratorium on conflict. "You should try one."

Danielle wanted to lean over the table and give her friend a hug. She fiddled with her cuff instead. "I'll stick with wine."

"Lightweight."

"Yep."

Cherry made a good show of juggling three cocktails and a clutch purse through the crowd. Midway through, Maeve jumped up to help. She snatched her glass and downed a good third of her cocktail before Danielle had her wine. Cherry lowered herself onto

Maeve's side of the booth, raised her glass in a wordless toast, and took a healthy swallow. Danielle pasted on a plastic grin and tried to stifle the nerves pinging around in her belly like bees in a glass jar.

If Maeve needed her to make nice to Cherry, she'd do her level best.

Cherry and Maeve giggled like high school girls, and Danielle tried to play along, with marginal success. They talked shopping and sales, since Cherry had spent all day working at Nordstrom's, and they debated whether it was too early for a shot of schnapps to warm them up. Danielle sipped wine and smiled. She sent up gasping prayers to whoever was listening that they'd get around to talking about the party.

About three sips into her wine, Chubb walked in, which turned the bees in her belly into a swarm of angry hornets. If Ryan came in behind him, things could get real ugly real fast. It was one thing for Maeve to deal with the idea of Danielle and Ryan as an abstract concept, but quite another to shove it in her face.

Besides, Cherry would freak out.

Danielle tried her best to steer the conversation toward New Year's Eve with only minimal success. Cherry waved at the waitress for another round. Maeve laughed and ordered a round of gin thingies and shots and *what was Danielle having?* Something about their frantic energy helped Danielle connect the dots. Ryan broke up with Cherry because she drank too much and wouldn't get help.

Well, Maeve was in trouble, too. Both women were dangerously out of control.

Danielle scowled at nothing in particular. A good friend would help. Once that good friend had time to process things. Danielle finished her wine and brought out her work face, taking charge and compelling the other two to focus on party planning. When she had as much of a to-do list as she could handle – and Maeve and Cherry were calling for another round – she made a polite excuse about a NICU project and some painting she needed to finish, and left them at the bar.

On the way back to her grandmother's house, she caught herself driving miles above the speed limit. Anger locked her jaw down tight and added extra weight to her foot on the gas pedal. She was upset with Cherry for being an idiot, and she was mad at Maeve because it was easier to be irate than to deal with the guilt and fear.

Beyond every other emotion, she was furious at herself for getting into something so straight out of high school.

That February 2nd flight couldn't come soon enough.

She headed down the hill onto Perkins Lane and took a deep, cleansing breath. Maeve and Cherry and all their insanity dropped away, as if nothing could really touch her down on this twisted road on the edge of the bluff. She made the last bend before the house. Ryan's truck was in the driveway, and she felt the beginnings of a foolish smile.

The fall-out might be making her crazy, but this young man sure made it worthwhile.

The porch light was on, and so was the floor lamp in the living room, but otherwise the house was dark. It was quiet too, lacking the rattle and hum that went along with Ryan's work. He'd talked about installing cabinet boxes in the kitchen, and that's where she found him, holding a beer, staring out the window at Puget Sound.

"What's up?" she asked, pausing in the doorway, reluctant to interrupt his private space.

He took a sip before answering her. "Didja have fun at The Pig?"

"Not especially." She rubbed her forehead, wondering how far to go. "Maeve and Cherry mostly wanted to drink instead of plan the party."

He snorted and crossed his arms. "The party."

There was just enough of an edge to his voice to send irritation zinging down the back of her neck. "The party." Danielle raked her hair out of her face and stayed in the doorway, uncertain whether she had the emotional resources to deal with Ryan's attitude.

"You sure you want to go to this thing?"

Danielle snuffed a laugh, almost quick enough. "No, not really." She took a couple steps toward him, hands out because she needed to feel him under her palms. "But it's important to Maeve, and…"

"Maeve? Who showed up here with your boyfriend?"

I need this attitude why? "I went out with him once, Ryan, and spent a good deal of time talking about you."

"Oh."

Danielle almost burst out laughing. With her focus on the game Maeve and Cherry were playing, it had never occurred to her that Ryan could be jealous of Christopher. She pressed her advantage right on into his body. "He's a nice guy." She stroked the rough shadow along his chin. "All he's worried about is whether he'll make money selling this house."

"You'd like to think so." He jerked his chin up. "That's not how he looks at you."

Deciding to pick her battles, Danielle pulled back a step. "If you say you don't want to go, we won't go."

"I really don't want to go."

Don't make promises you're not willing to keep. "Okay. I'll call Maeve."

Silence spread across the room. Danielle was doing her best to triage. If she had to tell Maeve she wasn't coming to the party, there would definitely be consequences.

"Except," — Ryan heaved the word out on a sigh — "I know my sister and my ex make a huge flaming deal out of this New Year's thing. If we don't go, they'll bitch about it for the rest of our natural lives."

She pinched the bridge of her nose. "It's your call."

To her utter surprise, he burst out laughing. "Is that right?" He grabbed her by the waist and pulled her against his body. "I think you just gave me the winning answer."

"What?"

Still chuckling, he backed her up until her butt hit the dining room table. "We'll go."

She eased back to let the antique cherry wood carry some of her weight. "We should take separate cars, because I don't think you want to get there to help set up at seven."

"We'll take separate cars," he said, taking control by sliding his thigh between hers.

"I'll totally owe you one."

"Don't leave, then."

His words knocked the breath right of her. "What?"

"Nothing." He pinned her to the table with his weight, no longer laughing. "Forget it." His hips jammed against hers, anger tightening the set of his jaw. "I'll go to this fucking party." He planted one hand on the table. "I'll fake it so Cherry doesn't freak out."He grabbed the back of her head with his other hand. "And you know why?"

"No," she whispered, wondering whether he was mad about the situation or whether it was personal.

"Because that's the only way I'll know for sure who's kissing you at midnight."

A little of both, maybe.

He followed up his words with a brutal kiss that lit up the desire in her belly like a torch. Burning with emotions she didn't want to examine, she gave it right back. She reached for his shirt, furiously ripping it off over his head and clawing at his muscular shoulders. She unbuttoned her own jeans, shoving them down over her thighs, then dragged his hand between her legs.

She wailed against his mouth when he plunged two fingers in deep and rubbed rough circles over her clit with his thumb, making her come so fast she lost track of everything but his strength and his urgency.

* * * *

Ryan pushed through the door of The Park, a boxing gym in a strip mall on a cleaned-up stretch of Aurora Avenue up north of the city.

The gym's manager stood behind the dinged up old front counter. "Well shit, O'Connor. Long time no see."

"Hey, Jackson." Ryan extended his hand to the green-eyed black man with blond hair and a scar across one cheekbone from a fight outside the ring.

As they shook hands, Jackson looked Ryan up and down in a way that would have made him uncomfortable if it had come from anyone else. "Looks like you've been working out somewhere."

"Twenty-Four Hour Fitness." Ryan snorted, a gust of frustration roiling him up. As crazy as things were between him and Dani, he needed more than his old gym could offer. "It's been a while."

"That's cool," Jackson said, cracking his knuckles. "We'll get you back in shape."

The cocky superiority in his tone made Ryan grin, and he reached for the clipboard to sign in.

Jackson took the clipboard from him but refused his debit card. "No charge today, man. I'm just glad to see you back."

Ryan thanked him and headed for the locker.

"Oh, and O'Connor?"

Ryan paused at the door to the locker room.

"Let me know when you're ready, and I'll hook you up with a sparring partner."

"Sure." Ryan nodded, his mouth damn near watering with the need to hit and get hit. "I'll be around a couple times a week."

"All right, man."

Ryan found an open locker and slung his bag in. He'd trained at The Park for years, from the time he was about fourteen until Cherry had talked him into working out with her at Twenty-Four Hour Fitness. She hated the 'boxing thing', as she called it. Yeah, a couple times he'd lost control, but not since he was a teenager.

There was a period of about a year, when he was eighteen or nineteen, when the partying sometimes blurred the line between what should stay in the ring and what shouldn't. Since then he'd learned to keep a lid on both the fighting and the drinking. It felt good to come back to the same bank of scratched and dented old lockers, the air in the room dense with layers of sweat, old blood, and musty showers. It felt like home.

The kind of home where he could hit something. Dani was under his skin, and every time he closed his eyes, his senses tricked him into smelling roses and vanilla, into feeling the soft swell of her breast and the silky weight of her hair, into tasting the secret hollows of her body.

Then reality would smack him like a slap to the back of the head.

He had some serious shit to work out.

In five minutes he was out on the main floor, dressed in baggy shorts and a worn tee shirt, like everybody else in the room. In ten minutes he was warming up on one of the bikes. In twenty minutes, he had his hands wrapped in cloth tape. Facing one of the bags, he started with a series of easy jabs.

His first punch might have been aimed at the face of a certain handsome real estate agent, but soon he found his rhythm and his conscious mind let go.

Chapter Fifteen

For Danielle, dressing for the New Year's Eve party was a losing proposition. If she dressed cute, Maeve would give her side-eye all night, worried about her hanging all over Ryan. If she dressed dowdy, Ryan would see her looking, well, dowdy.

Lose-lose.

She went for somewhere in-between, in a silver sleeveless mini dress with black tights, a beaded black cardigan, and the Heels from Hell. Festive, but not too short or too tight. Getting ready at the apartment, Maeve had insisted on twisting Danielle's hair into an up-do, because that's what best friends were for, and she lent her dangling rhinestone earrings when Danielle's own pearls were deemed boring. Some mascara and a touch of deep rose lipstick and Danielle was ready to go.

For once, Maeve was ready too. She fluttered around, lighting candles and setting out trays of snacks, her black sheath dress slit high on her thigh.

Cherry hid in the bathroom, putting the finishing touches on her hair and make-up. "I got the hottest little black dress ever," she said from behind the door. She leaned out, head and shoulders, like a burlesque dancer teasing her fans. "He's going to lose his shit."

Danielle knew exactly who "he" was, and Maeve confirmed her guess, her expression balancing irritation and guilt. Maeve started to say something, but closed her mouth in a tight line. Danielle sat crossing and uncrossing her legs, wishing she'd stayed home.

"I think we should do some shots!" Cherry called out through the open door.

"Not yet." Maeve lit the last candle, her perky tone at odds with her grimace. "It's going to be a long night, sister." She puffed her cheeks to blow out the match. "And I want to remember most of it."

Perched on the edge of the couch, Danielle tried to picture what the small living room would look like when it was full of people. Claustrophobic. She'd need to navigate without tripping over Maeve's suspicion, Ryan's anger, and Cherry's desperation. "I shouldn't drink yet, either."

"You guys are boring." Cherry stepped through the bathroom doorway. Her little black dress had stretch lace sleeves, a full, short skirt, and a neckline that plunged almost to her belly button. Her hair was a perfect drape of glossy mahogany, and her eyes were rimmed with kohl. She looked sophisticated. And sexy. And beyond beautiful.

Next to her, Danielle felt like a Sunday school teacher.

She added a second wish to her list. In addition to *don't piss anybody off*, she hoped *time would go quickly*. Because no one needed to deal with that much insecurity for long.

Cherry was still trying to coax them into drinking tequila shots when the land line rang, announcing someone at the main entrance. Maeve buzzed them in and Danielle put on her best plastic smile, determined to greet Ryan as if they were acquaintances who happened to have an old house in common. Their plan was to play it cool until everyone – mostly Cherry – was drunk enough not to pay attention.

A few of Maeve's coworkers came in, their natural fibers and geek-chic glasses making them look like extras from the set of Portlandia.

The land line rang three more times. Maeve opened the door three more times. Danielle flinched from the pinpricks of panic three more times. Some of

205

Cherry's friends came in, oozing Nordstrom's polish. More of Maeve's funky design-world friends followed them.

No Ryan.

Danielle was forced off her perch on the couch since everyone else was standing and she didn't want to be eye-level with a room full of people's butts. Maeve did a pretty good job of introducing her around and didn't force the issue when Danielle declined a glass of champagne.

The phone rang again. This time it was Christopher and his friend Jason. Danielle was so relieved to see someone she'd met before that she got carried away and hugged him with excessive enthusiasm. Christopher kept an arm casually around her waist and drew her off to one side, his smile broad enough to make the creases on either side of his mouth show.

"Where's your boyfriend?" Christopher pitched his voice low enough so only she could have heard him.

Still, Danielle's heart pinged in her chest like coins in a clothes dryer. "Haven't had one of those since high school." She hoped she came across as cool and disinterested instead of three steps from a seizure.

"Ah, I call bullshit on that." Christopher's hand traveled low enough on her hip to hit unsafe territory, and Danielle automatically eased away from him.

"See?" he said. "I made my point."

She burst out laughing. "What? Just because I don't want you groping me—"

"Right, right." He shifted his weight to open up space between them but kept a hand on the small of her back. "I thought Maeve's little brother was going to challenge me to a couple rounds in the ring when we showed up the other day."

Busted. Reaching up to rub her eye, Danielle remembered at the last minute how much make-up she had on and scratched the back of her neck instead. "No, he wouldn't…"

"Hmm. I know when I'm stepping on another man's territory."

Maeve stared at them from across the room, her expression unreadable, and Danielle Barbie-smiled back.

Christopher nodded in Maeve's direction. "She looks nice tonight."

Jason bounced up behind Maeve and wrapped his arms around her waist. Danielle would have had to have been a doorknob not to notice the tightening in Christopher's jaw. She stood on tiptoe, ignoring the squeal from the balls of her feet, and spoke right into his ear. "Ask her out, then."

Christopher followed Maeve with his gaze, the thoughtful twist to his lips letting Danielle know she'd guessed right. He draped an arm over her shoulders, and she was about to expand on the Maeve and Christopher idea when the front door opened. Joey and Chubb walked in.

No Ryan.

Danielle forced a grin. Christopher seemed like the kind of guy she'd like to have as a friend, and if this night was going to go down in flames it would be nice to have an ally.

"Tell me again why you don't ask Maeve out."

He looked up at the ceiling as if the answer would come from the old patched plaster. "Because I like her, but she's kind of a man-eater."

Not surprising. "A man-eater, huh?"

He swallowed a mouthful of whatever he had in his red plastic cup, but if he went on to elaborate on Maeve's man-eating tendencies, Danielle didn't hear him.

A hand dropped onto her shoulder, followed by a blast of hair product perfume. "My big bro sends his regards," Joey said.

Christopher made a big, obvious step back. "I know better than to wrestle with any of you O'Connor brothers." He raised his hands in front of his chest. "Let me go get you a drink, Danielle."

"Champagne."

"Got it."

She brushed a wayward strand of hair out of her eyes and waited to see what Joey would do next. She didn't have to wait long. He put his arm around her waist and nudged her back toward Maeve's tiny kitchen. She stopped digging in the Heels from Hell when he threatened to put her over his shoulder and carry her.

"You do that and I'll mess up your hair," she said.

Joey paused just long enough to smooth the side of his faux-hawk. He had on black jeans, a black crew-neck, a black leather jacket, and more eyeliner than Danielle ever wore. "Just cooperate."

She planted a hand in the center of his chest. "Cooperate? What the hell is going on?"

He laughed like he never took anything too seriously, which made her want to give him a lesson in messing with a grown woman instead of the college girls he was used to. Before she could, he had her backed up against the refrigerator, with Chubb blocking the doorway.

"Ryan doesn't want you talking to that guy," Joey said.

"Oh for God's sake." Danielle tried to push by him. "He can tell me that himself."

Joey caged her with an arm. "He'll be here."

"Fine." She grabbed his wrist hard enough to dig her nails in and shoved him out of her way. Chubb snorted a laugh as she passed, but didn't say anything. The stove clock said it was after ten o'clock. Danielle figured if Ryan didn't show up in another half hour, she was leaving. He could kiss his own ass at midnight.

She had no time for guys who bailed on her without a warning.

She escaped the kitchen and threaded her way through the crowded living room. Two steps in she almost bounced off Maeve.

"I was looking for you." Maeve's narrowed eyes telegraphed suspicion, but she didn't say anything outright.

"Yeah, um, I think it's time for a glass of champagne."

Maeve latched onto Danielle's hand. They ended up at the makeshift bar Maeve had created out of a bookcase and a cooler. "Shot?" Maeve asked.

"Nah. It's too early."

"Never." Maeve poured champagne into a red plastic cup and handed it to Danielle. "So where's Ryan?"

"Don't know," Danielle said through a sip of champagne. "His minions say he's coming."

"Might be better if he didn't," Maeve said, her voice vibrating with brittle energy. "Cherry's pretty hammered."

Down. In. Flames. Danielle gulped champagne, asking herself some hard questions. Where did a friend's loyalty end and a lover's loyalty begin? Because that's what Ryan was. Her lover. Too soon for boyfriend. Deeper than a temporary fling.

Her lover.

She pulled her gaze out of the cup, intending to say as much to Maeve.

Maeve preempted her. "Yeah, probably better if he stays away. You're my friend, Cherry's my friend, and right now I want to kill him."

Her words were hotter than just the tequila talking.

Danielle slapped as much of a smile as she could over lips that had all the pliability of steel straps.

"What?" Maeve asked.

"Nothing. I don't feel very good." *Time to cut my losses. If he shows up and I'm not here, it's not as big of a problem.* "I think I just need to go back to the house. Will your feelings be very hurt?" *Please understand that I'm trying to make the best of a shitty situation.*

"Nope." Her bitterness lashed at Danielle. "If he shows up, I'll tell him you said Happy New Year."

"Sure."

Danielle stepped around Maeve and ducked into the bedroom, looking for her purse. Chubb tried to block her exit, but she ducked past him and kept going, all the way down to where the Mini Cooper was parked on the street.

She started to cry right about the same time she got her seatbelt buckled.

The Mini's blasting heater dried her tears until she could brush the tiny crusts from under her eyes. Oncoming headlights made her blink. Onrushing memories made her blanch and start the tears again.

On its own, the Mini headed for her grandmother's house. She drove without turning the radio on, letting the hum of the engine and the soft hiss of her tires on the wet roadway soothe her ragged nerves. Ryan wasn't Braden, and Maeve would work things out for herself. They were making progress with the house, and she had a reservation for February 2nd.

Things could be a lot worse.

She only had to pull over once to cry.

The heavy darkness tamped down her hysteria, especially the stretch of road where Magnolia Blvd followed the water. Grand houses sat back from the edge of the bluff, the dark band of water far below, and in the spaces between the houses matte black clumps of trees absorbed the little light that escaped the overcast sky.

Darkness swaddled Grandmother's house, though all along Perkins Lane people were partying, playing music, and shooting off fireworks over the Sound. Danielle unlocked the door, hoping she'd remembered to turn on the heat. *No luck.* The air in the living room was barely warmer than the cold, damp night. She dropped her purse on the dining room table and kept her coat on, flopping down in the upholstered chair. A shiver rattled her. She'd had the oil tank filled for $800 and change. Another shiver hit. The cranky thermostat sneered at her. *Get up. Turn the heater on. Turn the lamp on. Do something.*

She sat, letting the chilly silence numb her head. Her cell phone chimed. Probably Ryan, calling to explain why he'd ditched the party.

Nothing she wanted to hear.

The cold clutched at her, dampening her ideas, driving the shivering deeper into her core. She wanted the cell phone to ring again and drag her out of the chair to answer it, to make her turn up the thermostat, to force her to listen to Ryan's excuses. The silence pushed at her ears, broken only by the occasional creek as the house settled and the random explosions from the neighborhood parties. After a big M80 boomed, she gave in and shifted forward, intending to get up and at least put the lights on, when footsteps came across the front porch.

She froze, waiting for a knock on her door. Instead, a key turned in the lock.

Ryan.

"You left," he said, mouth tight, totally furious.

Danielle sank down into the chair. "Things got complicated."

"How?" He crossed the room, catching her elbows and dragging her back to her feet. "I tried to reduce the drama by showing up late, and you didn't even wait for me."

"I thought you weren't coming."

His grip on her arms tightened. "Joey told you I was on my way." He shook her gently for emphasis.

For one long moment, Danielle searched Ryan's eyes. His frustration and honesty made her feel like an idiot. Instead of answering, she reached out and grasped the zippered edges of his leather coat, her numb cheeks warming up fast.

"By the time I showed up," he said, "you were gone."

"Oh." *A big idiot.*

"But instead of chasing you down right away, I stayed and made nice with my sister and gave my ex a midnight kiss because I wanted them to leave you the hell alone."

His body was rigid under his leather jacket, and her hands shook because his words put a pin in the balloon of tension that had been expanding inside her. She dragged him down close, his breath brushing warm against her face. Her sigh might have started somewhere under the foundation of the house.

"I screwed up." She tipped her face up until their lips were barely a breath apart. "Is it too late for a kiss?"

His response was forceful.

And non-verbal.

Danielle stood on tiptoe, draping as much of herself over Ryan as possible. He held her pinned to his body, tearing at her, wrecking her with his mouth. The heat between them brought the room temperature up to something close to a bonfire on a beach.

She would have stood there indefinitely, but with a throaty rumble Ryan pushed away, breathing hard, running his thumbnail along her cheekbone. "I'm still pissed."

"How can I make it up to you?" She let a touch of teasing into her voice. There were several possibilities, things he liked that would distract him from the current situation. She just wanted to hear which was at the top of his list.

He shoved her away. "Fuck if I'm going to let you stand there in your sparkly tiara and make this about me, like I'm some stupid carpenter who can't figure things out for himself."

"What are you talking about?" *Irrational much?* Danielle backed up farther, unsure how to handle the raw energy radiating from him. "It's my fault. I get it. I'm sorry."

Arms crossed and jaw tight, Ryan stared her down. "Are you sure?"

The flat-out distress in his voice made her hover on the cusp of uncertainty. "Yeah."

"Are you really sure?"

"You're not a stupid anything, and I'm not making this your fault." She reached out, moving slow the way you would with a dog who might still bite. "I shouldn't have let your sister talk me into the stupid party in the first place."

He clasped her hand and pulled her up against his body, a gesture as much about possession as it was forgiveness. "Okay, Princess, let's make a plan."

Her breath caught and stuttered. The buzz of energy between them was almost audible, like someone had thrown a switch. She wanted to pull off every bit of clothing and wrap herself around him.

His anger would warm them both.

Ryan cleared his throat. "It's about forty degrees in here, we're standing in the dark, the only bed is an air mattress, and it's almost one in the morning."

"Yeah, um, I was just going to…"

"What?"

"Put the heat on." She aimed for indignant, mostly missing the mark. "You interrupted me."

"I tell you what. I'm the boss in the bedroom, and that's where we're headed." He paused for a bitter laugh. "At least I think that's where we're headed."

"I hope so."

"Pack a bag. We're going to my house." He kissed her, his lips smoldering against her mouth.

Right. She shut up because to argue with him would move her behavior from 'moderate overreaction' to 'girl's gone crazy'. Giving him a tentative smile, she brought her cell phone out to check the time. "How many calls did I miss, anyway?"

"Six."

"Oh." She stifled an impulse to drop to her knees because she didn't want to overdo the apology thing. "I should make answering my phone into some kind of New Year's resolution."

"Ya think?" He said it with a smile, but the set of his jaw and the fierceness in his eyes told her he was still bitter. She laughed, fluttered a kiss on his cheek, and hoped he'd calm down if they had some really hot make-up sex.

Chapter Sixteen

Ryan woke up with the top of Dani's head tucked under his chin and her beautiful round ass pressed up against his morning wood.

Not a bad way to start a new year.

She stirred against him and he held his breath to see if she'd settle back to sleep. She did. He wasn't trying to avoid talking to her. The throbbing in his cock said he'd be waking her up sooner than later. He just wanted to lay there for a few minutes and not be frustrated.

He understood Dani's concern about Maeve, but he'd walked into the party angry. Telling his sister to mind her own damned business had been the high water mark for the night. Then that smarmy Christopher dude told him Dani had already left, and Ryan almost lost it completely. Dodging Cherry until midnight hadn't helped his mood.

But now Dani was in his bed, all soft and warm and smelling like roses and sex. He slid a hand over to tease one of her nipples, reaching down with the other to run his fingers along the warm, damp slit between her legs. Her soft little moan turned his morning wood into morning iron. He used his chin to move the hair away and kissed her neck. The kiss turned into a nibble, which turned into the beginnings of a hickey, which brought her around for real.

"Ryan." She wiggled away from him. "No love bites. I have to go to my uncle's for brunch."

He pulled her back against his body and thrust his hips a couple times. "You're not leaving yet."

"Not yet." She wrapped a hand around his shaft. "You should come with me." Her thumb teased the tip of his cock, her grip warm and firm and *god it felt good*.

"I'll be coming all right."

She stroked him a couple times. "No, I mean it. I'll call and tell him to set an extra plate."

"Sure." He rose up over her, resting on his elbows, his thighs between hers, dick poised at her entrance. He needed to grab a condom before going any farther, and paused to run his tongue up the valley between her breasts. She arched her back and he had to lock down every muscle in his ass to keep from thrusting into her bareback. He settled for toying with the soft skin of her throat, licking and nipping and sucking.

"Damn, young man." She shoved against his shoulders with a laugh that was way too naughty for first thing in the morning.

He let her push him to the side, using the opportunity to grab a condom from the nightstand. Her hair was a tangled mess and her mascara had turned into a raccoon's mask, but she was the most beautiful thing he'd ever seen. He got his raincoat on and pinned her down. "Are you sure we need to go out? I was kinda thinking we could stay here all day."

"You don't think you'll get bored?" She reached down to guide him in.

He thrust home in one stroke. Her tight heat felt so good he got lightheaded. "Nope."

* * * *

Parked in front of Uncle Jonathan's house, Danielle might have been perched on the edge of the world.

"We could still blow them off," Ryan said, even as he reached for the door handle. His eyelids slid to half-mast and he dropped his gaze somewhere in the vicinity of her breasts.

"Hey." She lifted his chin with one finger. "Save that for later. Right now we need to convince my uncle to convince my mother to spring for a new roof."

Ryan slung open his door. "Wouldn't it be easier to just ask her yourself?"

"Not if I want her to agree." Danielle hoped their morning games had shaken the rust out of her mental cylinders, because dodging Uncle Jonathan's well-meaning attempts to patch up the relationship with her mother added another degree of difficulty to the day. *Oh well.* She tightened her ponytail, straightened her shoulders, and climbed out of the cab of the truck.

Uncle Jonathan and his partner Robert lived in a big brick Tudor on the top of the Magnolia bluff only about a mile from Perkins Lane. They were farther from the water than Grandmother's house, but there were fewer trees, and the sky was huge.

Knee-high boxwoods lined the path to the front door, and a matched set of corkscrew hazels grew in huge Grecian-style urns on either side of covered entry.

"Come in, kitten." Robert held open the heavy front door, waving her in with a quick hug. His close cropped salt 'n' pepper hair matched his iron grey turtleneck. "Jonathan told me you were bringing a friend."

Danielle scooted past Robert. The foyer was bathwater warm after the raw, damp cold. Robert startled Danielle by lifting the coat off her shoulders. "Thank you," she said. "This is Ryan."

The two men shook hands, and Danielle vowed she'd keep her head in the present instead of picking at the past. Ryan laced his fingers with hers, a casual move that did a nice job of redirecting her memories. Better to think about the amazing things his hands had recently done, rather than how her mother had pointedly ignored

Danielle the day of her grandmother's funeral, turning an already bad scene into a grim nightmare.

"Go sit by the fire. Your uncle will be down in a minute." Robert waved them in the direction of the living room and disappeared down the hall.

The fire did its snap, crackle, and pop thing, and Danielle slid into the overstuffed lap of the love seat. Ryan bumped her hip on his way to claiming the seat next to her, draping his arm along the back of the couch and spreading his knees wide. Uncle Jonathan's house was all about contrasts. White stucco punctuated with heavy chocolate beams covered the exterior, and the interior carried on the theme. The floors were glossy, dark hardwood and the walls were white plaster. The furniture was antique teak and rattan, and the upholstery fabrics ran toward subdued floral in muddy coral, sand, and lime.

"I thought we'd call your mother while you're here." Uncle Jonathan blew into the room carrying a tray with three mugs.

Danielle straightened up and cleared her throat. Time to shut it down and turn into a manikin, or she'd never get through brunch without a lot of messy emotional overflow. Uncle Jonathan handed her a mug topped by a pile of whipped cream that smelled strongly of chocolate and mint. First round to Uncle Jonathan. Bring up her mother while handing her a cup of her favorite hot cocoa with peppermint schnapps. There'd be no way to avoid the phone call, and Danielle might as well minimize the collateral damage and move on.

"You remember Ryan, don't you?"

"Of course." Uncle Jonathan handed Ryan a mug and dropped into a chair, the cushion's *whoosh* echoing his sigh. "Much better." He took a sip from his mug, leaving a dab of whipped cream on the end of his nose. "But I thought you two weren't dating."

Ryan's chuckle vibrated against her upper arm, and Danielle's cheeks warmed up. As a distraction, she slurped enough whipped cream to find the drink underneath. *Cool. Keep your cool.* "We weren't before. We are now."

"Look how cute they are, Robert," Uncle Jonathan said.

His partner came through the door with his own mug. "Don't tease them, Jon," Robert said, perching on the arm of Jonathan's chair, his big black eyes and round cheeks making him resemble an intelligent squirrel. They'd been together for something like twenty years. "I know you won't get tired of the hot chocolate, Dani, but if anyone wants to switch to mimosas, just let me know."

"A mimosa sounds good," Ryan said.

Danielle tucked her nose back into her mug. Ryan seemed awful interested in making a good impression, as if two gay men weren't going to appreciate his confident smile and direct gaze. And his shoulders. *Duh.*

She sucked up the chocolate faster than she probably should have. Another mug or two and she could even handle the phone call Uncle Jonathan had threatened her with, though it would probably be better to get her other agenda item taken care of first. "So ... the house."

He raised his glass in toast. "To Mother's house."

Ryan and Robert raised their mugs.

"I'm just pleased you're taking care of things." Jonathan bent forward, resting his elbows on his knees, enough lawyer shading his gaze to put Danielle on her guard. She mirrored his posture, Ryan's hand resting on the small of her back.

"We're pretty much on schedule to get it on the market in the beginning of February," Danielle said.

"February?" Ryan asked, with just a touch too much surprise.

Danielle glanced at him. "Do you think we'll need more time?"

He waited a beat too long to answer. "No, I just—"

"What about some mimosas?" Robert hopped off the arm of Jonathan's chair. "Ryan, could you come give me a hand?"

Ryan and Robert headed out into the kitchen. Danielle took another hit of cocoa and gave her priorities a quick shuffle. She needed her uncle on board before she talked with her mother, but she needed Ryan more than either of the other two.

The fire gave an exceptionally loud pop. She twitched, slopping whipped cream down the side of her mug. "I'm going to try this again." The direct route would be the fastest way back to Ryan. "About the house."

"What?"

"It needs a new roof, and we'll get a better asking price if we do the work before putting it on the market." Danielle tried to relax against the loveseat. Now it was her turn to wait. She couldn't read her uncle's expression. His affable smile hadn't changed though a tiny note of tension began to hum.

"I guess you don't want to pay for a roof."

"My savings is pretty much tapped." She kept her tone casual, like she asked people to pick up a $25,000 bill every day.

"You know your mother is the executor of the will. Just ask her to cover the cost when you talk to her today." He raised his mug, toasting his own cleverness.

Of course that's what he'd say. "You know she'll say no, just because it's me asking. But if you ask her, it'll help my case."

"Hmm." Her uncle paused to take a sip of cocoa, his face a mask of lawyerly concentration.

Danielle did her best to stifle a grin. The longer he made her sweat, the more likely he was to agree. His refusals usually came swift and hard. After another few seconds, she decided to try to loosen him up. "Why is she always so nasty, anyway?"

Her uncle shifted, shrugged. "Maybe she doesn't want you to sell the house. Maybe she was hoping you'd stay here and live in it." He gave her a smile that was three quarters apology. "I'm sure that young man wouldn't mind if you stayed."

"What? Why?" Her family wasn't playing fair. "My job's in L.A. My life's in L.A. I've got a ticket for a flight home on February 2nd."

"February 2nd?"

Danielle jerked around. Ryan stood in the doorway holding a glass of champagne. His tone was mild but strained, as if anger and surprise almost overwhelmed his need to make a good impression.

Uncle Jonathan jumped out of the chair, his composure replaced by a boisterous grin. "I think I'll go help Robert in the kitchen."

"Wait, Uncle Jonathan," Danielle said, twisting around to follow her uncle's retreat, ready for one last shot before her ship completely sank. "If I ask her about the roof, will you talk her into it if she says no?"

Her uncle gave Ryan a pointed glance on his way through the door. "Oh, sweetie, you've got other stuff to deal with right now."

Ryan took a careful sip of champagne. "I guess I didn't realize you actually had a ticket."

Danielle blinked a couple times, wondering how she'd been so completely clueless. "I'm sorry."

He met her gaze for a brief moment, then looked away.

She scraped at a loose strand of hair. An absurd mix of frustration, sadness, and humor weighed her down. "You knew I was leaving."

"Can't fault me for hoping."

His half-assed smile squashed the humor, leaving her with the perfect recipe for tears. She went to him, running her hands up his arms to lay her palms on his face. "Let's just enjoy what we've got, okay?"

He closed his eyes, then wrapped her in a hug. "Sure."

Her words had an undercurrent of desperation, but it matched the fierceness of his arms around her shoulders.

* * * *

The shock of hearing Dani say she'd bought a plane ticket pretty much destroyed Ryan's appetite. He kept his arms around her until Jonathan called them to the dining room, because it was easier than figuring out what to say.

She didn't seem interested in letting go of him, either.

Her uncle called them a second time, and Ryan tugged gently on her ponytail. "Would have been easier to just stay in bed."

Dani gave him the briefest smile and tipped her head to rest her forehead against his chest. "Yeah."

"For the record, I knew you were leaving, but it surprised me to hear you'd bought a ticket," Ryan said.

She took a step back, her expression hardening into something artificial. "I guess I should have mentioned it."

"I guess." Ryan matched her cool smile with one of his own. He made a show of offering her his elbow and escorted her down the hall to the dining room. They sat down to platters of bacon, poached eggs on toasted brioche, and individual corn soufflés. Fortunately there was more fresh squeezed orange juice and an open bottle of champagne.

He could have used something stronger, but another mimosa was better than nothing.

Dani's uncle kept the conversation going with a bunch of questions about the house project, and her silence forced Ryan to talk. Somewhere between his second helping and third mimosa, a realization slid into place.

For ten years with Cherry, he'd put up with limitless shit.

No more.

He liked Dani a lot, but that didn't give her an open pass. Her reluctance to be up front about their relationship had turned Christmas Eve into a disaster and New Year's Eve into a shit-storm. Even little surprises, like *"oh, I already bought my plane ticket home"* stung.

Baseball only gave each batter three strikes.

She was at two and counting.

He took a long swallow of orange juice, a bleak sense of freedom helping him relax. Robert asked him where he worked out, and he made a joke about Gold's Gym. The whole table relaxed after that, and Dani even reached over and squeezed his thigh, her hand about two inches higher than was polite.

On the way back to Perkins Lane, he stopped at Magnolia Park so they could watch the tide go out. This time when her hand landed on his thigh, he dragged it up toward his bullseye, and she did a sweet job of distracting him when he didn't want to think.

Chapter Seventeen

Tuesday morning they both got up early; Ryan had to go to work at his day job, and Danielle wanted to deal with the stack of increasingly hysterical emails from her boss, Sharon. The telephone conversation with her mother had gone about like Danielle figured it would. Mom was pissy, Danielle was cranky, and Uncle Jonathan finally had to step in and talk them both down. Her mother did agree to shift funds around to pay for the roof, relieving Danielle of that particular worry.

Though that emotion couldn't compare with the happy free-fall she'd felt when Ryan finally smiled at her again.

The coffee pot rumbled and the shower squawked overhead. Danielle opened email after email from her boss, who wanted to know whether she'd finished several projects and if she was willing to start others. She'd gone through about six of them when her laptop made a weird little chirp. At first she ignored it. The chirp happened again. This time a small square popped up in the bottom corner of her screen. The pop-up was from her Skype program, telling her someone was trying to call in. She opened it up and Sharon smiled at her from a thousand miles away.

"Good morning." Sharon's perfect pixie cut had gone from coal black to silver in the years Danielle had worked for her, but her tailored suits and perfect posture hadn't changed.

"Abbie and I were just starting the year off with a friendly meeting," Sharon said. "She said she could tell you were online because you were on Facebook."

Damn. "I wasn't, I mean, yeah, I guess I opened Facebook." Danielle hunched down to limit Sharon's view to a head shot. Underneath Ryan's old sweatshirt she was naked except for a pair of thong panties, a look he appreciated but which wasn't the best ensemble for work.

Abbie, another assistant manager, stuck her head into the screen. "Happy New Year!"

"Yeah, same to you guys." The shower stopped.

"Listen," Sharon said. "I know you're really busy with the house and all, but I just wanted to see where things stood with the insulin guidelines."

Danielle brushed a floppy strand of hair out of her eyes with a mental message to Ryan to stay upstairs. "Insulin guidelines? I don't remember…"

"I thought you were taking that on." Abbie claimed the screen again. "We talked about it at that meeting right before Halloween."

Danielle scrambled for an answer. Halloween might as well have been back in college. Over the last couple weeks, she'd paid less and less attention to work.

Because she was on leave. Trying to get the house ready to sell. And oh yeah, Ryan.

Periodic floor squeaks cued Danielle that Ryan was moving around upstairs and she had to hope he stayed there. It's not that she didn't want her colleagues to meet him, just not at seven in the morning when she was half naked.

Danielle still hadn't come up with a response to Abbie when Sharon spoke up. "Do you remember telling some of the girls you'd get them feedback on their poster presentation? Their deadline for submitting it is next week."

"Oh, shit." She scratched at her hair again, embarrassed to have forgotten something that important. With all the pots she had on the stove, she was bound to burn one of them. "I'm really sorry. I meant to get comments to them before the holidays."

Heavy steps pounded down the stairs. Danielle's nerves pinged. Half her mind focused on the computer. The other half dropped into panic mode, words crowding in the back of her throat unable to make it past her embarrassment.

On the L.A. end, the meeting continued. Sharon muttered a quick aside to Abbie, then came back to the screen. "It would be awesome if you could get them something this week. Then they'll have time to tweak it before the deadline."

Ryan blew into the dining room, laying a kiss on Danielle before she could react. "I smell coffee," he said, reaching down to cop a feel before stepping away.

"Um, Danielle?" Abbie grinned so hard she all but popped out from the laptop screen.

"What the—" Ryan glanced at the computer.

Danielle came very close to crawling under the table.

Ryan took a big step back toward the kitchen. "I'm just ... going to go pour us some coffee."

"It's a work thing," Danielle said to him with a strained pseudo-smile, and while Abbie was laughing, Sharon was definitely not.

"Danielle?" Sharon looked like she wanted to say something more but had no idea what.

"I'm sorry, that's ... uh ... Ryan. He's been working here."

"He sure has," Abbie said, and then she cracked up, falling away from the screen.

Sharon took a deep breath, puffing her cheeks out as she exhaled. "We can do this another time." She gave Danielle a hard look. "I need you back February third, ready to go to work."

"Of course." Danielle gulped like a teenager. "I'll get the comments on the poster presentation done by the end of the week." She gestured at the piles of paper on the table. "I'll finish up this other stuff, too."

"All right. Talk to you later, then," Sharon said, Abbie still giggling in the background.

The Skype window closed. Danielle stared at her computer desktop for a minute, trying to assimilate what had just happened.

Ryan set two mugs on the table next to her. "Sorry, Princess."

He didn't actually sound that sorry.

"Oh shit. Oh shit. Oh shit. Oh shit." She snatched up a mug, sending a splash of hot coffee onto her thigh. The coffee didn't burn nearly as hot as the embarrassment racing from her brain to her belly and back again. "Ouch." She made a fist with the end of her sleeve and scrubbed at the spill. "I can't believe that just happened."

His hands were solid and strong and warm on her shoulders, and he pressed a kiss onto the top of her head. "What?"

"They saw you. Sharon. My boss. Abbie." She set the coffee back down and rocked her head back against his belly, an unholy trio of shock, surprise, and embarrassment taking potshots at her pride.

"So?"

"You kissed me."

Ryan ran his thumbs up the back of her neck. "Again, so?"

"It's just…" She pulled up one of his hands to nip his knuckle. *What was the problem, exactly?* "I'm wearing a thong and I smell like sex and Abbie, at least, jumped right on that."

"Well, they couldn't smell you and I'ma guess they couldn't see your bare ass, or things would have been over before I showed up." He pinched her cheek and reached over her shoulder for a mug. "And what the hell were they bugging you this early for, anyway?" He brought the coffee to his lips, then flinched and moved it away. "You're on leave."

"Honestly?" She blew at the steam rising from her mug, mortification fading to an awkward pang. "If I left things until I got back, I'd have to work eighty-hour weeks for months. It's just easier to keep some of it going."

"What the hell kind of job have you got?"

"Good question." Danielle took a cautious sip. "Very good question."

"Yeah, well, I'm going to go to work before your boss turns up again." Ryan's dimple disappeared and the shields went up in his eyes. "Don't want her to think you're sleazing around."

"What?"

He almost said something but gave her a quick kiss instead, his freshly showered Irish Spring scent catching her breath, his cool expression adding to her irritation.

Fine. Be a dick, then. She grabbed her notebook with both hands and showed him her to-do list. "There's enough here for me to work fulltime from now until I fly back to L.A."

Ryan raised his hands, palms toward her. "Sounds like bullshit to me, but it's your gig."

Danielle clamped her molars together. She didn't owe Ryan an explanation, why the combination of Sharon's persuasion and Braden's approval had cornered her into a manager's position in the first place; how deftly playing unit politics had turned her into Sharon's eyes and ears and spunky right hand; how keeping herself too busy to think had helped her cope.

"I didn't used to think so." She dropped the notebook next to the laptop. "Now I don't know."

Ryan's expression warmed up some. He came over and brushed his knuckles across her cheek. "You'll figure it out, Princess."

She cupped his hand, holding it against her face. "Thanks."

"I'll be back after work."

"Hopefully I'll have made some progress by then." On something besides NICU work.

Danielle was pretty sure Sharon's attempts to keep her working violated all kinds of HR policies, and for possibly the first time ever, Danielle wanted to push back. Management had never been a career goal until she got involved with Braden. He'd hated having her work night shift, and no one would fault her for taking a day job, especially if it made her partner happy.

Would they?

She'd never been the kind of woman who made decisions to keep a man happy. Right? Because otherwise, she was in trouble. God only knew what she'd do for Ryan.

* * * *

"Are you going to the gym?" Niall asked from his seat at the dining room table.

Ryan loaded one last glass in the dishwasher and closed the door, giving it a hard shove to make it latch. "Shit. Forgot soap."

Niall got up and brought an empty coffee mug to the sink. "Stick this in there, too."

Ryan snorted but grabbed the cup, reaching under the sink for the box of dishwasher detergent. He kept his eyes – and his mind – on the task, ignoring where his brother's expression was headed. He'd worked hard all week, and didn't have the patience for a lecture. "Before I start this thing up, do you see any more dishes?"

"There might be a science experiment or two in Chubb's room, but otherwise I think you got 'em." Niall leaned back against the counter, crossing his arms over his chest. He reminded Ryan of their father, gearing up to lecture him about making babies or doing drugs or something.

In no mood to deal with whatever his brother had in mind, Ryan jammed the dishwasher door shut. It hummed to life. "I was thinking I'd head over to The Park and pound on a heavy bag for a while."

"Can I tag along?"

All the O'Connor boys knew how to box, although only the two of them had ever taken it seriously. Niall kept himself in pretty good shape for a guy of thirty-five, and Ryan figured a good workout would help his brother deal with some of his frustration with his soon-to-be ex-wife.

"Sure, man." Ryan ducked into the hall, heading for his room. For the moment, he'd dodged whatever conversational bullet Niall had been aiming at him.

His brother called his name, and reluctantly Ryan paused. "Yeah?"

"How come you're not over at Dani's?"

Because if I'm not around her, she won't get tagged with her third strike? Ryan came up with a half-hearted fib instead. "Dani's got stuff and I wanted to get in a workout."

Niall gave a subtle jerk of his head, a move that might get some freshly-arrested thug to keep talking, but Ryan wasn't playing. "What? That's it."

"Nothing, bro. Just wondering what the deal is with you and Danielle."

His tone of voice made Ryan glad he'd be hitting a bag soon. "I like her and for some reason she likes me, too."

"For some reason … she's the same age as Maeve, right?"

"Oh for Christ's sake, Niall." Annoyance turned to anger the deeper it crawled into his gut. "You know the answer to that. If you have a problem with Dani and me, remember it's *your* problem, not mine."

"I didn't say it was a problem."

Ryan hated when Niall used his reasonable voice. "Good." Ryan took a step back and let go of a breath, promising himself he wouldn't punch anything with a pulse. Including his brother.

Niall must have picked up his vibe, because he sighed and rubbed a hand over his freshly-shaved head. "Kinda soon after Cherry."

Ryan flexed his knuckles a couple times. "Cherry and I have been done for a couple of years."

"You say that now."

"I'd have said it a year ago." His fist rapped the door frame, a piss-poor pop-off valve. "You never asked."

Both hands raised as if declaring a truce, Niall started and stopped a couple times before finally responding. "You're right."

Ryan paused, eyes narrowing, shoulders tense. His oldest brother was too much of a cop to give in that easy.

"You know, on Christmas Eve I was pretty much a zombie," Niall said. "And even though you and Danielle weren't officially together, looking at you two made me want to kick something."

A whoosh of laughter escaped before Ryan could shut it down. "I know I'm ugly, but…"

"Yeah you are, but you're happy, too, you bastard, happier than you've been in a while."

Ryan didn't know what to say, so he kept his mouth shut. Next thing he knew, Niall would be trying to hug him or something. He met his brother's gaze. After a few beats, Niall nodded. Moment over.

"So, um, The Park?" Ryan's voice was gruff enough he had to clear his throat to get the words out.

"Yeah." Niall interlaced his fingers and stretched his arms high over his head. "We can grab a pizza or something on the way home."

"We could hit the Pig." Ryan grinned, still leery that Niall would start to hassle him again. Chubb was likely to be at the Pig too, unless he'd hooked up with some no-life video gamer friend. Hanging out in pubs wasn't really Niall's style, and Ryan felt bad for his older brother. Being lonely sucked.

Maybe he'd give Dani a call later, too. They'd agreed to take an evening off, but she was in his blood, and he wanted her down to the marrow of his bones.

The strength of his feelings freaked him out a little.

Hell, it freaked him out a lot.

* * * *

Over the course of the week, Danielle reached another conclusion. She enjoyed working on old houses. She might have started out motivated by guilt, but things had changed. She'd become fascinated by the hundreds of tiny gestures she'd made over the first two months at her Grandmother's house, each move aimed at repairing a solid decade of neglect on top of several generations of wear. Working on the house took a different kind of discipline than caring for preemies, but the attention to detail felt familiar. Really, if a nurse did a good job with a baby, the baby got seventy-five years out of the deal.

If a carpenter did a good job on a house, it could take care of a family for generations.

Apples and orangutans, but rehabilitating a house had its positives.

Friday afternoon, Danielle worked on painting the two front bedrooms upstairs a shade of cream with a hint of sage, which gave her plenty of major muscle group action and freed her mind to think. She finished the last wall, wrapped the rollers and brushes in plastic, and covered the paint cans, ready to go for tomorrow.

By the time Ryan's headlights sliced across her big front window, she'd progressed to slouching in the wing chair, debating whether the ache in her arms was a deal-breaker for starting a new project. Any half-assed ideas about what to do next died a fast and painless death when he carried in a couple bags from Panda's Chinese Kitchen instead of his toolbox.

"We're taking the night off," he said, dumping the bags on the dining room table, daring her to cross him.

Danielle curled up and rested her elbows on her knees. "I've been painting."

He took an exaggerated sniff. "Your new green highlights were my first clue."

"Shit." She tried to rake her fingers through her ponytail, but they got stuck hard enough to make her eyes water. "I need a shower."

He took a second exaggerated sniff. "Yep."

"Shut up."

He grinned hard enough to show both dimples. "Food'll get cold if you shower now." He spread the top of one bag and lifted out a couple small white boxes. "Cashew chicken." He set the boxes on the table and took out two more. "Smoked pork. Rice." He opened one box and lifted out a small browned pocket of meat. "Pot stickers."

Danielle's shoulders hurt. Her neck was stiff. She had blisters on her thumb from wielding the paint brush. But when Ryan lifted the pot sticker to her lips, it didn't hurt at all to open her mouth and take a bite. The fabulous mix of crisp and soft, salt and savory made her stomach growl. He fed her a second pot sticker, nodding encouragement as she ate. He lifted a six-pack of beer out of the second grocery bag, opened her one, and passed the bottle over. She downed about half, washing away the paint stink stuck in the back of her throat and loosening some of the tension in her jaw.

"Thanks, babe," she said.

Ryan rested against the table and his smile grew. "Anything for you, Princess."

"Shut up."

He raised an eyebrow, a totally sweet and sexy gesture. His five o'clock shadow was heavier than normal, as if he hadn't bothered to shave in the morning, and his hair fell in messy curls. Sensual curls. Bedroom curls. He grabbed a pair of chopsticks and picked up one of the white boxes.

"Here." Slowly, he lifted a chunk of chicken from its pool of rich, soy and spice broth.

She allowed him to feed her one bite, and another. Hand feeding her Chinese food was its own kind of sexy. "Why are you being nice to me?"

"Because I'm hoping you'll suck my dick."

Danielle giggled, all but choking on her chicken at the abrupt change of subject. "You could have just asked."

"Okay." He cupped his hand over his crotch. "Now I'm asking."

"Don't you want to eat first?"

His dimples deepened some more. "I'm not starving." He reached over and traced her lower lip with the tip of his finger. "I want your mouth on me."

"In the dining room?" Every possible objection made a party in her head. "There's a big window and no drapes."

"It's dark outside. Nobody's going to see us."

Says the voice of reason.

Except, he was right. Very few cars tackled Perkins Lane, and unless someone was looking, they wouldn't see anything behind the laurel hedge. The gruff edge to his words wore down her resistance. All the negatives – anxiety, embarrassment, fear – were trumped by a craving to taste him, to take him down deep.

She sank down to her knees, jaw chattering, shivers running deep in her belly. He eased back, bracing himself against a chair. She lowered his fly, and he did a little shivering of his own.

Drawing out his thick cock, she stopped to admire it, running light fingertips along the knotty veins. He thrust toward her and groaned softly, his enthusiasm paying her a high compliment. She drew the smooth pink head to her lips, tracing the rounded edge with her tongue. He gasped and his hands flexed, gripped, and held.

"More," he said, his voice stripped raw.

Danielle ran her tongue along his shaft. She couldn't swallow it all, so kept hold of the base with one hand. The other she trailed up his thigh until she reached the thatch of dark hair surrounding his balls. She took as much as she could, set up a rhythm, synched her mouth to her hand, and caressed his balls.

Ryan's jeans slid down around his thighs and he sighed from somewhere deep, rocking his hips in time with her motion. He scooted the chair out and sank to the edge of the seat. Her awareness was wrapped around him, his strength as he thrust against the back of her throat, his musky smell, the heavy velvet of his balls. He dug his fingers through her hair, his other hand clutching her shoulder.

When he gasped again she stopped, cupping both hands around his shaft and teasing the head with little bites. She flicked the band underneath with the tip of her tongue and grinned at the determined thrust of his hips. "'S good?"

"Shit."

She opened up and took him deeper than before, increasing her pace, prompting Ryan to let loose a stream of muffled curses. For every *shit* or *damn,* there were multiple variations on *Oh my God. So good.*

She did feel good, amazing even. Ryan's pleasure bathed everything from her soul to her sex in a giddy, warm, sweet sensation. Ryan's hips lost their rhythm at the same time that his cock pulsed in her hands.

"I'm going to come." He gritted the words out on a ragged exhale.

Her instinct was to draw back. She'd never let a guy come in her mouth before. But then, she'd never had a guy like Ryan before, a guy so real and so strong. A guy who tweaked every one of her expectations. A guy she might one day be able to love.

Instead of finishing with her hands, she swallowed him down, loving the taste of his salty release.

Ryan folded over her, landing on his knees. He lifted her chin and clamped onto her lips, sucking her tongue into his mouth. Her own need jumped up and claimed her attention. Desire soaked her panties, and she wanted nothing more than to lay back on the grubby hard wood floor and let him pound into her.

"Upstairs," he said, pulling her onto his lap, nuzzling her neck, and stroking any part of her he could reach. "It's going to take me a minute to get ready again, and while we wait, I want to return the favor."

"Oh." *Stop blushing!* Having his mouth on her sounded like the best idea ever. She scrambled up and offered him her hand, grinning as she led him up the stairs. Now she knew his secret. For a guy who wanted to be the boss of the bedroom, he was pretty docile after having his dick sucked.

Totally worth remembering.

* * * *

An hour later, Ryan lay on the air mattress, Dani stretched out against him, his hand tucked around her waist. Between working hard all day and loving her hard all evening, a sweet, narcotic relaxation pinned him down. He loved being in her bed, loved the feel of her naked curves against his body, loved the addictive smell of roses surrounding her.

He nuzzled the soft spot under her ear, nipping the tender lobe. "It's early to go to sleep for the night."

The rumpled sheet muffled her giggle. "I'm not asleep."

He pulled his hand free of hers and reached up to cup her breast, his lips still pressed to the side of her neck. He sucked in a small mouthful, likely hard enough to leave a mark, then grinned as she squirmed away from him.

"Stop."

"Well we should get up then, because I'm in that kind of mood."

"What time is it?"

He reached across her, grabbing her cell phone from the floor beside the air mattress. "Eight o'clock."

He reached over her again, deliberately crushing her into the mattress with his body, a position very similar to one they'd both enjoyed a few minutes earlier. He set the cell phone back on the floor. Almost immediately it started to chirp.

Dani groaned. "Make it stop."

Ryan picked it up and rolled onto his back. Answering would make it stop. He glanced at the screen, recognized his sister's avatar, and tossed the phone onto Danielle's chest.

She held it up long enough to see the screen before answering, her voice husky, muted. "What's up?"

He shook his head, trying not to look as irritated as he felt.

"What?" she said. "No, I'm not asleep. Just … hanging out."

He reached over, running a thumb over her nipple. He stroked back and forth, Up and down. He gave it one…two…three strikes.

She slapped his hand away.

He reached for his jeans.

"I've been painting and stuff." Her voice was colder, sharper, like she'd turned into a bitchy movie goddess for real.

He sat up and flipped on the squatty little lamp that sat next to the head of the bed. The light brought out hard lines in her face.

"No, I just want to hang out here tonight." She scooted over to the edge of the mattress and pushed herself up, turning her back to him.

Ryan got out of bed and pulled on his jeans. Part of him thought he should leave, give her some privacy. Part thought he should leave before he said or did something they'd both regret.

Part of him refused to go anywhere until she was off the phone.

"Ryan's not here."

Ryan's fists tightened, though he had no right to get upset. So what if she lied about him to his sister? So what?

Her hunched shoulders shut him out more effectively than anything else she could have done. She sat for a minute after ending the call.

He waited, anger and pain fighting a death match, tearing him up.

"She's mad at me." She kept her back to him, her voice faded, distant.

"Really?" For some reason he needed her to spell it out.

Her shoulders rotated, twisting her upper body and giving him a profile view. "She wanted me to meet her at the Pig." Her vacant expression didn't match the tension in her body. "I hate lying to her."

"But you did."

"And you're pissed."

"Damn straight."

"I'm sorry I don't want to tell her I sound like I'm asleep because I'm in bed with her brother." Danielle scraped the hair out of her face, her eyes tough, cold, and angry. "Damn it." She let go and put her palms behind her head, hair falling down to shield her face.

"Damn it."

She might as well have stabbed him in the effing heart. He was some dirty secret to her, not good enough to introduce to her friends from work, not someone she'd choose over his sister. A guy probably needed a sports car and a six-figure income to meet Dani Jacobsen's standards.

A thunder clap of emotion broke over him, blasting his core like a bolt of lightning. "You know..." He stopped and cleared his throat, barely able to choke the words out. "I care about you a lot." He had such a tight grip on his sweatshirt he could have drilled his fingertips through the fabric. "And you're treating me like a fucking booty call."

That snapped her attention to him. "What?" Her gaze burned through layers of defense, leaving him naked.

"I spent the last two years dealing with Cherry's crazy." He crossed his arms, a lame attempt to protect himself from the shattered anguish in her face. "I can't do it again, Danielle. I'm sorry."

Though it carved him up with the worst pain he'd ever experienced, he left the room. He left the house. He left the woman he'd been in love with since he was nine years old.

Climbing into the truck with his shoes in his hand and his sweatshirt tucked under his elbow, he'd never felt so old.

Chapter Eighteen

The bubble of numb lasted through the weekend. On Monday, pain and shame moved in, grinding against the tension in Danielle's chest, sapping her determination. She'd had an Eamon moment and tried to avoid the wrath of Maeve. *Stupid.* Ryan's ongoing silence had become a weight, like a collar made from sandbags and wet cement. She didn't doubt he'd meant it when he said he was done.

Her only hope now was that he'd change his mind once his temper cooled.

She also tried real hard not to compare her state of mind with those days six months ago right after Braden left. At least Ryan had given her a reason. Sort of.

About ten o'clock Monday morning, Danielle's phone chirped with the text from Maeve.

Meet me for lunch.

Lunch with Maeve. Now that was an interesting idea. Interesting in a more-awkward-than-a-gynecological-exam-but-slightly-better-than-amputation kind of way.

In the end, the chance to get out of the house decided for her, though the chance to see someone connected with Ryan was also pretty compelling. Danielle promised herself she wouldn't mention his name. At all. Not even once. No matter what Maeve said.

I'll be there at noon.

Maeve responded by directing her to Cutters, the restaurant next door to her design firm.

To fill the empty hours, Danielle went from room to room, jotting down notes on everything that still needed doing. The list was long enough that even if Ryan worked fulltime until the end of the month, it wouldn't be done. She hadn't heard from him since the Chinese Food Debacle, and though she'd never expected a man to be her foundation, the house was a heavy load without him.

Right before noon, she parked the Mini up the hill from Cutters and dashed through the rain to join the lunch crowd.

Maeve stood in the lobby, arms crossed, bright coral nails popping against the forest green wool scarf wrapped around her shoulders. "They said there'd be a ten-minute wait."

"That's fine." Danielle couldn't find anything else to say, so she counted hexagonal tiles on the floor, feeling like she'd raced outside naked and lost her keys. A thought slid across her mind; she could tell Maeve about Ryan and deal with the side effects. Maeve hadn't been happy to hear about them dating, and who knew how she'd respond to hearing they broke up. Danielle would have to throw those dice at some point. Maybe this was a good time. It would be her penance. Sort of like going to confession, without the Catholic part.

Or she could do her best to get through lunch without losing her best friend, too.

"What'd you do this weekend?" Maeve asked.

Spent the whole time curled up in bed. "Not much."

Another awkward silence built, and Danielle shoved her work-shredded fingernails in the pockets of her down jacket. She used to be as pulled-together as Maeve, before she'd launched her life to Mars.

What the hell happened?

They made two more conversational false-starts before the hostess seated them at a table with a view of the water. Or rather, a view of the mist and low-hanging clouds hiding everything but the boats tied up on the dock nearest to them, which stood out black and clear against the soggy pewter backdrop.

Maeve chased the hostess off with a you-can-pour-water-later frown. "Did you hear what happened New Year's Eve?"

Danielle slow-blinked to clear the image of Ryan pinning her to the bed. "No."

Tossing her scarf over the nearest chair, Maeve gave Danielle a catty grin. "Fucking Cherry." A soft shadow of hurt fell over her eyes. "About one-thirty I caught her in the bathroom with Jason. He was straddling the toilet and she was straddling him."

Danielle applied every ounce of control she possessed to keep her expression neutral. "No way."

"Right?" Maeve planted her elbows on the table, fists clenched, jaw tight, pride stung. "All these years we've been friends, and she totally plays the slut card right in front of poor Ryan." She smacked the table. "If she goes near him again, I'll rip her tits off."

"Mm-hmm." The conversation definitely wasn't helping Danielle's appetite. Though Maeve might not have been seriously interested in Jason, friends didn't do that kind of thing to each other. Nevertheless, trash-talking Cherry could very well come back to nibble on Danielle's ass. She swallowed a couple variations of *Gee, I'm so not surprised* and tapped her fork against her knife, desperate to change the subject.

The hostess helped her out by showing up with the water, accomplishing her mission despite Maeve's go-away glare, and the waitress showed up right on the hostess's heels, further delaying their conversation. Danielle asked for the Thai chicken salad and a glass of iced tea. Maeve took a long hard look at the wine list but ordered iced tea also. Danielle was too much of a nurse not to notice the tremor in Maeve's elegant fingers. She knew a red flag when she saw one.

Maeve leaned forward, keeping her voice pitched low like they were discussing a threat to national security. "And Ryan's going nuts, too. I heard from a little bald birdie that he's been running around like he's got barbed wire up his ass."

Their waitress chose that moment to deliver their drinks. Danielle grabbed her tea and started to gulp, trying to find something like composure before she responded. No luck. Clutching at her promise not to mention his name, she wasted another thirty seconds wiping condensation off the glass. Niall was living with Ryan, so he'd have the birdie's-eye view.

Danielle got to hear about it, thanks to the O'Connor Family mafia.

"So since Cherry's old news, I guess you and Ryan are it." Maeve said, pulling Danielle back into the conversation with a sardonic smirk.

"Oh." *Not going there. No effing way.* Sometimes the best defense was a frontal assault. Danielle schooled her face and kept her delivery smooth. "Do your hands always shake like that?"

"Shake? What?" Maeve showed Danielle her empty palms. Both hands had a very slight tremor.

"Like that."

Maeve pressed her fingertips against her forehead, creating a defensive shield for her eyes. "I guess they do sometimes. I went to the Pig last night and probably had one too many."

Alcoholics depended on denial, so Danielle didn't want to push too hard. At least she'd managed to get the conversation off Ryan. "What was going on at the Pig?"

"The usual. I just stopped in after work." Some of the tension faded from Maeve's shoulders. "I hung out with Christopher for a while."

Danielle couldn't help but grin. "That's cool. You should go out with him."

"Christopher? No way. He's a player."

"Oh, it's okay for me to go out with a player, but not for you?"

"That's different."

Danielle snickered, and after a minute, Maeve joined her. It was a short laugh, tentative, with a dash more sarcasm than Danielle usually projected. But they were laughing together. The way friends do.

"And if you're rehearsing a Maeve-drinks-too-much speech, don't bother," Maeve said. "You'll have to get in line behind Mom and Dad and Niall." Maeve made a disgusted snort. "Even Eamon takes a swing at me every now and then."

"Do you think they're wrong?"

"Hell no." An echo of sadness carried through Maeve's defiant words. "I'm just not ready to do anything about it."

The waitress with the amazing timing arrived with their salads, and both women thanked her. They picked at their food and reminisced about high school, and Danielle left in a marginally better mood.

At least until she got to the house and realized Ryan wouldn't be coming over.

* * * *

Ryan drove straight home after the day job. Again. No stop in Magnolia. He was done with that. As much as he liked Dani – hell, maybe even loved her – he couldn't deal with another woman who played games. Cherry had cured him of that.

Traffic didn't suck too bad, and when he got home, Niall and Chubb were camped out at the dining room table. Chubb's shit-eating smile suggested he'd made a new friend sometime in the recent past. Niall grinned like a kid, as if Chubb's success gave him too much vicarious stimulation.

"What was her name?" Ryan asked.

Niall faked a cough to cover his laugh, and Chubb sat up straighter, removing his feet from the neighboring chair.

"Whose name?" he said. "What makes you think I'm talking about a woman?"

Ryan flicked the hickey on his roommate's neck on his way by. "Lucky guess."

Niall's guffaw earned him a flying bird from Chubb.

"I need to make you rub my bald head, dude, so some of your luck will rub off on me," Niall said.

Ryan had to agree. Niall's soon-to-be-ex-wife had done a serious number on him. A little recreational sex would be a good thing, though he wasn't sure his conservative older brother would ever be ready for Chubb's freak show. "Be careful what you wish for, bro."

Chubb rested his elbows on the table and kicked a chair in Ryan's direction. "If you weren't Mr. Monogamy, you might have fun, too."

Ryan ignored them both and went to the fridge for a beer. Coming back into the dining area, he grabbed the chair Chubb's feet had freed up and straddled it. Niall and Chubb compared notes on the best places to go to meet chicks, and Ryan nursed his beer, running back through the scene at Dani's for the seven-hundredth time. The memory was about as comfortable as scraping sandpaper over sunburn. He wasn't really threatened by her ex, could have dealt with hiding things from Maeve, and even hiding things from her coworkers in L.A. It was the flat-out lie over something stupid that drove him into his present mindset.

Right now he needed space more than he needed to bury himself in her body. Though it likely wouldn't take long for him to go crawling back.

"What are you doing here, anyway?" Niall knocked against Ryan's elbow, bringing his attention back to the present. "Don't you have some nails to pound?"

"Heh. Nails." Chubb snickered into his bottle.

Ryan tipped his beer for a long swallow before he answered. "I'm taking a break."

"Your hammer all worn out?" Chubb smacked the table with an open palm, all kinds of amused at his own joke.

"My hammer's fine."Ryan stood, weary joints whining at the effort, too tired to put up with Chubb's bullshit. He could finish his beer on the way to the shower.

Niall put a hand on Ryan's forearm. "No, seriously, what's up? This is the second evening in a row you've been home early. Everything okay with Danielle?"

Ryan shook his brother off and headed for the door. "We're done."

Ignoring the variations on 'what the hell?' from his brother and his best friend, Ryan downed another long swallow of beer on his way down the hall. They'd keep up their chatter, a couple of old nanny goats who'd bonded over skeevy women and now had him to pick apart. They could have at it as long as he didn't have to listen.

In the four days since Ryan had last talked to Dani, he'd gone from frozen pissed to aching angry.Now, he just wanted to crawl into bed next to her, to lose himself in kisses that were soft and fierce at the same time, and to wrap himself in her rose scent.

Nope, he was done. No more gorgeous redheads for him.

His dick had other ideas, snapping to attention as he slid out of his jeans. Somehow he always ended up with a hard-on, whether she was with him or not. He dropped onto the edge of his bed, stroking himself up further, channeling all his anger and frustration into a vicious orgasm that left him drained.

And exhausted.

And lonely.

* * * *

Wednesday, Danielle sanded and primed. Thursday, she painted. The heavy rain made it easy to spend time indoors, though even the steady activity and the old oil heater couldn't warm her core.

Or else the cold was from the hole Ryan left.

By Friday morning, it rained hard enough and long enough that the news-geeks' chatter had turned to mudslides. A section of the rail line between Seattle and Everett was closed because of a slide, and the morning news pelted viewers with stories about past disasters.

Perkins Lane was featured prominently in all of them.

Danielle wanted – no, needed – a latte, but between the winding road and the heavy rain, steering the Mini was like navigating a submarine. Branches drooped into her field of vision, water weighing them down.

Coming out of the Magnolia Coffee Company with her prize, Danielle had a near-manicure experience. Three doors down from the coffee shop, LuAnn's Nails called to her. Danielle made it as far as the door before deciding to wait until she'd finished painting. Why trash a perfectly good manicure with taupe semi-gloss? She'd put manicures on hold until she'd settled the house deal.

Hell, she'd put her life on hold until she settled the house deal.

Instead of a peaceful hour in a nail salon, she went back home and picked up the to-do list. She came close to calling Christopher to ask if he knew a good carpenter. She already had a good carpenter, though without him the rest of her life had turned into an endless tunnel of bleak.

Danielle hunched over the laptop, jabbing the keys, pretending to look for a roofer. The heavy overcast outside funneled straight into her belly, dragging her low, and in her head, she argued with Ryan.

I didn't mean to lie.

Imaginary Ryan crossed his arms and scowled. *Except to Maeve. About me.*

No. I mean, you know why.

I told you I hated games. Imaginary Ryan's smile was all heavy and disappointed, and Danielle wanted to slap him.

A tiny headache spread up the back of her neck, clinging to the muscles the way ivy sticks to brick. Part of her acknowledged that going along with Maeve had been a mistake. The rest of her was pretty convinced Ryan needed to get a handle on his temper. The current drama was not all her fault.

Oh. Wait. Yes it was.

The rain rotated between sprinkling, spattering, and downright pouring, and Danielle threw a presto-log in the fireplace, trying to take the edge off the chill. She was too tired to paint, too sad to find motivation, and too frustrated to deal with the house. Instead, she dragged the wing chair close to the fire, made a nest out of blankets, and opened her laptop to her Pinterest page.

Her redecorating fantasies were interrupted by a burst of thunder, a rare event for a city with its reputation built on rain. The thunder went on and on, longer than it should have, louder than a low-flying jumbo jet. The noise vibrated in her bones. Confused, she jumped up and went to the window, only to be knocked back by a blast that slammed into the wall of the house.

Mud.

It smashed through the window, a heavy, sludgy mass studded with rocks and tangled roots. Glass shards flew out like a spray of foam above the wave. Each one stabbed down into the floor, the wall, or the muck. Thick, wet dirt rolled over the fire, smothering it. The wing chair got shoved against the fireplace, only one of its ball feet on the ground. The floor lamp went down hard. Danielle stumbled out of the way, landing on her ass in the dining room.

Then the noise stopped.

The flow lost its force right at Danielle's feet, leaving her stunned at the edge of the wave. She shook her head and scattered shards of glass from her hair. Something warm trickled down her cheek. Blood from a cut near her temple. Mud splattered the fireplace tile she'd spent hours cleaning. Streaks marred the chair rail molding under the window. A layer several inches deep covered much of the living room floor.

Wind and rain blew through the broken window. Danielle hugged herself, shivering from a combination of the cold and the shock wrapping around her head like cotton batting. Her teeth couldn't chatter much harder.

The Mini's car alarm shrieked, a perfect soundtrack for the scene.

The wing chair lost its fight with gravity and toppled over. The laptop slid out of the seat into the sludge, its screen going black. She let them sit, disbelief slowing her responses. The newscasters claimed the City had done amazing things to stabilize the bluff, and mudslides wouldn't be a problem anymore.

Wrong.

Danielle's L.A. experience kicked in. If an earthquake had done this much damage, she'd expect to evacuate. She'd shut the power and water off and go someplace safe. If a patient had an emergency at work, she'd take the necessary action and deal with the emotional stuff some other time. Power. Water. Something to cover the window.

Move it.

She went downstairs, grabbing a dishtowel on her way through the kitchen to wipe the blood off her face. At the bottom of the steps, she tried not to notice the new cracks in the basement's concrete floor. She flipped the breaker, cut power to the house, and went in search of the water shut-off, keeping the towel pressed to the cut that hurt the worst. She could call Maeve. She could call Ryan. Her hands were too numb to manipulate the phone.

Back upstairs, she avoided as much of the mess as possible, rounding the edge of the living room into the foyer. The intermittent shrieking of the car alarm stabbed at her composure, and she grabbed her car keys on the way by. When she turned the knob, the front door popped against her hand, the weight of a knee-high hill of gravelly sludge pushing through and splattering at her feet. The stream of debris had been funneled through the driveway, tearing up the laurels closest to it. One of the tall shrubs lay on its side, tangled roots torn from the earth, its leathery green leaves plastered with dirt.

Even sadder, her Mini was canted up against the garage, rear wheels higher than the front end.

Despite her careful navigation, her shoes were soon caked with mud. Her fingers were numb from cold and shock, and it took four tries to hit the 'silence' button on her key fob. When the Mini's alarm finally stopped, the quiet echoed.

To the north, the road was completely blocked. Who knew how long it would take the city to clear it? She forced back the image of the cracked basement floor. Later she could worry about the damage to the house.

Worry. Later.

The stream of mud had come down the bluff to the north of Grandmother's house. The big new-construction faux-Craftsman next door jutted up from a pool of black, its baby rhododendrons mashed up against the front wall. On the south side, the 1940s box was pretty clear. If the slide had started a little more to the south, most of it would have run into the laurel hedge, which would have at least slowed things down and protected Grandmother's house. The owner of the '40s box, however, would be standing in her living room surrounded by smashed windows and piles of mud.

It was all so random.

The Mini wasn't going anywhere, but Danielle was going to have to. She didn't have time for a big sob-fest, so she stuffed the tears away until her gut filled with sadness and she could barely move.

It would take months – years even – to get rid of it all.

After packing her injured laptop and a few essentials in an overnight bag, she tacked one of Ryan's plastic drop-cloths around the broken front window with a staple gun. She grabbed a wool cap and pulled on a jacket. Carrying her bag with the strap diagonally across her chest to keep her hands free, she started out.

She forgot to put on gloves, and soon her fingers were reddened and numb. The smell of damp earth surrounded her and the water view was obscured by a heavy curtain of rain and mist. Walking the mile to Uncle Jonathan's was likely going to be an excursion through several levels of hell.

Even worse, it gave her too much time to think, when she wasn't dodging emergency vehicles trying to make their way down to the slide. Thoughts about all the money she'd spent. Gone. Thoughts about her grandmother. Gone. Thoughts about Ryan. Gone.

The first couple of policemen who passed her delivered the evacuation order. She had to fight to keep from laughing in their faces.

It was that or start screaming.

Chapter Nineteen

Robert installed Danielle in the guest room, or at least that's how it felt, like he'd lifted her fragile self from the entryway's tile floor, leaving behind a pile of soggy packaging and carefully carrying her upstairs. He was too reserved to strip her down, but he gave her some privacy and brought her sweat pants and a cable knit sweater from his own closet. He knocked softly on the door and passed in the clothing, then took her wet things away.

When his one question about Ryan went unanswered, he left the subject alone, giving Danielle another gift to be grateful for.

Over the weekend, both Robert and Uncle Jonathan treated her gently. They fed her, set up a desk in the guest room, and let her borrow a laptop when they determined hers was beyond help. They didn't ask about Ryan. Maeve called once or twice, but Danielle let voicemail pick them up, despite her New Year's resolution to answer all calls. She spent the weekend on the jagged edge of tears, a swarm of saline crystals she couldn't seem to shed. There was no point in crying. She had three weeks before her flight back to L.A., and everything she'd accomplished since the beginning of November had turned to shit.

Monday morning, Danielle sat at the desk with a mug of Earl Grey tea and very little hope. Perkins Lane was still closed to vehicular traffic. Every hour that the mass of wet earth sat in the living room was damaging. Even if the blunt force trauma of the slide hadn't knocked the house off its foundation, the ongoing exposure to water meant more repairs: replacing the plaster and lathe walls with sheetrock, putting down new hardwood floors, bringing the plumber and electrician back out. She would be starting from scratch.

Danielle kept browser pages open for each of the local news channels and watched a #Seattle twitter stream, hoping to catch the first announcement when Perkins Lane reopened. The mud had to be cleared from the road, and city inspectors had to go through all the houses first. A green tag meant the house was safe. An orange tag meant it needed work. A red tag meant the homeowner had a problem.

She opened a new browser page to the PubMed website and typed "preterm infant" and "insulin" into the keyword search. The NICU hadn't shut down, and there was always more work to be done. When the mudslide hit the window, she'd caught some glass with her face, but her sweatshirt protected her arms and her hands came through without injury. If she could type, she could work.

Her phone rang while she scrolled through the list of journal article hits. She almost ignored the call. At the last minute, she answered. The number on the screen was from work.

Abbie greeted her with way too much enthusiasm and a huge project. "Thought I better warn you Sharon's decided we're running a skills lab in March."

"Awesome," Danielle said. She could picture Abbie sitting at the desk on her side of the office they shared, her long wavy hair doing the ombre thing from light to dark, her nails painted with a perfect French manicure.

"Yeah, I knew you'd be excited."

Running a skills lab meant organizing presentations and teaching stations. It meant scheduling staff and listening to people whine about the extra work. It was an enormous pain in the ass.

"Oh, and Sharon said to remind you about evaluations," Abbie said, still just as upbeat and enthusiastic as could be, like she didn't know she was some kind of Monday morning nightmare come to life.

Danielle refreshed the twitter feed, distracting herself from the onslaught of work by looking for news of the mudslide. Nothing. "Yeah, um, they're due at the end of May."

Abbie paused, and from the subtle hiss in her ear Danielle guessed she was taking a hit off her ubiquitous bottle of diet soda.

"The hospital wants them by then," Abbie said, pausing a few seconds for another slurp of soda, "but Sharon wants ours done by May first, May fifteenth at the very latest. She wants extra time to log them all in."

Danielle couldn't find the words to respond. Getting the evaluations done early reflected well on Sharon, but organizing evals for thirty-five nurses in two months would be almost impossible. From Abbie's glib tone, Danielle guessed who the job of Sharon's spunky right hand now belonged to.

"I mean, do you really need to stay in Seattle until February?" Abbie asked. "You got that carpenter dude running around. Put him in charge."

"Yeah, well…"

"I was kinda surprised to see a guy like him crawling all over you the other morning. Braden was more the sapiosexual type."

Abbie's harsh giggle convinced Danielle they'd never really been friends. "Yeah, well…"

"Sharon and I just got a quick look, you know, but boy howdy he was hot."

"Yeah, well … he was." Danielle couldn't quite keep the hitch out of her voice. The hard crystal tears threatened to go off like a cloudburst.

Abbie must have accomplished her mission, because she got off the phone before any real emotion got out there between them.

Danielle set the phone down on the desk, moving carefully in case her world was in imminent danger of shattering.She closed the PubMed browser page. She refreshed the Twitter stream. She sat with her hands in her lap, staring out the window at the distant view of the Sound.

On the plane flight up from L.A., it had all seemed so simple: get in, get dirty, get back to real life. But right now she didn't know what real life meant. Could she be having a mid-life crisis at the age of thirty-three? She picked up her tea and rubbed the warm mug against her cheek. The citrus and nutmeg scent should have been calming. It wasn't. More than anything else, she wanted to get back into her grandmother's house, to assess the damage, and to wipe the mud off the damned fireplace tile she'd worked so hard to clean.

That did it. Her tears fell, long and hard and wet. She didn't stop crying until Uncle Jonathan tapped on her door, asking if she wanted to drive down to Perkins Lane to check on the progress.

* * * *

"We won't know anything until the inspectors are done." Uncle Jonathan pointed at Danielle with his fork, speaking over the muted crowd of diners. "I know it sucks, but we're just going to have to wait."

"I'm an ICU nurse. I'm not good at waiting."

Jonathan had insisted on going out for Thai food before heading down to Perkin's Lane. Danielle stirred the curried vegetables on her plate. She wasn't hungry, the spicy smell choked her, and the gurgling fountain got on her nerves. Even the drooping orchids provoked her.

Her uncle grinned like some kind of benevolent Buddha come to life. "Patience, Grasshopper."

"If I had patience I'd work in a rehab unit."

"You won't be waiting forever, you know."He spoke carefully through a mouth full of curry.

"I just…" She set down her fork and massaged her temples. "There was meat in the freezer and the power's been off long enough that I'm sure it's rotted. I'll probably have to have someone haul the fridge to the dump."

"Why don't you ask your friend Ryan to help?"

Uncle Jonathan's expression stayed benign, but Danielle came close to shouting *A-ha!* This whole lunch thing was a search for information about a subject she really, really wanted to avoid. She took a swallow of her Thai iced tea and waited until she could respond rationally.

The silence between them lasted long enough to make Danielle twitchy. Uncle Jonathan seemed content to let her stew, the bastard. After another swallow of tea, she finally caved. "Ryan won't be helping me anymore." *There. See? No tears.* "He won't be around at all." *And the reason is none of your business.*

Her uncle tilted his head, but otherwise his Buddha smile stayed fixed in place. "That's too bad."

"Yeah." She made another half-hearted swipe at the curry with her fork. "Can we pack this up and go? Please?"

He tipped his head at the waitress. "He didn't seem like the type to do something stupid enough for you to give him the heave-ho."

Ooo-kay. "As much as I'd like to blame this one on him, it's me who screwed up." Danielle paid strict attention to the fountain, because it was easier than meeting her uncle's gaze. "Wasn't meant to be, I guess. I'm leaving, anyway."

"You could always stay long enough to make it right."

Danielle snorted a laugh with so much bitterness it burned on the way out. "Sure."

"I don't suppose you've called your mother since the slide."

More laughter. More bitterness. More burn. "Nope, Uncle Jonathan. There's a limit to how much drama I can deal with."

He shifted in his seat, not nearly uncomfortable enough in the face of Danielle's anger. "How long has it been since you've talked to her?"

Danielle pushed her plate away. "Five years. Except for New Years, I mean."

Uncle Jonathan's slow blink gave Danielle a good idea of how frigid she sounded.

"She called me one night five years ago, drunk, and begged me to forgive her for hiding me away from my father." Danielle squeezed her lips tight because a small Thai restaurant at lunchtime was not the place to unload a lifetime of hurt feelings. "When I asked his name, she said she couldn't tell me because it would screw up my childhood."

Her uncle's cheery expression faded in response to Danielle's barely-contained rage.

"As if our long-distance relationship wasn't screwed up enough."

"If I had to guess," Jonathan said sadly, "you're probably better off without him." He laid a tentative hand over Danielle's. "The men she brought home back in those days were pretty rough, and she never even brought this guy home."

"Fantastic." She shut her eyes and bent her head. After a minute, she took hold of her uncle's hand. Her own parents might have been effed up, but Uncle Jonathan and her grandmother had done a lot to get her through.

Half an hour later, they were in Jonathan's Mercedes, driving around the curve by Magnolia Park. A bag of Thai food sat on the back seat like a cilantro-scented air freshener. Fighting her jittery nerves, Danielle all but held her breath against potential disaster.

She'd have to hold it a while longer. A cop had parked his car sideways across Ray Drive, the street leading down to Perkins Lane.

"Damn it." Danielle said.

Uncle Jonathan pulled off to the side and parked along the gravel strip near a stand of madrona trees. Danielle popped out through the passenger door. "Where are you going?" He raised his voice because she was already three steps away from the car.

"To ask when the road'll be open."

She took off before he could reply. Five minutes later she climbed back into the sedan, spewing a torrent of HBO-worthy profanity. "Officer Dickhead doesn't know when we'll be able to get down there."

"Best not to let him hear you talk like that."

She was pretty sure her glare would peel the bark off the nearest tree.

"Hey, I'm not a public defender." Her uncle rubbed his mouth like he needed to hide a smile. "That guy's probably sucking up some overtime, bored out of his mind, and up to his balls in bitchy homeowners."

"Oh, and now I'm bitchy." She slammed the heavy door with a solid thunk.

Uncle Jonathan put a hand on her knee. "Now come on, Dani. I didn't mean you."

She cooled down some because of the underlying compassion in his tone.

"It's those other stressed-out crazies that got to him first," he said.

Danielle's sigh turned into a laugh, and her uncle joined in. When the giggles threatened to exceed her control, she tipped her head back against the leather seat, swallowing hard before the laughter morphed into sobs.

* * * *

Later that afternoon Danielle got a text message from Maeve.

Giving up on work. Pedicure?

Lunch with Uncle Jonathan had put a dressing over the worst of her hurts, so instead of ignoring Maeve, Danielle responded *when & where?*

When was as soon as she could get there, and *where* was the nail salon next to Pagliacci Pizza in the lower Queen Anne neighborhood. Hoping to capture just a little bit of normal, Danielle borrowed Robert's Prius and headed out.

The trickiest bit was finding a parking place on busy Queen Anne Avenue. By the time she reached the salon, Maeve was already in one of the big vinyl chairs with a built-in, foot-sized Jacuzzi tub.

A tiny Asian woman greeted Danielle with heavily accented enthusiasm. "Pick a color," she said. Danielle grabbed a deep spicy red, slipped off her down jacket, and dropped into the chair next to Maeve's.

"Danielle's here. Yay!" Maeve said, her voice rising to a squeal. "How come you didn't call me back this weekend?"

"I don't know, sweetie. It's been…" Danielle fussed with her seat rather than answer, unable to explain to her supposed best friend how hard it was to talk when everything sucked. Maybe *normal* had been too much to hope for. Maybe get-through-an-hour-without-tears was more realistic.

The salon girl came from the back room and took the polish from Danielle, then helped her remove her shoes.

"You want a manicure too?" the girl asked.

Danielle gave her shredded fingernails a quick inspection, more than ever conscious of the contrast between Maeve's glam jeans and tunic combo compared with her borrowed sweater and the one pair of jeans she'd worn out of Grandmother's house the day of the mudslide. "Not yet."

"Here, my dear." Maeve passed her a Starbucks cup. "The latte you wanted." She leaned into the word *latte* like it was the clue to the Maltese Falcon.

Danielle tried not to look too perplexed and took a tentative sip. "Mm … coffee." With a kick.

Warm water frothed around Danielle's ankles and she eased back in the chair. Maeve had spiked the coffee with at least Kahlua and Baileys, and possibly also vodka. Danielle tried another sip. Then another.

"I've been calling you all weekend," Maeve said. "Niall says your house was damaged by the slide. How bad is it?"

Danielle hit the Starbucks cup again, letting the alcohol soothe her fraying composure. "It's bad. Mud came through the living room window. I don't know how much damage was done."

"Oh my God, that's terrible." Maeve patted Danielle's arm awkwardly, as if someone along the way had told her physical contact was appropriate, but she wasn't quite sure how to make it happen. "What does Ryan think?"

Now *there* was a question Danielle had no intention of answering. She really, really didn't want to get into the whole Ryan thing with Maeve.

The salon girl squatted on a stool in front of Danielle and lifted one of her feet out of the water. She used the activity as an excuse not to respond.

"Dude, come on."

Maeve yelped loud enough to make Danielle wonder if she'd had more than one *latte*. "What?"

"What's that bandage on your face for?" Maeve asked, leaning over the armrest as if she could force Danielle to respond.

Relieved at the shift in emphasis away from Ryan, Danielle answered. "A cut from the flying glass when the window broke."

"Oh shit. No one told me you got hurt."

"I'm fine. Uncle Jonathan and Robert have been taking good care of me."

"Well, if you get fed up with hanging out with old men, let me know." Maeve's grin promised good times of the party-girl variety. "You can always crash with me."

After that, Maeve let the subject of the mud slide drop. Christopher had taken Maeve to a movie, and while Danielle had her toenails trimmed and her heels buffed they discussed the significance of the event. Was it a just-friends date, or a date-date? Maeve was uncertain. Danielle was amused.

Neither had the nerve to call Christopher and ask.

With a pink-jacketed worker massaging each hand, Maeve's smile got a little abstract. "Since you're kind of homeless, I'll take you out to dinner tonight," she said.

"We could just to go Pagliacci's next door."

"Sure." Maeve's concession was simply a feint, her relaxation an act, allowing her a moment to launch another attack. "Now, back to the house…"

Danielle kept her gaze on the table top, exasperated by getting caught off-guard.

"When will you and Ryan get to take a look at it?"

All out of dodges, Danielle tipped her head so a few strands of hair covered her face. "Ryan's not working on the project anymore." Staring at a scuff on the floor was easier than meeting Maeve's gaze.

"Why not?"

Danielle didn't bother to unravel the threads of surprise and concern in Maeve's tone. Lying had caused her trouble. More lying would make things worse. "You know, the other night, when you called?"

"Yeah?"

The salon's floral acetone scent made Danielle lightheaded. "After we hung up, he got mad and left." She paused to catch her breath, the echo of his angry words slamming through her chest, amplifying her feelings of desertion. "He said I was treating him like a booty call."

"That's crazy." Maeve rocked her head back, her gaze fixed on the big-screen TV on the back wall of the salon.

"I guess I screwed up, made him feel like I didn't want people to know we were together." Danielle rubbed a palm across her brow. "Which sucks because Ryan and I had something good."

"Okay." Maeve lifted her hands, palms aimed at Danielle. "You know I don't want to hear details, right?"

"Whatever, Maeve. I really cared about him." The words burst out, almost against her will. "A lot."

Danielle had to stop and clear her throat. "He was an amazing part of my life."

Maeve interrupted her. "You're using past tense."

"What?" Danielle asked. She'd been too focused on blinking back tears to listen.

"Past tense. You're talking like you *used to* have something, you *used to* care."

"He busted me lying, and he left." Danielle went back to wrestling with the tears. She'd had plenty of time over the last few days to scrutinize Ryan's motivations. "He's always been pretty clear that he didn't want to be with another woman who played games." She shrugged, more a gesture of defeat than anything else.

"Patty Perfection admits a sin," Maeve muttered.

"What did you just say?"

"Nothing." Now it was Maeve's turn to stare at the floor.

Embarrassment, anger, and hurt converged, curdling the cocktail and pretty much ruining Danielle's mood.

Maeve paused for several beats, arms crossed, body stiffening. "Did you really try to keep it a secret?"

"No." Danielle directed all her attention to the young woman massaging her calves. She was buying time, scrambling for an out. "Except at first. With you."

"Oh." Maeve sat back, hard. "Oh."

"It was stupid. I should have just been honest from the beginning."

"Shit." Maeve stared at a foreign language soap opera playing on the big screen. She didn't move until the woman working on her toes tapped her ankle and asked if she liked the color.

Maeve's pause gave Danielle plenty of time to shrink and shrivel and wither. To imagine life without Ryan. To imagine life without her best friend since high school. To get her brain around the situation's inherent stupidity.

"So is this where I tell you I'll talk to him," Maeve said, her mouth a tight line, "and then we have a Hallmark moment?"

Righteous exasperation broke through Danielle's normal restraint. "I haven't asked you to do shit, Maeve. I'm doing my best to keep you out of it."

Maeve turned completely around, jerking her left foot away from the woman with the nail polish. "Did you just snap at me?"

She looked crazy, with her spikey hair and wild eyes and the streak of red across the top of her foot. Danielle hunted up all the reasons Maeve was crazy, and then she started to laugh.

Because instead of Maeve's sins, all she came up with was a list of the things she'd lost: Grandmother, Braden, her love-affair with her job, all the work she'd done on the house. Ryan.

Provoking Maeve was the overload, the one thing that dropped her to the very bottom. From way down there, Danielle surprised herself. Laughter came easier than tears.

"Why yes," she said between snickers, "I guess I did snap at you."

Maeve's mouth pinched like she was constipated, and then a smile broke free. "I meant it when I called you Patty Perfection."

"Bite me."

"What. Ever." Maeve waved her hands in apology at the woman painting her nails. "I'll give him a call." She rolled her eyes at the ceiling. "Just don't tell me about the make-up sex."

Danielle rubbed her cheeks with her palms, equal parts relieved and despairing. "I'm not asking you to do anything, but thanks."

"That's what best friends are for, I mean, that's what family's for."

Danielle lost the battle with tears.

* * * *

Maeve called at eight o'clock Tuesday morning to tell Danielle Perkins Lane would be open by noon. "Niall heard it at work," Maeve said. "He doesn't have your phone number, and he wanted me to pass the word."

Danielle was awake but hardly ready to face the day. "I'll see if I can borrow Robert's Prius again."

"Not even," Maeve said with a bulletproof giggle. "Christopher and I will pick you up at 11:45."

Danielle didn't have the energy to argue with her.

When the black Saab pulled into the driveway, she jumped up, threw on her jacket, grabbed her bag, and hit the door. Concerns about her grandmother's house pushed every other drama far down on the list.

"Ready to go?"Christopher kept one hand on the steering wheel and turned his shoulders to give her a sober smile.

She slammed her door shut in response, his friendly attention more irritating than anything else.

He turned the engine back on and put the car in reverse.

"Good thing I don't have to pee," Maeve said.

The drive to Grandmother's felt like it took about three hours instead of ten minutes. The heavy overcast dragged Danielle down, forcing time to move in slow motion. Evidence of the storm grew more obvious as they drove the last bit downhill on Ray Drive to Perkins Lane.

Downed tree limbs had been stacked along the side of the road, pine boughs tangled with glossy rhododendron leaves in a crazy quilt of chaos. Whole trees had come down, their convex root circles tilted up, exposing the frayed edges to the harsh light and air.

Closer to Grandmother's house, mud had been scraped off the road, looking like black snowdrifts studded with rocks and torn shrubs. Everywhere, fluorescent orange markers showed where the City crews had been working; strips tied to branches or stakes stuck in the mud. The road was passable, but restoration would take a lot longer.

The laurel hedge lay in catawampus piles and the continuous rain had cut mini canyons in the mud heading down to the beach. The Mini was more-or-less level, though the hood was wrinkled up like a sneer. Footprints leading to the front porch pockmarked the mud-covered lawn, and the plastic sheet Danielle had stapled over the window flapped free on one corner. Christopher slowed to a stop in front of the house, idling the engine. From there, they could see the tag on the front door.

Orange.

Chapter Twenty

The ridge of mud left by the city repair crews who cleared Perkins Lane blocked the entrance to Danielle's driveway. Since the road was about a car and a half wide, Christopher couldn't park in the street or none of the other desperate homeowners would be able to get through. He drove a block past Grandmother's house to a turn-out and left the Saab there.

Faced with the actual devastation, Danielle's meager clean-up enthusiasm got lit up by indignation. This was her house. Her house. Hers.

Even when she sold it, she'd do it knowing she'd finished the job.

Maeve walked partway with them, until she figured out she didn't want to navigate the mud. "You guys go take a look," she said, lifting a heel to let them admire her choice of footwear, "and I'll see you when you get back to the car."

"Her heart's in the right place," Danielle said as soon as Maeve was far enough away not to hear.

Christopher lifted one of his feet, giving Danielle a look at a shoe that hadn't likely cost much less than Maeve's. "So's mine."

"You don't need to come in with me." Danielle navigated the pile of dirt and stones and broken shrubbery that blocked the end of the driveway. The air was cold and salty, and the steady breeze coming in off the ocean grabbed at her hair and her jacket.

"It's cool." Christopher went right on up beside her. "I've got more where these came from."

Danielle slipped, landing hard on the edge of what looked like a broken piece of brick. Christopher stutter-stepped down the other side of the mud heap and offered her his hand.

"That hurt," she said. "Thanks for the assist." Soggy denim stuck to her knee, and she half-skidded down to where Christopher stood.

He gave her fingers a squeeze and released her, the way a friend would, and Danielle had a moment of gratitude for having met him.

"Is everything okay over there?" Maeve yelled from the road about halfway between the house and the car.

"All good," Christopher called out, and Danielle waved with as much confidence as she could gather. An orange tag was better than a red one, but it still meant damage.

"ServPro is meeting me out here in an hour or so," Danielle said, taking careful steps through the dense mud. She'd called the local branch for the company that specialized in cleaning up after Mother Nature as soon as the road opened. "And the insurance guy should be here about the same time."

"I can hook you up with some people, too." Christopher followed her, the mud caking his fancy shoes. "And then you go back to L.A. in a couple of weeks, right? Want me to see if I can find someone to supervise the job for you?"

Maeve must have said something about Ryan, but Danielle didn't have time for embarrassment. "Probably should." Danielle gripped the railing to half drag herself up to the front porch.

Christopher steadied himself with a hand on her elbow. "Any chance you could get more time off work and do it yourself?"

"You mean stay here?" Danielle brushed a stray strand of hair out of her face, leaving a smudge of dirt on her cheekbone. "I seem to be the only one who thinks I should go back to L.A."

He cocked his head, laughter mixed with evaluation in his eyes. "Better put it to a vote, then."

"Be quiet." She glanced down toward the beach, the faint rhythm of the waves as familiar as the color of her hair or the damp cold of a January day. "I love this house and it's kind of a bummer to see all my work wasted." She glanced over his shoulder in Maeve's direction. "And I do have friends here." She licked her fingertip and made an attempt at wiping the smudge off her face. "And you know, there's … other things." Leaving would make the split with Ryan permanent.

They had to shove on the front door to force it open, the bottom edge scraping over mud and debris. The smell in the house was a powerful mix of soil and mold, and something scary in the kitchen.

"As much as it hurts me to give up a commission," Christopher said, "I can see you living here."

Danielle assessed the living room, with its carpet of mud and moisture stains at least knee-high up the walls. "Right."

"I mean, when the ServPro guys are done."

Danielle gave him a tired smile and planted her fists on her hips. "Think I should start at the top and go down, or the bottom and go up?"

Christopher rifled through his wallet and handed her a card. "Either way, call my friend Nicky. He and his guys can be out here tomorrow with a backhoe to clear the mud out of your front yard."

Danielle didn't watch Christopher plow back through the mud. She was too busy taking stock of the damage to the house.

* * * *

Ryan got lucky. His boss sent him out on a job in suburban Bellevue to deal with a nice-looking Mid-Century Modern house with an original floor plan constructed around the "warren of rooms" concept. The main floor was a series of interconnecting boxes, and the new homeowner wanted to open it up, creating a single family/dining/kitchen area.

The walls had to come down.

When he arrived on Tuesday morning, Ryan left his toolbox in the truck and brought out his sledgehammer. After a whole lot of wall destruction, he'd almost reached a place where he could talk to people without taking their heads off. The laborer who'd been assigned to help him with clean-up had skipped out at lunch. He claimed to have a headache, but Ryan was pretty sure the guy was just tired of dealing with his surly ass.

Despite the cold, raw day and the thermostat set at about sixty, sweat poured down Ryan's back and around his face. He took a break about two o'clock, setting his sledgehammer against one of a pair of king studs that framed a doorway between rooms. They stood like lonely sentinels in the field of debris. Because they were weight-bearing, he'd need to reinforce the cross beam before he could knock them down.

He grabbed a piece of scratch paper and the stub of a flat carpenter's pencil to make some notes for the next day. The process was interrupted when his cell phone rang.

It was Maeve.

He came *this* close to letting it go to voicemail, but in case she was calling to tell him one of his parents was in the hospital or his brother had been shot on the job, he answered.

"Ryan."

Maeve had her *shut up and listen voice* on. Awesome.

"Maeve."

"We fucked up."

He bit back a snarky comment. The fastest way through this was to let her have her say and hang up. "Yeah?"

"I…" She paused, as if she was having trouble getting the words out.

It threw him off, so he kept his own mouth shut.

"You and Danielle had a thing."

She didn't make it a question, and he didn't give her an answer.

"And Danielle knew I didn't want to hear the details."

He knocked his knuckles gently against the stud, stifling the pain and sadness that tried to ambush him. "I wonder why."

"Shut up, already. I said we fucked up."

He took a deep breath and let it out slow to keep himself from smacking something. "So…"

"So her grandmother's house is covered in mud, and she's stuck with her crazy uncle, and, and, and…" Maeve's voice hitched to a stop.

Ryan almost dropped the phone. This side of Maeve almost never came out to play.

"And she needs your help," she said, pausing to give him time to anticipate her big finish, "for more than just the house."

A punch to the gut would have hurt less. He stared at the piles of broken sheetrock and stacks of used baseboard he'd planned to take to the dump before he knocked off for the night. "So I should drop everything and come running?"

"I don't know about the running part, but could you call her?" Maeve's voice took on its usual aura of sarcasm. Ryan almost felt reassured by the change.

"I'll think about it," he said, damned sure he'd think about very little else. Having Maeve's permission didn't change the fact that Dani lied about him.

But it sure changed something.

* * * *

Danielle had a Come-To-Jesus moment while she waited for the guys from ServPro to show up.She checked the power – it was out – checked the basement – there was a puddle of water in one corner – and considered her options. She could get on an airplane on February 2nd, prepared to fight her way back to the top of Sharon's heap.

Or she could stay in Seattle and finish what she'd come here to do.

Both choices required commitment. Both choices required hard work. Neither gave her any guarantees.

And Ryan didn't figure into her consideration.

At all.

Sure.

A high overcast gave the day a silvery sheen, like the underside of the scallop shells washed up on the beach. Between phone calls, Danielle tried to picture herself walking back into the NICU, but she couldn't see it. If she'd been less strung out she might have gotten the joke. On New Year's Day, when Uncle Jonathan suggested her mother wanted Danielle to stay in the house, she'd shot him down. Now here she was, actually considering it.

Would she be making a decision to please her mother? Braden? Anybody else?

Not really.

The restoration team showed up about an hour after Christopher and Maeve left. A matched set of half a dozen men in blue coveralls with ServPro embroidered on the back cleared the mound of debris that blocked the driveway and backed their shiny white van up close to the house.

Their ringleader was distinguishable by his salt 'n' pepper goatee. He came over and introduced himself while his partners unloaded a pile of equipment.

"So first I'll take a quick look around," Mr. Goatee said, "then give the boys their assignments."

Danielle grabbed a pencil so she could take notes while he inspected things. "The upstairs is in okay shape, but there's a puddle of water in one corner of the basement."

Mr. Goatee stuffed his hands in the slash pockets on the hips of his coverall. "Lights still out?"

"Yeah."

"Tried the plumbing?"

"Not yet, but I've got an electrician and a plumber coming out tomorrow."

"Good job." He took an exaggerated sniff. "Our other truck will drop off a Sani-Can out front, and I'll put a guy on cleaning out your fridge."

"Oh, I can do that," Danielle said, though now that he called her attention to it, the aroma of spoiled food was pretty overwhelming.

Mr. Goatee rubbed his chin. "Nah, we'll do it. You can show the guys how to get down to the basement so they can set up some fans."

A loud rumble started up outside, making Danielle twitch.

"Generator," Mr. Goatee said.

Someone knocked on the front door and Danielle left the ServPro team to their work. She spent an hour with a nice man from her Grandmother's insurance company. The details of rolling the policy over to Danielle were sort of blurry, though having her in-house lawyer-slash-uncle on speed dial certainly helped.

In between giving the insurance agent a tour and signing paperwork, Danielle kept track of the living room progress. The workmen hauled out the mud, rocks, torn up shrubbery, and shattered glass from the window. Underneath, the hardwood floor was buckled and warped, the finish bubbling up like blistered skin.

After seeing the insurance guy out, Danielle caught up with Mr. Goatee.

"We're gonna have to pull all that up," he said, gesturing to the floor.

"Looks like."

"The molding, too."

He said it like it was no big deal, but Danielle jerked like someone had stabbed her. "What?"

"See how the wallboards are wet, almost up to knee level? They gotta come down, and the trim will come with them."

But Ryan said the original trim made his dick hard. Danielle exhaled hard through her nose, ending with a harsh hiccup where the tears tried to break through. Such a stupid thing to cry over. "What about the built-ins around the fireplace."

"Them too. The bottom of 'ems all warped out."

"Oh."

Danielle stood in the middle of the living room, dimly aware of the workmen moving around her. With a dual-fisted effort, she grabbed hold of her attitude and stuffed the sadness away for another time. "Yeah, well, you gotta do what you gotta do, I guess."

"We'll put up new stuff." Mr. Goatee patted her shoulder awkwardly.

It just won't be the same.

"I could do it." A familiar baritone spoke from the doorway, a voice that came with dimples, biceps, and a killer sense of humor.

And strength. Not just the kind that comes from the gym.

Danielle closed her eyes, not willing to believe Ryan was there, offering to help. This had to be some sick delusion brought on by stress and the stink of rotten food.

There were footsteps, the warm brush of his presence bypassing her, and his silhouette kneeling in front of the fireplace. An "ah shit" almost too quiet to hear.

Danielle couldn't respond. Ryan turned to Mr. Goatee. "I've been working here part-time, and if Dani's okay with it, I'll pull the molding down and disassemble the built-ins, see what can be salvaged."

"Danielle?" Mr. Goatee asked.

Danielle nodded, a creaky jerk, and managed to rasp out the word "yes".

"Okay, I'll start my guys on pulling up the floor," Mr. Goatee said.

"I'll go get my tools."

She turned in time to see Ryan's shadow pass through the door. Everyone seemed to have a job except for her, and she desperately needed to pull her head together. He looked thin and hard, like he'd lost some weight, and his loose curls were sloppier than normal. She went upstairs for some private time, sat on her soggy air mattress, and forced herself not to overreact.

She'd still lied. He'd still left.

She'd somehow have to keep her hands in her pockets whenever he was around.

Chapter Twenty-One

Driving over to Magnolia, Ryan figured he better be ready for anything. Still, the damage to the house hit him like a shot to the kidney. Cheap. Painful. Potentially disabling.

He showed up just in time to hear a guy from ServPro tell her they'd need to trash all the trim in the living room. She'd had her back to the doorway, but Ryan could read the tension in her shoulders as easy as the raw edge to her voice.

He'd practically run out of there to get his tools, because otherwise he would have ambushed her with a full-body lock.

He started with the chair rail molding, strips of mahogany circling the room about hip-level. It was in pretty good shape, so after laying down a heavy drop cloth, he stacked the strips on the cherry wood table. Prying eighty-year-old nails out of solid hardwood chewed up his fingers, and at times he had to step between the floor joists, because the ServPro crew was pulling up the floor. It didn't take long, though, before they laid down some plywood and promised to return in the morning.

Ryan kept working.

The house got real quiet, save for the soft pulse of the waves out back. Ryan's fingers were numb enough that scrabbling with ornery wood and nails no longer bothered him. He got down on hands and knees to pull up the baseboards, noting the soft squeak of footsteps overhead. Those footsteps came down the stairs, and he sat back on his heels.

Dani cleared her throat. "So, um, I guess this is where we—"

"Don't." A bead of blood welled up on one of Ryan's knuckles and he took a second to suck it off before he continued. Being near her was like sitting an inch too close to an open fire; uncomfortable and threatening serious pain. "It'll probably take me until tomorrow to get the rest of this taken care of. Once it's all pulled down, I'll be able to figure out if I can save any of it." He might have made the first move, but he wasn't ready to for the conversation she wanted to have.

She kept quiet, and he caved in to his need and shifted around to face her.

"The baseboard's pretty waterlogged." He went on like she wasn't staring holes through his heart. "I'll let it dry out, but we might need to chuck it."

"Okay." She raised a hand, palm out. "Right. Just let me know what you think … about the trim, I mean."

"Sure." He reached for his crow bar. "I told my boss I'd be out here at least a week, but you've got ServPro here already, so maybe you don't need—"

"No, I mean … yes." She pressed her fingertips into her forehead. "Please. I don't know what the hell I'm doing out here."

The crack in her voice found an answering weakness in his defenses. He stood slowly, groaning at the creak in his knees. "What do you mean, Dani? You're doing great."

She took a step back and flapped her hands like she didn't quite know what to do with them. "Yeah, sure, I've got it." A hunk of hair slipped out of her ponytail. She tossed her head to get it out of her face. "Listen, it's, like, seven o'clock, and you've been working all day. You should take off."

"Right." He funneled all his self-discipline into staying put and not following her across the floor. "Looks like your Mini's pretty messed up. You need a ride somewhere?"

"I can call my uncle."

He tossed the crowbar in the direction of his toolbox. "C'mon. I'll give you a ride home, at least."

She gave him a brittle smile, and in a few minutes they took off for the coldest, quietest, longest one mile drive of his life.

* * * *

The next morning Robert brought Danielle and her latte down to the house. The ServPro crew was already pulling down the old lathe and plaster walls in the living room, their matching uniforms still mostly clean. Danielle expected to do a meet-and-greet with the plumber and the electrician, and if she was lucky, Christopher's landscaper friend was going to show up with a backhoe. She had a source of caffeine and a list to work from, and even Ryan's arrival wouldn't mess her up.

Until he walked through the door, hair damp from the shower, sideburns kind of raggedy, and with enough of a smile to show off his dimples.

She gulped like some kind of bad seventies sit-com actress. "Um, hi."

"Figured these guys would beat me here." Ryan shook hands with Mr. Goatee. "I'll pull out those built-ins as fast as I can."

"Take your time. We'll work around you." The guy headed for the basement, and with a quick nod at Danielle, Ryan carried his tool box to the fireplace.

She made a lame attempt at rubbing out the tension in her neck and went to the kitchen, where horrors awaited. A couple of the ServPro guys had emptied out the refrigerator and freezer, but it still stunk like the nastiest part of a landfill. Danielle figured she's scrub it out with bleach, then cover the insides with a baking soda paste to see if she could get rid of the smell.

She was still at it a couple hours later when Ryan called her name.

"What?" she said.

"Your uncle just pulled in."

She wiped her reddened hands on an old towel and went into the living room. Her uncle's Mercedes was parked behind Ryan's truck in the driveway. Uncle Jonathan got out.

Mom climbed out the other side.

Danielle dropped the towel. She couldn't feel it anymore. Hell, she couldn't feel her fingers anymore. The whole flight-or-fight response took over, jacking her heartrate to the moon and pulling every bit of extraneous blood to her body's core. Her capacity for trouble officially overran its banks, leaving her standing up to her knees in shit. Somewhere a higher power had to be laughing.

Danielle pretty much didn't get the joke.

Her mother's hair framed her face with blowsy bleach-blonde curls, and she wore an honest to God fur coat and dark brown boots with three inch spike heels. *Because that's how we dress for a disaster.*

Danielle's thirty-three year old self engaged in a brief and bitter fight with her inner child over whether they should greet Mom or not. *Oh for pity's sake.* Her adult self won. Danielle brushed her grubby hands on her dirtier jeans and went to the door.

The fur coat padding deflected any actual physical contact, but their awkward shoulder-clutching hug made Danielle wince.

"You're making progress," Uncle Jonathan said, giving her an apologetic side-arm squeeze. "When she heard about the slide, your mother booked a flight, didn't you, Patricia?"

"Obviously." Mom's gaze stopped on each element of the trashed living room – the torn-up walls, the plywood floor, the partly-disassembled bookcases around the fireplace. "You were right, Jonathan. This view from down here is stunning. I'd forgotten."

Nice one, Mom. Despite her stress level, Danielle kept her sarcasm to herself."Before the slide, we had the main floor pretty much fixed up. It's a mess now, but the upstairs is in okay shape." She bit down on the tip of her tongue to shut off the babbling. She was caught in a real-life version of one of those embarrassment dreams, the kind where her skirt flew up and all the boys could see her panties. Embarrassment wasn't the right word. More like failure. Failure to rebuild. Failure to properly honor her grandmother's memory. Failure to be the kind of daughter her mother could love.

The gauge on her emotional gas tank flipped over toward zero, and she was grateful when a new roar came from the yard. Danielle ducked out in time to see a backhoe start in on the mud in her front yard. She ran out to talk to the guy, and by the time she returned, Ryan was giving her mother a tour. She tagged along, making a point of showing off Ryan's work.

He went back to it and the rest of them ended up in the dining room around the cherry wood table, glaring at each other over the piles of mahogany molding. Her mother drilled Danielle with a million questions before finishing off with the big one. "And you're still planning to sell?"

Danielle kept her gaze on her uncle. Watching Mom was too hard, and watching Ryan was impossible.

"Not anymore." She stopped, surprised. She poked at the decision. It felt seamless, true. "I think I'm going to stay in Seattle, at least until the house is done."

"Wait a minute," Mom said, completely ruffled. "You can't give up that good job, can you?"

Irritation did a whipcord swipe through Danielle's gut, and she stuffed her fists deeper into the pockets of her coat. Even if Mom did want her to stay in Seattle, she just couldn't go along with one of Danielle's decisions. Her crazy consistency would probably make Danielle laugh, like, when she was warm and dry and had had a cocktail. Right now though, it made her want to smack something. Even Uncle Jonathan looked at his sister like she'd come down from Mars.

"I'm a nurse. I'll find another job." Standing still allowed the sweat to dry. Danielle's teeth chattered, either from the cold or the smell or her frustration with her mother.

"Of course you will." Uncle Jonathan reached over and grasped Danielle's forearm. "I think it's marvelous."

Uncle Jonathan's attention veered to something over Danielle's shoulder. "I'll email my boss tonight," she said, pausing to glance at whatever distracted him.

Ryan stood in the doorway with his hands on his hips, his expression so cagey she almost changed her mind.

"Well, Ryan," her uncle said. "How long do you think it'll take to get this place ready for Dani to move in?"

Ryan jerked a glance at Danielle, expressionless. "Move in?"

"Well, it's her house," Mom said, hands folded on the table in front of her. "Leaving it to Danielle was Mother's way of punishing me."

Danielle stifled a groan. No way she had the bandwidth to throw a pity party for Mom.

Her uncle stepped in to rescue her. "That's not fair."

"But it's true," Mom snapped. "I wouldn't live my life on her terms, so this is my reward."

Danielle blinked to cover her spontaneous eye roll. *Nice irony, Mom.*

"Now, Patricia." Uncle Jonathan put some starch in his tone and locked her mother in a steely gaze. She looked away first, and with a satisfied smirk he rattled on about Danielle's impending move, extrapolating ideas out of thin air. Ryan kept looking a question at her, even as he eased his way closer to her side.

He ended up propped next to her, fists on the tabletop. The breadth of his shoulders and his mix of clean sweat and soap scent drove most rational thoughts to the back of her mind.

Finally her uncle took pity on her. "We'll see you later," he said, one arm around Mom to steer her out the door.

"Yeah." Danielle didn't quite manage to make any sound, as if making a noise might chase Ryan away.

The car doors' slam carried over the grind of the backhoe, the guys working in the living room, the fans in the basement.

"That coat makes your mother look like she's dressed for a date with Chewbacca," Ryan said.

"If Mom's a Wookie, does that make me an Ewok?"

Ryan gave her ponytail a gentle yank. "Yep." His voice was husky, soft, restrained. "You're the little cute one."

"Shut up." Now that it was just the two of them, Danielle's body pretty much turned to jelly. "I really didn't mean to hurt you," she whispered, reaching up with wrap her fingers around his wrist. "I'm sorry."

"It's okay."

Their hands shifted 'til their fingers intertwined and they stood quietly. From the other room, Mr. Goatee called Danielle's name.

She blew through a shuddering exhale. "I better go see what he wants."

"And I better get those bookcases pulled apart."

Danielle stood, and though the natural progression of things might indicate it was time for them to get closer, she held off.

Ryan squeezed her hand. "Yeah, if I kiss you now, we're gonna give those ServPro dudes a show."

Her cheek muscles tightened, as close to a smile as she could get given the range of feelings racing through her. Relief buoyed by happiness chased away fear, pain, and sadness. "A show."

"But you could come home with me tonight."

His words held so many kinds of promise Danielle almost melted on the floor. "Yes."

Chapter Twenty-Two

Over the course of the day, the icy restraint binding them faded away, and by sunset, Ryan knew three things. Dani was in the front cab of his truck, he had to grip the steering wheel hard to keep his hands off her, and his cock was ready to go off like a jackhammer. The combination made for some pretty tough driving.

At the last red light before leaving Magnolia, she wordlessly reached for his hand. He let her take it, although the feel of her slender fingers laced with his damned near topped his limit for concentration. Then she made it worse. She lifted his hand to her mouth and kissed the ticklish skin on the underside of his wrist.

She might as well have tossed a match on a can of gasoline. "Do that again and I'm likely to drive off the road." He drew his hand away. It was that or pull over and jump her.

They caught the early edge of rush hour, which gave Dani plenty of time to mess with him. She made a game of it, and more than once he had to ease away from her, let go of her hand, or put a stop to her traveling fingers as they wandered up the fly of his jeans. "I'm going to owe you for this," he said, need spreading from a taste on his tongue to a clutch at the back of his throat. "Paybacks are a bitch." Need traveled farther, settling like hot coals deep in his belly.

She just laughed.

They pulled into his driveway. No lights. No cars. No one home.

Not that it would have made any difference.

He shut the door and tore off his jacket in the same motion, then reached for her.

She buried her face in his chest, shuddering a sigh.

"My room. Clothes off," he said, desperate enough to take her over the banister.

He followed her upstairs, distantly aware of the curve of her ass and her drifting flowery scent. Other details were lost in the waves of violent desire crashing over him. He needed her in a way so deep and primal it blurred everything else.

As soon as they were through the door of his room, he dragged her against his chest. The impact of his mouth on hers drove him wild. Her feral little groan spun him higher. Her skin was soft and yielding, a high contrast to the fierce clench of her hands on his shoulders. He got a grip on her neck and an arm around her chest. He straightened to his full height, pulling her up on tiptoe. He didn't want to play nice. Not this time. He wanted her off-balance, open, and vulnerable.

She opened, sucking his tongue about halfway down her throat and dragging his hand under her shirt to cover her breast. He pinched her nipple and she squealed against his mouth. She jerked away from the kiss, found a soft spot at the base of his throat, and bit.

That did it.

He forced her face up, crushing her lips with a kiss, his power carrying them across the room. He pinned her against the dresser, her breasts crushed against him, and grasped her hands behind her back.

Dani lifted her chin and grinned at him, slow and naughty. "You're playing rough."

"Is that a problem?"

"No."

Her dark-eyed stare sliced away the rest of his restraint. "Okay." He jerked her around toward the dresser and pushed down on her shoulders. She braced herself with her hands, and he reached around her waist to undo the fly of her jeans, rocking himself against her ass.

"You know the good thing about that long drive home?" she asked, her voice breathy, as if the fire consuming them had burned away some of the sound. "I'm *so* ready for you."

He shoved her pants down and reached between her legs.

Soaking wet.

He drew in a harsh breath and ripped open the fly of his jeans. He slid himself back and forth through her slick folds, each time spending longer at her opening. She arched and ground her hips against his. With a sharp shove on her back, he adjusted the angle. She scrabbled for a grip on the dresser. Poised at her entrance, he wrenched her jeans down past her knees, then forced her thighs even wider apart.

He drove deep with his first thrust, deeper still with the second. She wailed his name, but he couldn't stop, wouldn't stop. He pounded hard enough to lose track of himself, silencing the voice that kept him in line. The world narrowed down to her silky rose-gold hair and raspy cries, to his bruising grip on her hips and the whirlpool of velvet heat he plunged into again and again and again.

She broke underneath him, clawing at the dresser, her wordless scream sending liquid lightening shooting from the small of his back, through his ass, and into his balls. He shattered, falling into her, holding tight.

* * * *

Danielle came back to herself, bent from the waist, her bare butt in the air, her cheek mashed against Ryan's rickety dresser.

And she'd never felt better.

"Damn, young man."

Easing himself out of her, his muttered 'shit' clashed with her mood.

"What?" Looking over her shoulder to see his face took almost more energy than she had left.

He pulled them both up to standing, wrapping his hands around her ribs and turning her gently. He tipped his head to rest it against her forehead. "Went bareback. I forgot."

She laid a palm against his cheek, chuckling from some deep and very satisfied place. "Oh well." She tipped her head back to kiss him, her lips tender after his ferocious attack. "I'm clean, and I'm on the pill."

"I got tested last month." He folded against her and pulled her close.

They fumbled out of the rest of their clothes, their brief attempt at conversation fading away. They'd gone at it hard, found a place so raw and open that in the afterglow, Danielle didn't know how to get back to safety. Showing Ryan her naked body had been no problem compared with showing him her naked soul.

"Do you want a shower?" Ryan asked, sitting on the edge of his bed, as perfectly gorgeous as some Italian Renaissance statue.

She sat down next to him and put her hand on his thigh. "Later." They needed to talk, and she had a sense that if she left the room now it would take them a long, long time to handle this level of intimacy. "Are you okay?"

He flopped back on the bed, his arms spreading out over his head. He either sighed or swore, then lay quiet. Danielle stretched out next to him, supporting her head on her hand. The low light played up the bricks across his abdomen and the scattering of dark curls over his chest. She bent her leg across his thighs, bringing her lips right up close to his scruffy sideburn. "So you want to hear what I think?"

He flinched like her breath tickled. "Sure."

Was Ryan okay? "For something like ten years you dated a woman with an alcohol problem. I don't remember much from my psych nursing classes, but I do know addicts are terribly unreliable. They say they'll do something, and then they flake." She paused, giving him time to interrupt, tuning in to the depth of his breathing and the earthy, sexy smell of his body. "Your experience with Cherry taught you the value of a person's word, and now you're kind of a freak about it."

"Yeah."

That one, heavy syllable walloped her. She wanted to cuddle him close and kiss all the bad stuff away.

"And then you thought I was messing with you."

His hand moved up over her thigh, tugging it higher to cover his groin. She slid it back down, pretty convinced they both needed for her to keep going.

"You've been so straightforward, and all I could think about was why it wouldn't work. Mix in your temper, and we have a clusterfuck."

"I don't think I've ever heard you drop an eff-bomb before."

She burrowed in closer, her head on his chest. "The last couple weeks pretty much earned it." Putting a sideways kiss on the closest available bit of his skin, she looked up to get a read on his expression. "Is my assessment good?"

"Yeah."

The same syllable, but much lighter. He hugged her tight. "I might have overreacted a little. I do have a temper."

"You do."

"So do you still think it won't work?" he asked.

Tough question. A momentary chill brought her down. "I'm always going to be nine years older than you are." She nuzzled the dark hairs on his chest, allowing the contact to warm her. "But I'm not going back to L.A. And Maeve's not a huge fan, but she's getting over it."

Ryan shifted again, drawing her in for a kiss. His knuckles brushed her nipple, and the tamped-down heat in the pit of her belly flared up.

"Lemme finish." She tugged his hand away from her breast. "I think part of the reason I keep throwing excuses at you is because of the way Braden left." She sighed and nuzzled and reached for the guts to spell it out to him. "He just … left, after over five years."

"Damn."

"I mean, at least I know if you ever leave, you'll tell me why."

Ryan wrapped his arms around her and pulled her tight against his chest. "So maybe that's our promise. If either of us is going to do something crazy, we gotta tell the other one why."

Danielle thought for a moment, then raised her fist.

Ryan bumped it gently with his. "Are we done talking now?" he asked, rubbing up against her, his cock hard and full.

"Already? Stud."

He rocked his hips up and pushed down on her thigh, pinning his cock between his belly and her leg. "I don't have to put it in you if you're sore. We can find other ways to play."

"Or we can do this." She scrambled up and coaxed him into leaning against the headboard. She straddled his thighs, a position that exponentially increased their intimacy. Face to face. Belly to belly. Heart to heart.

He teased her sex, flicking and stroking with strong, calloused fingers.

"Oh my God you're good." Shivering an exhale, she ran her tongue along the edge of her upper lip.

His eyes were half closed and he had just enough of a grin to show one small dimple. She reached out and stroked him, long and strong and steady. "You're letting me tell you what to do."

The other dimple made an appearance. "Maybe."

"I think you are." She rose up on her knees, grasped his shaft, and poised herself over him.

"Maybe I want you to think that."

He might have had more to say, but she dropped onto him in one extended slide. A guttural sound, deeper and heavier than a groan, vibrated through him.

"Izat right?" She rocked her hips against him, let him spread her, fill her, stretch her. She flowed back and forth, up and down, making small circles with her hips until a glow started building down deep. "You're not all that bossy." She came off her knees and pulled him up, wrapping her legs around his waist, taking him deeper. She met his gaze and allowed him to see the scope of her feelings. "Maybe I'm in charge after all."

With a wild cry, he flipped her onto her back. "Gimme these." He gripped her calves, setting her legs against his shoulders and driving himself in. "I." He thrust again. "Am the." And again. "Boss."

His cheeky grin undercut the severity of his words.

He set up a steady, rocking pace, and she clenched her jaw to keep from screaming. For all her independence, she secretly loved feeling overpowered, possessed. If they came home, she didn't want Niall and Chubb to hear her yell *you feel amazing and you move like a maniac and oh my God you're going to make me come.* She especially didn't want them hearing her yell *I love you. I love you. I love you. I love you. I love you.*

The glow swelled until it took over. A warm buzz drove out thought, and all she wanted was more and harder and deeper. On a breath, she tipped over into a climax so absolute it was nothing and everything at once.

He kept moving, giving her a cornerstone to rebuild herself around. When she could peel her eyes open, his expression almost stopped her heart. His feelings for her were right there to see, and while neither had come out and said the 'L' word, it was present, as close as the slick sweat sliding between their bodies. He rolled against her, a driving wave, each thrust a little harder, deeper, and faster. Abruptly, the motion stopped. He went totally rigid, head bowed, brows drawn together, and lips opened in a soundless scream.

Danielle caught him as he came down from his climax, hands in his hair, legs down around his waist. On each exhale, she hummed, purring like a very satisfied cat.

"You're going to move in," Ryan mumbled. "This is a thing now. We're a thing."

"But you've got a houseful of people living here."

"They can sleep on the damn street. I'm kicking 'em out after dinner." He pulled her closer, one hand casually cupping her breast.

"What about the cat?" She grinned into the dark.

"Chubb's cat." Ryan's words came out slurred, like he was on the cusp of falling asleep. Then his stomach rumbled, and he struggled to sit up. "Are you hungry? I'm thinking Indian food. There's a good restaurant down on Roosevelt."

"Sure. Indian food sounds good." Danielle couldn't help herself. She started to laugh, real amusement fueled by a bright, elemental joy beyond anything in her experience.

* * * *

"Anybody need another beer?" Ryan asked, hoping no one took him up on the offer. He shoved the front door with the flat of his hand, shutting it with a bang.

Chubb lounged against Eamon's Nissan Leaf with a grin designed to get under Ryan's skin. "I want one."

"You can get your own."

Ryan was the last one to join the party on the front lawn because he'd made a final sweep of his house. Even though it was the end of February, the weather had cooperated with their project and granted them a day of warm weather. Eamon sprawled across the grass, Niall had parked it on the front steps, and Dani and Maeve sat side-by-side on the open tailgate of his pick-up, a funky Goth girl hanging out with a movie star.

Ryan was pretty damned proud that the star would be going home with him.

They'd spent most of the day moving Niall's furniture from the house he'd shared with his ex to Ryan's old house, but for the last hour or so, they'd loaded the back of the Ford F250 with most of Ryan's possessions.

He and Dani would unload the truck at her grandmother's house.

Maeve and Dani got into a wrestling match over Maeve's phone. "Don't lie to me, girlfriend," Dani said, with a giggle that prompted an echoing smile from Ryan.

Maeve held her phone as far away from Dani as possible. "Bitch."

"You're totally texting Christopher." Dani lunged across Maeve's lap, her hoodie flapping open to give Ryan a sneak peek at her curves. Heat started to build, down deep, fueled by the excitement of taking their next big step.

"I am not." Maeve's squeal had a snide echo from Chubb.

The women kept bickering, and Ryan downed the last of his beer. He wanted to leave, to get down to Perkins Lane, to start the next stage of his life.

"I was reading an email from Mom," Maeve said. "She wants to know if any of us want to go to Joey's graduation in June."

"I said I'd go," said Eamon.

"Well since we've all seen you graduate how many times, I guess it's fair," Maeve said.

Eamon's raised eyebrow told her exactly how little he cared for her snark. "I'm pretty sure I only saw you in the audience once."

Ryan jumped in to defuse their bickering. "I'm thinking about going." His inflection made it a question, and his eyes were on Dani.

"Sure." Dani's wide smile pretty much promised to follow him anywhere. "Where are we going again?"

"Notre Dame," Ryan said.

Maeve left off glaring at Eamon when her phone buzzed.

"It *is* a message from Christopher," Dani said, delighted. "I told you so."

They went back to wrestling, and Ryan downed the last of his beer. "I'm thinking we should head over to Magnolia soon, Dani, so we can get stuff unloaded before it gets dark."

"Aw…" Dani stretched her arms up over her head, unconsciously teasing Ryan with an even better look at her curves.

"Can't we sit here in the sun for a little while longer?" she said.

"I'll follow you down and help you unload," Niall said.

Eamon scraped a hank of hair out of his face. "I can help for a bit, too."

"All right." Dani hopped off the tailgate, leaving Maeve and her phone and lifting into a whole-body stretch that momentarily distracted Ryan from his afternoon agenda. Eamon and Niall climbed into Eamon's Leaf and after a moderate amount of complaint, Chubb climbed in the back.

"I gotta go … do … something." Maeve jumped off the tailgate and headed for her car. "I'll see you all later."

Ryan cut her some slack, figuring she'd only bitch about him living with Dani anyway. He took one last look at the house, tossed his key to Niall, and climbed into his truck. "You ready?" he asked Dani.

She buffed his cheek with a kiss. "Yes."

"This is your last chance to back out."

"Back out?"

Her laughing surprise reassured him more than her words.

"I can't wait," she said.

"Good." He put the car in gear, flustered by how right things felt between him and Dani. This might be the first night they'd officially share an address, but as far as Ryan was concerned, he was in it for good.

For better. For worse. Forever.

The End

www.liv-rancourt.blogspot.com

Evernight Publishing ®

www.evernightpublishing.com